THE
DARKEST
PATH

JEFF HIRSCH

THE DARK

EST PATH

SCHOLASTIC PRESS | NEW YORK

Library of Congress Cataloging-in-Publication Data

Hirsch, Jeff.
The darkest path / Jeff Hirsch. — 1st ed.
p. cm.
Summary: Since he was captured by the Glorious Path, a militant religion based on the teachings of a former soldier, fifteen-year-old Cal has served the Path in its brutal war with the remains of the United States government, and tried to survive and protect his younger brother, but when he kills an officer to protect a stray dog, Cal is forced take his brother and the dog and run.
ISBN 978-0-545-51223-7
1. Dystopias — Juvenile fiction. 2. Militia movements — Juvenile fiction. 3. Cults — Juvenile fiction. 4. Survival — Juvenile fiction. 5. Escapes — Juvenile fiction. 6. Brothers — Juvenile fiction. [1. Militia movements — Fiction. 2. Cults — Fiction. 3. Survival — Fiction. 4. Escapes — Fiction. 5. Brothers — Fiction.] I. Title.
PZ7.H59787Dar 2013
813.6 — dc23

2013004367

10 9 8 7 6 5 4 3 2 1   13 14 15 16 17

Printed in the U.S.A.   23
First edition, October 2013

The text was set in Trade Gothic.
Book design by Phil Falco

For Gretchen

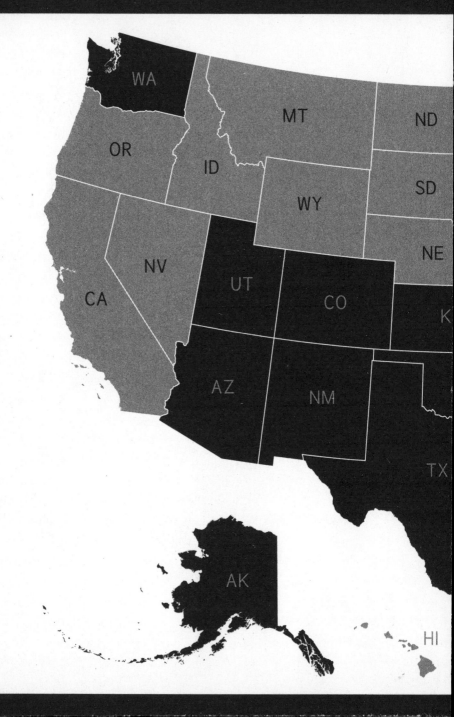

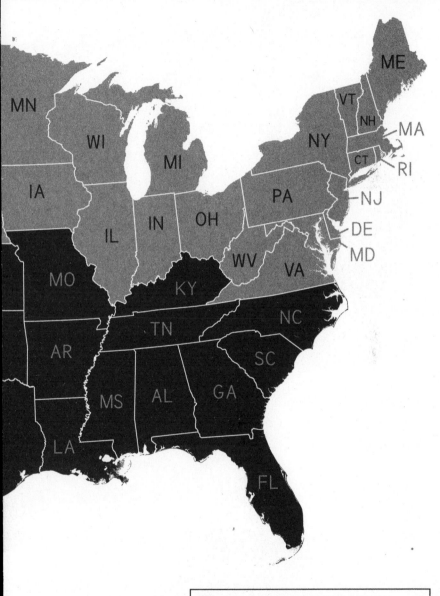

CONTROLLED BY THE U.S. FEDERAL ARMY
CONTROLLED BY THE ARMY OF THE GLORIOUS PATH

PART ONE

1

When I woke up in the examination room, I was handcuffed to the bed. A loop of steel circled my right wrist, holding it fast to a guardrail. My left arm lay throbbing by my side, the skin swollen taut from where Sergeant Rhames had broken my wrist with a baseball bat.

My head swam as I lifted it off a thin pillow. The room was nearly empty, nothing but the cot I was on, a discolored sink, and a few cabinets. A rush of air kicked on from somewhere above me. I searched the ceiling and found a single dusty vent. Air-conditioning.

I've done it, I thought. *I'm here.*

I closed my eyes and thought about James, hoping my little brother's face would ease the pounding in my chest. I pictured him moving through our barracks, turning the chaos around us into folded clothes and tidy stacks. He said that cleaning calmed him and, even though I made fun of him for it, the truth was that seeing him do it calmed me too. The day before I left, I didn't make my bunk, just so I could watch as he tucked the sheets beneath the mattress and then smoothed the wrinkles flat with the palm of his hand.

My pulse stilled. I breathed. A door opened and someone shuffled into the room.

"Well, you must have *really* pissed somebody off."

I didn't move. Didn't speak.

"Multiple shallow cuts as well as bruises over your chest and arms and face. Your wrist is fractured. I think I can put a cast on it, but I can't spare any pain meds. Your friends in the Glorious Path are to thank for that."

I opened my eyes. The doctor was short, with thinning brownish-gray hair. An awkward belly poked out of his white lab coat and hung over his camo fatigues.

"They're not my friends," I said.

"Ah, the dead arise. It's a miracle. What's your name?"

"Where am I?"

"Okay," he said, making a note on his clipboard. "Path John Doe it is, then."

"I'm not Path," I said. "Not anymore."

"Funny," he said. "The Army of the Glorious Path isn't exactly known for its revolving-door policy."

My tongue darted out over my cracked lips. "Can I have some water?"

"If I can have a name."

"Callum Roe. Cal."

He lowered a canteen to my lips. I drank until he pulled it away from me.

"You're in the infirmary at Camp Victory," he said. "I'm Dr. Franks. One of our patrols found you out in the desert and brought you here."

"I need to see your base commander."

"Oh, sure," Franks said with a chuckle. "I keep my sidearm in my desk — maybe you'd like to take it with you."

I glared at him until he chucked his clipboard onto a nearby table with a sigh.

"All right," he said. "Why do you think you need to see the commander?"

I swallowed hard. Could I really do this? Would he even listen? My pulse raced, but I made myself think of James moving through our barracks, slow and deliberate, setting everything in its place.

"Because if you don't let me see him," I said, "everyone in his camp is going to die."

2

Dr. Franks led me from the chill of the examination room into the hundred-degree blast of the California desert.

Camp Victory was smaller than I thought it would be. I counted no more than ten dusty buildings, a mix of repurposed civilian houses and corrugated-steel huts. They didn't have much in the way of vehicles, just a couple Humvees with .50 caliber machine guns on the roof, a troop carrier, and a single decrepit-looking Apache. What they lacked in mobility, though, they made up for in perimeter defense. The whole place was surrounded by a high wall — a mix of concrete slabs, sandbags, and steel fencing. Gun emplacements sat every ten to fifteen feet, each one manned by a team of hard-looking Fed soldiers.

While most of the base was military, there was also a sizable civilian population that must have been drawn from the two small towns the base protected. The civilians seemed to be acting as gofers and nurses and mess-hall attendants. I felt sick just looking at them. They had no idea what was coming.

We stopped at a small plywood building at the center of camp, and Franks conferred with a guard. I stepped back, looking up at the red, white, and blue flag of the Federal Army, whipping about in a dry wind.

I shivered as we moved out of the heat and into the chill of the commander's office. A small air conditioner teetered in the window above his desk. Below it was a computer, an electric lamp, and a handheld calculator. I stared from one to the other, tracing their contours like they were relics from some lost world. Nathan Hill said it was reliance on things like these that made the Pathless so soft. Followers of the Glorious Path were stronger, he said. They didn't need toys.

Franks shackled my wrist to the chair and sat me down. My arm itched under a plaster cast that ran from just below my elbow to halfway down my palm. My fingers, bruised black and red, stuck out at the end. On top of that, the simple walk from the infirmary had every one of my injuries throbbing at once, igniting a headache at the base of my skull. Franks handed me two aspirin, and I chewed them like candy.

"You just tell him what you told me," Dr. Franks said. "Answer his questions and you'll be fine."

The door behind him opened and a gray-haired man swept in. He wore a standard camo uniform, no rank insignia, just a stars-and-stripes patch and a tag that said Connery. He sat down across from me without a word.

I've always been small for my age, five feet five, and so thin you could see my ribs through my T-shirt. Still, I cringed down into my chair, trying to make myself look like even less of a threat. If I had learned anything in the last six years, it was that there was nothing people like Connery enjoyed more than feeling big. Give them that and they just might listen to you.

"So," Connery said, regarding me with watery blue eyes, "I hear you have things to tell me."

I took a shaky breath and let it out. Here we go.

"There are nearly two hundred Path soldiers a little over ten klicks to your east," I said. "They have armor and air support and they'll be here just after midnight."

There was no change in the stony composition of Connery's face. His thin lips were set and straight. Painful seconds passed and then he turned to his computer. He tapped a key and sent a blue glow over his face.

"Thanks for bringing him in, Dr. Franks. That will be all."

"Sir," Dr. Franks said. "Don't we have to at least —"

"If there was a significant force of rebel fighters on my doorstep, I think I'd know about it."

"You know how they work," I said, struggling to keep my voice calm. "They scatter their forces, put them in small groups that can't be discovered. They only join up at the last minute and then —"

"Son, even if the Path did have a force that size in the area, they'd be headed to Greenfield. It's a far more strategically valuable piece of land. If you want to control the region, you go there."

"They're not trying to control the region."

"No?" Connery said with a condescending chuckle. "Then why are they here?"

I leaned forward as far as the handcuffs and my injuries would allow. "They're here to give you the Choice."

Franks made an anxious little noise behind me and then fell silent. Connery's chair creaked as he sat back. His hand fell to a folder on his desk. He moved it idly back and forth, making a sandpaper rasp against the desktop.

"And you came here to tell us this out of the kindness of your heart?"

"My brother and I were visiting our mom's family in Phoenix when we were kidnapped and made to serve the Path. I was nine. James was seven. Since then we've seen them give the Choice to Bowling Green and El Paso and Marietta."

A silence fell, as it always did when someone mentioned Marietta.

"You were at Marietta?"

I nodded. "I've seen what Nathan Hill's men do to people who choose not to embrace the Glorious Path. I didn't want to see it again, so when I got a chance, I ran. Path security caught me. I guess when I passed out, they figured I was dead."

Connery glanced over my shoulder.

"Corporal Tate's men picked him up a few miles from here," Dr. Franks said. "He was beaten badly enough that if they hadn't found him, I'm pretty sure he would have died."

"I left my brother alone with those people to come here and help you," I said. "So I am not leaving until you listen to me. Your base is dangerously isolated. They've got you beat three to one on men. They have four Apache gunships to your one, and six armored Humvees. If you move now, you can evacuate your men and the civilians. Like you said, there's nothing to be gained here."

"Look, I'm not about to bug out just because some kid —"

I drew a folded-up piece of paper out of my back pocket and tossed it onto his desk. It was stained with dirt and flecks of my blood.

"I stole their com frequencies and encryption codes before I left," I said. "If you don't believe me, then take a listen. They're out there."

Connery stared at them, the muscles in his jaw and neck tight as cables.

"Please," I said, nearly in a whisper. "You're running out of time."

He glanced out the window by the air conditioner. The sun was already starting to fall. Connery swept the papers off his desk, then strode past us into the outer room. The door slammed shut behind him.

I sank back into the chair, weak and exhausted, wishing it was over but knowing it wasn't. What if he still refused to listen? What if he decided to be a hero? Then all of this would be for nothing. I thought of James alone in our barracks, and my head began to pound.

"So, the Choice . . . it's really what they say it is."

I couldn't turn to face him. "You should take your family and go while you can."

"I can't abandon my post," Dr. Franks said, voice quivering. "They need a doctor. I —"

"Your family needs you too," I said. "Up to you which is more important."

The doctor said nothing. Minutes later the door behind him swung open and Connery walked in, carrying a long roll of paper. He passed us without a word and sat back down at his desk. After moving aside his electronic toys, he unrolled the paper in front of me. It was a map.

"Show me how to get away from them," he said.

It was just after dawn when the convoy pulled into an abandoned parking lot near the shores of a small mountain lake.

We had driven through the night, Connery's few armed vehicles bracketing a column of civilian cars and trucks and RVs. The Apache that shadowed us throughout the trip had just peeled off in search of fuel, with a promise to return as soon as it could.

When we came to a stop, civilians cracked the doors of their vehicles and stumbled out into the morning light, dazed. I watched one family flee their broken-down RV, the mother and father sweeping two young boys and a teenage girl up into their arms, all of them crying. It was happening everywhere, tears mixed with sudden bursts of relieved laughter. And why not? They had escaped the Army of the Glorious Path. They were all alive. All together.

I was in the lead Humvee with Connery. As soon as he left to tour the camp, I took off too, winding through the parking lot toward the edge of the lake. I was halfway across when I heard a voice behind me and felt a tug at my shirttails. One of the boys from the RV. He was seven or eight, with a pinpoint nose and brown hair in a shaggy bowl cut. He was holding a white plastic box out toward me.

"Here."

"I don't . . ."

"My mom said you were the one who came to warn us," he said, and turned the case over. On the other side, there was a small glass screen surrounded by brightly colored buttons. "It only has Starfighter 3 on it right now. But it's still pretty fun."

He tried to push the game into my hands. "No, you keep it. I didn't —"

The kid's brows dropped, making a single confused wrinkle between his eyes. I didn't know what else to say, so I turned from him and hurried off. He called after me, but I kept my eyes fixed on the dark blue of the lake and strode toward it. Soon, the buzz of the camp faded behind me. The rising sun was warm on the back of my neck. I reached the pebbly beach and started down the length of it until I found a sliver of shade behind a group of boulders. The lake in front of me was vast and slate-gray, perfectly still.

My arm and ribs ached from the bounce of the long drive. I would have killed for more of Franks's aspirin, but I couldn't go back to all those people. Not yet. I picked a handful of stones and threw them into the water one by one. For a moment I imagined myself on the shore of Cayuga Lake, surrounded by moss and autumn trees instead of rock and sand. Mom and Dad and James were just a little way ahead, around the bend in the shore. My chest clenched at the thought of them, and I had to snap the image away.

I lifted my hand to throw another stone but froze at a crunch of boots on the sand behind me. The reflection of two soldiers appeared in the lake, dark pillars to each side of me. I threw the stone, shattering their reflections. When the water stilled, they were sitting to either side of me. Corporal Johnson, a beanpole redhead, was on my left.

On my right was Sergeant Rhames.

"Anything unexpected?"

I shook my head. Rhames pulled the mic off his shoulder and reported in.

"Huntsman One, this is Huntsman Two. Bloodhound reports all clear. Repeat, we are alpha charlie."

"Understood, Huntsman Two. We are go."

Rhames replaced the radio, shaking his head. "I swear, I never thought it would work. I mean, a commander hands over his entire base because some skinny kid tells him to? I can't believe it's taken us so long to beat this bunch of cowards."

I skipped a rock across the lake. "He was just trying to protect his people," I said.

Rhames laughed. "And that's why the Pathless will lose," he said. "They don't think there's anything worth dying for."

After a short prayer, Rhames and Johnson pulled out their MRE rations and tore open the brown packaging. Johnson's was spaghetti. Rhames had meat loaf. They offered me one, but I refused.

"You should eat," Johnson said. "You'll stunt your growth."

"Too late for that," Rhames said with a snort.

I watched Rhames's reflection as he ate. He was a piggish-looking man with a blunt nose and deep-set eyes. A scar at his temple made a part in his trim salt-and-pepper hair and ran down one cheek. I looked away, remembering how I'd cringed as he towered over me. How he'd barely checked his swing when he'd shattered my arm with the bat. He said it had to look real if it was going to work.

"How much longer?" I asked.

As if in answer, a black spot appeared over the mountains and dropped soundlessly into the lake's valley. As it drew closer, I saw it was the returning Fed Apache. It was about a mile out when the smoke trail of a Path Stinger missile streaked across the blue sky. The Apache tried to dodge, but the missile struck the helicopter broadside and it went up in a furious explosion.

Behind us came a gasp and then the sound of rushing bodies as the evacuees ran to their vehicles. But it would be too late for them too.

Just do what they tell you, I thought. *Do what they tell you and everything will be all right.*

Rhames and Johnson said another prayer and then finished their meals. When they were done, they set about meticulously tidying up, putting the MRE wrappers back into their packs, brushing crumbs from their uniforms and checking for stains. One of the first things we learned after we were taken is that Path soldiers existed to set an example for the Pathless, so no detail was too small. So said Nathan Hill.

There was a firecracker chatter of gunfire from the direction of the parking lot, then two explosions that sent tremors through the ground.

"They'll be given the Choice," I said. "All of them. That was the deal."

"You didn't make a deal," Rhames said as he stood. "You followed an order."

Rhames strode away, but Johnson hung back.

"Want to go witness?"

I stared at the edge of the lake and shook my head.

"Arm okay?" Johnson asked, softening his voice now that Rhames was out of earshot. I drew the cast to my chest and said it was. "I hear Captain Monroe is going to make you and James citizens because of this."

I nodded weakly.

Johnson knelt beside me. "Look, Rhames is just — he's Rhames, right? You drew a tough assignment, Cal. We all know that. You just have to understand that some of the things we do . . . you have to put them behind you. Heck, a few years from now the whole country will be on Path, and people will barely remember that things like this happened. It'll be a whole new world."

I stared up at the sharp lines of his face until they shifted into a brotherly smile.

"You brought people to the Path, Cal. You should be proud."

I forced myself to nod, even muscled up a paper-thin version of a smile that seemed to satisfy him. Johnson cuffed my shoulder.

"It'll be over in about an hour," he said as he started back to the parking lot. "Choppers will be leaving twenty minutes after that. We'll be back at Cormorant before Lighthouse."

The crunch of Johnson's boots faded and I was alone again. Soon a beacon would be standing in front of the survivors, all smiles and pious concern, to administer the Choice. Unite with the Glorious Path or receive Nathan's Blessing.

Seconds ticked away. The soldiers would be moving through the crowds now, separating the new converts from the rest and leading them away to their new lives as novices and companions of the Glorious Path. Once they were safely away, the ones who had opted to remain Pathless —

The roar of automatic weapons shattered the lakeside quiet. My body seized, folding in on itself. I tried to drive out the sound with thoughts of Mom and Dad and James, but the firing went on so long that it was useless. Everything in me and around me was wiped away by that one awful sound.

And then, all at once, the firing ceased. I sat in that tense after-action silence, staring into the dark of my closed eyes.

I lifted my head, blinking away the glare of the sunlight. The lake was a glassy calm, reflecting a pale blue sky and streaks of clouds. The shadow of a Path Black Hawk flew over me, its rotors kicking up a cloud of tan dust.

I stood by the lake until my legs steadied, and then I walked back to the lot.

3

We made it to Arizona just before dark. Beacon King was waiting at the landing pad when the Black Hawk touched down. Hunched over and mouth covered with a cloth to keep out the dust, he hustled us all through Cormorant's operations center.

There was the usual rush of activity around us as uniformed men moved in and out of the plywood-and-corrugated-steel command buildings. Radios blared and vehicles roared. Electric lights shone everywhere.

The noise lessened when we reached the canvas tent that stood at the edge of the ops center. There, soldiers turned over their weapons and radios and any other bit of the modern world on their person. Once that was done, we followed Beacon King inside.

The tent was lit with candles and smelled faintly of sandalwood incense. We dropped to our knees before Beacon King and bowed our heads.

"I am a blade in the hand of God," we intoned. "To walk the Path he has set for me, I must put my hand to worldly things. This is a sacrifice I make for my brothers and sisters. When his kingdom has come, I will forsake these things and be clean again."

Blessing over, Rhames announced that they were going to squeeze in an after-action meeting before evening Lighthouse began. I saw him looking for me but managed to slip through a gap in the tent wall and disappear. A sentry at the gate that separated the ops center from the rest of the base nodded and let me pass.

My steps lightened as I moved into the residential district. It was quieter there. No coms buzzing, no grind of engines or turn of rotors. No glare of electric lights. I passed the soldiers' and citizens' barracks and made my way down the hill to the novices' district.

A group of companions came up the road from their own barracks on the far side of Cormorant. There were ten of them, huddled close together, ghostly in their white robes and veils. I moved off the path and stood, eyes cast down, as the shepherd at the head of the flock hurried them along.

When I looked up again, one of the companions had paused on the road and was staring at me. Her eyes were wide shadows beneath her veil. She raised one hand gently to her cheek and I understood. The bruises. The cast. I must have looked as bad as I felt. I waved her away and she glided up the hill with the others.

Two oil lamps sat just inside the door to our barracks. I lit them both and was relieved to find the place empty. Our fifty or more barracks mates were either finishing up the day's work or already wolfing down dinner in the mess before it was time to go to Lighthouse.

Standing in the doorway, I cast my eye down the two lines of steel bunk beds. I saw what I was looking for immediately. Top bunk. Last row. A single cardboard box. I grunted from the pain in my side and shoulder as I reached up and pulled the box off the bunk. A single folded piece of paper sat on top.

To Callum Roe:

Please report to Captain Monroe, Base Commander, at 0900 tomorrow morning. Kennel Master Quarles has been informed that you will be late arriving to your duty assignment. This meeting will be to discuss the future duty assignments for yourself and your brother, James Roe.

Yours on the Path,

Hemet Walker, adjutant

I dropped the note and tore open the box. Inside were two stacks of MREs. I shuffled through them. Meat loaf. Burritos. Chicken teriyaki. As hungry as I was, I set them aside and dug until I uncovered the three asthma inhalers hidden beneath. I held my breath when I saw them. For novices like me and James, medical care meant herbal tea and prayer. These inhalers might as well have been made of solid gold. I couldn't imagine the look on James's face when I put them in his hand. Never mind when I told him about the rest of Captain Monroe's promise.

Citizenship.

For years the word had seemed too impossible to even speak, but here it was, a day away. Better jobs. More access to medicines. A private room with actual beds, doors, and windows. After six years of struggling, James and I would finally have a place we could make our own.

Outside, the Lighthouse bells began to toll. I pocketed one inhaler, then hid the rest of them with the MREs under my bunk's mattress.

I stopped at the shared latrine on my way out, hoping to scrub the grime off my face before Lighthouse. The line of sinks and mirrors gleamed in the lantern glow. I turned one of the faucets, thankful that the Path didn't consider hot running water as corrupting as radios and electric lights. I leaned over the sink to fill my hands but drew them back when I saw the white of the cast Dr. Franks had put on my arm.

I stared down at the cottony fringe where my fingers emerged from the plaster, each one bruised black and blue. A dull throb built in my head and I felt a sick whirl in my stomach. The flow of the water through the chrome rose in pitch until it sounded like a chorus of screams. I lurched forward to turn it off, striking my cast against the fixture. My body shook with the pain of it, and I nearly called out before I managed to pull back and stagger away from the sink.

I closed my eyes, forcing myself to breathe slow and deep, willing the shaking to subside. When I opened them again, a stranger's face glowered at me in the mirror. My eyes were surrounded by kaleidoscopes of black and red and blue. There were two crusty gashes on my cheeks, and bruises on my neck and shoulders. I moved my fingers lightly over the wounds, wincing at their tenderness. The faces of Camp Victory crowded the edge of my mind. Connery. Franks. The little boy who was so eager to thank me for saving them all. I could hear their voices. The gunfire —

Citizenship. I imagined the word carved into a stone door that I pulled closed, trapping any other thought, any other memory, on the other side. My fingers traced the body of the inhaler in my pocket until my heart quieted.

The bells tolled again and I left the barracks, striding up the hill to the Lighthouse.

•   •   •

The Lighthouse was full by the time I got there. I pushed my way through the ranks of shuffling novices to my place in the rear of the hall. Down below, the soldiers and citizens were laid out in a fan around the simple wood-plank altar. Beacon Thomas hadn't appeared yet, so I turned and looked for James. He should have been behind me, just ahead of the white-robed companions who haunted the very back of the Lighthouse, but I didn't see him. Jimmy Wayne and Rashid James, officers' valets just like James, were there, but I couldn't catch their eye to ask where he was.

Beacon Thomas came out onto the stage below, and a hush spread through the crowd. The soldiers and citizens took their seats on the rows of benches, while us novices and the companions remained standing behind them. We folded our hands before us, our heads slightly bowed.

Beacon Thomas took his copy of *The Glorious Path* off of the altar and opened it.

"With these words, I consecrate my life to the Glorious Path," he recited.

"With these words, I consecrate my life to the Glorious Path," all of us echoed, beginning the call-and-response opening to service.

"God, lead me to my Path. Let me be a light in the darkness and the rod that falls upon the backs of the defiant. The lives of my brothers and the lives of the Pathless are in my hands. If I allow them to fall into the darkness, then so must I. Their loss is my loss. Their death is my death."

Once the congregation fell silent, Beacon Thomas set the book down and lit a single candle in the center of the altar.

"There is but one God and he sent us Nathan Hill to light the Path that leads to his kingdom."

Beacon Thomas continued the service while Beacons Quan and Rozales stalked the aisles, their eyes sharp for the insufficiently reverent. I dropped my head as they passed, my eyes closed tight. Looking distracted during Lighthouse was a ticket to hours of hard labor. Of course, seeming too enthusiastic led to the same thing if a beacon decided you were mocking the service. I had fallen on either side of the line more times than I could count. James was the real master. Over the years he had figured out how to play the game perfectly. Back flawlessly straight, his copy of *The Glorious Path* open before him, his eyes boring into its pages as if he was searching for the subtlest meanings buried in Nathan Hill's words. No one would ever guess it was all an act.

Once Quan and Rozales passed, I turned and caught Rashid's eye. I nodded over to James's spot, but he shrugged and went back to praying. My stomach sank. There weren't many reasons why a novice would be allowed to miss Lighthouse.

My hand went to the inhaler in my pocket. One day the previous April, I had returned to the barracks to find James clawing at his chest, nearly purple from lack of oxygen. Had it happened again? Was he at the infirmary? The attendants there wouldn't know anything about the deal I made with Captain Monroe. They'd just stand there mumbling prayers while James struggled to breathe.

The beacons had now descended to the front of the Lighthouse to help Thomas with the Receiving. The soldiers and citizens stood up and moved toward the central aisle. One by one, Beacon Thomas lifted a lit candle to their foreheads and said a prayer. The novices and companions would follow. If I had a chance, this was it. When the time came for our row to move into the aisle, I pretended to retie my boots, fumbling with the laces because of my cast.

Novices huffed and jostled by me, putting me at the end of our line. I shuffled up the aisle between the rows of companions making for the back entrance. My fingers hit the door handle, and a voice stopped me in my tracks.

"What are you doing, Mr. Roe?"

Beacon Quan stood in the aisle behind me, frowning, his shaved head gleaming in the lantern light.

"I'm, uh . . ." I mumbled, hoping to buy some time. "I wasn't feeling well. I thought —"

"You thought you would skip the service and head to the infirmary without informing anyone."

"No. I mean . . . I guess I'm a little light-headed." I held up my cast. "My arm was hurting. I wasn't thinking. I can —"

"I think you can figure things out while you're digging latrines tomorrow. Wait here and I'll get Beacon Rozales."

Quan passed me and headed down the aisle. My heart pounded, thinking of James in the infirmary, suffering and alone.

I lifted my cast and slammed it into the corner of the pillar next to me. The pain was an explosion that flipped the entire Lighthouse upside down. My knees turned to jelly, and the ground slammed into my side and then into my head. The last thing I saw before passing out was Beacon Quan running up the aisle toward me.

4

I sat up in the infirmary cot, pushing away the third cup of herbal tea a companion had tried to force on me in the last hour.

"Look, I'm fine. Could you please just tell me where my brother is?"

"I don't know your —"

"Roe. James Roe. He has trouble breathing. He should be here somewhere. You have to —"

"Cal?"

James was running down the aisle toward me. He was still in his valet's uniform, its blue lines pressed just as neat as they were the last time I had seen him.

"James? What are you — are you okay?"

"Uh, you're the one in the infirmary, Cal."

James nodded to the companion and she drifted away to another patient. He sat down on the edge of the empty cot next to mine.

"I came here looking for you," I said. "You weren't at Lighthouse and then —"

"I had to stay late with Monroe. Why did you think I was in the infirmary? And what happened to you? Your arm —"

He reached for my cast and I pulled it back. "It's nothing."

James laughed, putting an accusing finger in my face. "It was that Rottweiler again, wasn't it? The same one that knocked you down on the last work detail Quarles sent you on."

I paused, remembering my cover story for the last couple days. "The detail was fine. I just . . . I had an accident, that's all." James narrowed his eyes at me, but I pulled the sheets back on the cot. "Look, forget it. Let's get out of here, okay?"

"I think they want you to stay till morning."

"Seriously?"

"You're aware that you puked all over Beacon Quan when he carried you out of the Lighthouse, right?"

"I don't actually remember puking."

James threw the blankets back over me and helped me sit up.

"You been to the barracks?" I asked.

"No. Why?"

I scanned the infirmary floor. Two companions and a citizen medic were at the far end of the room. They were presided over by a single beacon who looked busy with some paperwork. I slipped my hand beneath the sheets and into my pocket.

"Give me your hand," I said.

"Why?" James asked. "Is it a bug? Are you going to put a bug in my hand again? Honestly, Cal, that stopped being funny when I was five."

"Just do it."

James held his hand out and I pushed the inhaler into it, closing his fingers around it fast. He drew his hand back to his waist and opened it.

"James, this is — where did you get this?"

"It's not contraband. Don't worry."

"Then how —"

"I got it from Monroe."

"From Monroe?" James looked from the inhaler to my cast and the bruises. His face went gray as ash. "If this is what it took to get this, then you should take it back. I don't need it."

"Oh, really? You and the beacons gonna pray the asthma away?"

James gritted his teeth. His fingers went white, curled around the inhaler.

"You're Monroe's favorite, Jim. The guy couldn't tie his shoes without you. I promise, it didn't take anything more than me asking nicely to get the meds. All this . . . it's nothing you have to worry about. I swear."

"Nothing that's going to get you in trouble?"

"Scout's honor, little brother," I said, holding up my busted left hand.

"You were never a Boy Scout," he said. "I wanted us to be Scouts, but you said it was for weenies."

"I know. It was a mistake. You would have fit right in."

James tucked the inhaler away, but his face was still scrunched up and dark, his lips tight.

"Come on," I teased. "James . . ."

"I just don't want you to get off Path again."

"I'm not. Look, come here," I said, waving him over. "Keep it between you and me for now, but there's more, okay?"

"More what?"

"I'm meeting with Captain Monroe tomorrow."

"So?"

I glanced back at the beacon, who was still absorbed in his paperwork. "We're getting moved up."

"Moved up?" James said. Then it clicked. "You mean . . ."

I nodded. "I told you you're his favorite."

"But —"

"We've been here six years now, James. With everything you do for him, it's not even that far ahead of schedule."

James still looked wary, but I could tell there was excitement bubbling underneath it.

"When?"

"Soon, I think, but I'll know more after the meeting tomorrow. We'll talk between breakfast and morning Lighthouse, okay?"

I almost laughed at James's openmouthed speechlessness.

"Who's the best big brother in the entire universe?"

"Well . . ."

"How about within a five-foot radius?"

James finally laughed but a companion cut it off, appearing just behind him. He nodded and she stepped away.

"Cal, I don't . . . I don't know what to say."

"Music to my ears. Just go home and start packing our things."

"Want me to lead a prayer before I go?"

James had his copy of *The Glorious Path* open in his lap. I checked over his shoulder. The beacon was on the far side of the room and out of earshot.

"It's okay, Jim," I said. "No one's looking."

There was a second's pause and then something inside of James seemed to shift. "Yeah," he said, snapping the book shut. "Right. Of course. I'll see you later, okay?"

"Get some sleep," I said.

"You too. And try not to puke on yourself again."

"I'll do my best."

James tucked the book back into his pocket and walked away down the line of beds. Companions moved through the infirmary, snuffing out candles. I lay back on my cot, staring up into the dark, fantasizing about what job I might get once we were citizens. Surely they wouldn't make me keep mucking out the dog kennels with Quarles. That was a novice job, and a bad one at that. Could I be a cook's apprentice? A mechanic? It seemed impossible.

Of course, whatever duty I pulled, the important thing would be me and James in our own room in the citizens' barracks — two beds side by side, with four walls and a door. Inside that room, there would be no beacons, no Lighthouse, no Army of the Glorious Path, just us.

I tried to banish my impatience for the morning with a prayer of my own, one that was composed of a single word written in stone.

5

I nearly knocked over a lieutenant when I staggered out of Captain Monroe's office the next morning.

"Watch yourself, novice."

"Yes, sir," I mumbled automatically. "Sorry, sir."

I stumbled down the stairs and out onto the street, shielding my eyes to block out the glare of the sun. A Humvee laid on its horn and blew past me. Cormorant had come alive in the hour since I had been inside. Soldiers grunted up on the training field and the air was thick with dust and diesel exhaust.

I fell into a stream of citizens who were bustling from their barracks to mess. They were all talking and laughing. I thought of how each had slept that night in a private room in a real bed.

"Hey, Cal!"

I turned to see James peeling off from a group of friends and rushing toward me.

"Get to mess, James."

"How was your meeting?"

"Later. I have to get to work."

"But —"

I whirled on him and shouted, "Just leave me alone!"

James nearly toppled backward. I shoved my way through the rest of the crowds and left him. My head was pounding and it only got worse when I reached the crest of a hill that led down to the kennels. I could already hear the rolling growls of the dogs and the rattling fences down below. The air was thick with the smell of meat, urine, and fur. I stepped into it, pushing through the stink and noise until I found Quarles out back on the edge of the training ground.

"The hell you been?" he croaked.

Quarles was balding and fat, dressed in layers of greasy wool despite the heat and sun. His blotchy skin sported a constant growth of stubble.

"Ops," I said. I was about to remind him that I'd been with Monroe, but I couldn't make my lips form the man's name.

Quarles glanced down at my arm, then up at my face. "Should have figured," he said, rolling the words around in his mouth like wet gravel. "Only a matter of time before someone decided to put a beating to a kid like you. Useless to me busted."

"I'm fine. Let's just get going."

Quarles stared me down with his rheumy eyes. I was close to insubordination, but sending me off for discipline would mean he'd have to see to the dogs alone that day. Quarles broke and nodded toward the kennels.

"Feed 'em," he growled. "But half rations! I want those monsters blood hungry this morning."

The kennel was a narrow concrete-floored room lined with cages, ten on each side. Each steel mesh cage was barely two by three feet with an exit on either side, one leading to the yard and one into the kennel's central aisle. I heard Quarles out in the yard, setting up the dogs' practice dummies. I looked up at the pull chains hanging across from the back door. One pull and every cage would open at once, leaving him surrounded by twenty starving animals. Of course, with my luck I'd grab the wrong chain and send them all into the kennel with me.

The ammonia stench of urine clung to my skin as I crossed the kennel and found the bucket of kitchen scraps. It was a gloppy mess of day-old meat, rice, and rotten vegetables. I grabbed a scoop off the shelf and stepped into the aisle, kicking the bucket ahead of me.

The dogs threw themselves against their cages and howled. I just wanted to feed them as fast as possible and get out of there. My arm and my head were screaming. I tossed half rations into each cage, which blunted their frenzy for the ten seconds it took to gobble it all down. I paused at the doorway, looking back at the dogs as they threw their scrawny bodies against the steel, eyes wild, jaws snapping.

Disgusting as Quarles was, Monroe put up with him because he knew how to train an attack dog and how to do it cheaper than any kennel master Cormorant had ever had. Most of the dogs came in as skinny strays, scared and hesitant. They left with a streak of violence running through them like an electrified fence.

I glanced out the door at Quarles, then threw an extra scoop of food into each dog's cage. They fell to it savagely. I felt heroic for half a second, before I realized that there's nothing heroic about giving an animal what it deserves.

"What now?" I asked, standing in front of Quarles on the practice field. "Want me to clean the cages?"

The sun was high and Quarles was sweating heavily, his skin blotchier than usual. He sneered at me. "You'd rather muck out cages than watch them tear apart a few dummies. What's the matter, Roe, feeling a little delicate this morning?"

"They don't perform well when I'm here," I said. "You know that."

Quarles considered a moment. I looked back and saw a company of men kicking up dust as they descended the hill.

"They're almost here," I said.

Quarles scooped a dogcatcher pole off the ground and handed it to me. It was a long stick with a sliding handle that tightened a noose at the end.

"Got report of a stray out by the highway. Go see if you can bring him in."

"With my arm like this?"

A stiff-backed sergeant appeared out of the glare. His men were arranged around him.

"Are you ready, Mr. Quarles?"

Quarles's own back went straight. "Yes, sir!" he announced, his voice without slur or stutter. "We're ready whenever you are."

The sergeant directed his men into the kennel. When he was gone, Quarles looked at me, his hand resting on his belt, between his black club and his revolver.

"Go get that mutt or you're gonna be down one more arm," he said. Then he climbed the dusty hill, up to the range.

An abandoned shopping center sat on a little-used highway at the edge of the base. There was an old supermarket. A gas station. A pawnshop. All the windows had been shattered and their signs were bleached to ghostly shades by the relentless Arizona sun.

I stepped onto the cracked parking lot, then circled around to the back, where scrubby weeds gave way to desert. In the far distance were the tops of rock-pile mountains. No dog in sight.

It had taken me nearly an hour to walk to the lot, which meant the soldiers had at least another hour of training to do. There was no way I was going back until they were done. I propped the dogcatcher over my shoulder and walked onto the hard-packed dirt. It was like wading into the ocean, the asphalt shore and sun-bleached bones of the shopping center at my back, an endless plain ahead.

I dropped onto a gravel-and-dirt hill, broiling in my dress uniform and my shined shoes. I hated myself for every second I had spent in the mirror that morning, combing my hair, brushing my clothes. I wanted to look so on Path. The picture of a citizen. I dug into my pocket and pulled out a small metal token. A sunburst bisected by a razor-sharp line. It glowed, growing hot in my palm.

"I have wonderful news," Monroe had said, standing up behind his great oak desk as I entered. "Quite an honor."

I stood there, grinning and attentive as a fool, ready for that single word to part his lips. I wanted to hear it so bad I almost swore I had, but then Monroe slid the token across his desk, and the illusion was shattered. I stared at it, my world collapsing down onto that gold pin.

"Generally we make novices become citizens first," Monroe said. "But your work yesterday was so exemplary, so indicative of a young man on Path that you are excused from that requirement."

I tore my eyes from the pin. "Sir?"

Monroe beamed, clearly pleased with his own generosity. "You're our newest recruit, son," he said. "You are now Private Callum Roe in the Army of the Glorious Path. You'll be assigned to Sergeant Rhames's platoon."

He paused there, waiting for . . . what? Joy? Thanks? I knew that was what he expected and what I needed to give him — for me, for James — but I couldn't find it inside me. When I finally managed to speak, my voice was small and shaky.

"And I'll . . . be doing what I did at the last base?"

Monroe nodded. "Exactly. Sergeant Rhames will be taking his men on an indefinite campaign into California. You'll infiltrate a town, preparing it for Rhames and his men. They'll lead the assault, bringing whoever they can to the Path before moving on. You've seen it done, so you know how it works. You leave in three days." Monroe stuck his hand out across the desk. "Congratulations. It's an incredible honor."

"But James," I said. "He'll still be made a citizen."

Monroe dropped his hand. "Callum . . ."

"You said —"

"I prayed hard on this, son. Believe me. Your brother is a fine valet. Best I ever had. But as much as I may want to, I cannot grant citizenship to someone with his . . . difficulties."

"But you gave him the medicine. If he takes it —"

"Giving him that medicine was a sentimental weakness on my part. I shouldn't have done it and I apologize."

"But, sir —"

"Each man walks his own Path, Cal. You got where you belong and your brother will do the same in time. You have to trust in that."

A helicopter flew by, toward Cormorant, kicking a cloud of dust into the empty lot and snapping me back to the present.

The pin lay in my hand like a bit of molten gold. My arm ached to hurl it into the dunes, but I knew I couldn't. I needed to fix it to my collar and present myself to my new commander. To Rhames. I closed the metal in my fist and got up to go.

That's when I saw him.

The dog was standing on a nearby dune, watching me intently, his short legs tensed, ready to flee. He looked like a Doberman but at about a quarter of the size. He was deep black with blazes of copper on his legs, chest, and muzzle. Rust-colored pips sat above each eye, giving him expressive little eyebrows. His tail had been docked into a stub, and he had enormous ears that stood straight up.

The dogcatcher was inches from my fingers. He flinched as I went for it but didn't run. He leaned forward instead, curious, tongue out and panting. I imagined him back in Quarles's cage, cowering amid monsters twice his size, and pulled my hand back from the dogcatcher.

"Go on," I called. "Get out of here!"

When he didn't move, I kicked a cloud of dirt at him. He held his ground, so I grabbed a small rock, sure a glancing blow to his side would send him running. I lifted the stone, ready to throw, but my arm went weak.

The dog crept down his hill and then up mine. His muscles were taut, ready to flee if I made another wrong move. When he reached the top of the hill, his eyes darted over me, sharp and alert, the color of amber.

"Go on," I said again but softer this time.

Close up, I could see his ribs standing out as bold as a range of sand dunes. His short fur was filthy, matted with dried mud. I held out my hand tentatively and he sniffed at it. His nose, cool and wet, prickled the hair on my arms. He licked a patch of sweat off my forearm and then came closer. There was a barely healed wound on his side.

"You in a fight?"

He dipped his snout into my face and there was a metallic clink under his chin. I found his narrow pink collar and turned it around. There was a silver tag with two mostly scratched-off phone numbers on one side and a single word on the other.

Bear.

"Why would anyone name a dog Bear?"

"Rrrrr-Rup! Rup rup!"

I turned back to the grocery store, thought for a minute, and then started toward the entrance. The grocery store was abandoned but not completely empty. I walked up and down the aisles, Bear's claws clicking on the cracked linoleum behind me.

"Sorry," I said, standing in front of the cleaned-out pet section. "No Alpo left."

I spied a couple dusty water bottles left in a far corner. I took them along with the spare-change dish from the front counter, then went back outside. The second I got the dish full of water, Bear was on it, lapping hungrily and panting between gulps.

"Yeah, you're thirsty, all right."

While he drank I ran one hand along his side until it came to the gash. Something with claws had gone after him. I cracked open another bottle of water and knelt beside him. Bear growled when I poured water over the cut.

"Take it easy."

Bear's copper brows scrunched together as he eyed me, but soon enough he returned to his water, and I returned to the wound. I trickled water down his side, then swept along after it with an open palm as gently as I could, wiping away dirt and crusted blood. Long and shallow, it didn't look quite as bad as I had feared. After refilling his water dish, I moved farther along his flank, washing off the dried mud.

Once I was done and Bear drank his fill, he turned and stepped up into my lap.

"Hey. Wait. You —"

He ignored me, spinning a few times before dropping down and laying his snout across my knee. He yawned and then the thump of his heartbeat slowed against the side of my leg. I leaned over him. His fur smelled warm and haylike. My palm fell on his side and I petted him with long, even strokes.

"Mom said when me and James got back from Phoenix, we'd go to the shelter and pick out a dog. But then we never came back."

Bear huffed and squirmed. I looked over him at the emptiness that stretched north and east. Somewhere on the other side of all that was home.

Ithaca.

For years I had pushed thoughts of it, along with thoughts of Mom and Dad, out of my head as fast as they came. I was afraid they would sweep me away, back to the terrified kid I was six years ago. But sitting there with my hand on Bear's side, I felt anchored in place and I let the memories draw near. When I did, I realized how indistinct they had become, like photographs faded in the sun. Had Mom's hair been fully blond or was there brown in it too? Who was taller, Mom or Dad? What exactly was the tattoo on Dad's right arm, and what kind of guitar was it that he would play for us every night after dinner?

I wondered if I'd reach the day when the memories of them would fade entirely and I'd be left with just my years in the Path camp. What would it be like to look backward and see nothing but stretches of desert and the stubbly, bloated face of Benjamin Quarles? How would it be to trade the sound of Mom singing Joni Mitchell songs to the strumming of Dad's guitar for the chop of helicopter rotors and the bay of starving dogs?

How much longer would it be before I lost them forever?

There was a rush of wind as a beat-up supply truck appeared on the highway, kicking up a trail of dust as it headed into Cormorant. Bear lifted his head.

"Rup! Rup rup! RRRRR-RUP!"

"Well done," I said. "You really scared them off."

Bear jumped up and headed toward the parking lot. He rooted about in the debris by the gas station until he discovered a length of black rubber. He brought it over and dropped it between us.

"Rup! Rup rup!"

"I don't want to play," I said.

Bear wouldn't take no for an answer. He edged the stick of rubber toward me with his nose and barked until I tossed it away halfheartedly. Bear exploded across the parking lot and dove on top of it, tumbling over onto his side and then trapping it under his paws like a fleeing squirrel. Once it had been subdued, he took it in his jaws and proudly dropped it at my feet.

"Rup!"

I laughed and snatched it up again. Bear leapt up onto his hind legs and danced in anticipation, his forepaws clawing at the air.

"Oh. Bear. Like a dancing Bear. I get it now."

I threw it out into the desert, each time farther and farther away. We played until I collapsed into the sand. My wrist ached underneath the cast, but it felt distant now, muted by exhaustion. Bear protested my idleness with a few playful growls, then dropped down beside me, nestling into the crook of my arm, his front paws on my chest. He held his head erect, scanning the desert, his ears on alert, panting happily. I raised one rubbery arm and took his silver tag in my fingers.

I saw him then as the family dog he must have been once. Curled up on a couch and sleeping with his family. Eating from a bowl with his name on it. Nothing at all like the monsters kept by Quarles, whose eagerness for anything other than blood and violence had been starved out of them ages ago. I ran my fingertip over the scratched-out phone numbers on the tag and wondered if Bear still thought of his old owners and his old life. Was he trying to get back to them, or had he given up too?

Bear dug his snout beneath my hand, urging me to pet him. I cupped my palm against his cheek and drew it back over his ears. His fur was smooth and warm.

We dozed a moment and when I opened my eyes again, the sun had dipped into the west. What time was it that Quarles had sent me away? Nine thirty? Ten? I realized with a shock that it had to have been hours ago.

I jumped up and started back toward the lot. Bear trotted along behind me and when I stopped to pick up the dogcatcher, he planted himself in front of me, eyes bright and expectant. I dropped the dogcatcher and took his head in my hands.

"You can't come with me," I said, a dull ache growing in my chest. "It's not a good place."

Bear shook himself away, dancing backward like we were playing again. When I didn't follow, he stood there, staring back at me.

"You're going to have to find your way back home, okay? It can't be far."

I wished he could understand me, but I knew it was pointless. Nothing could change what had to happen next. I had to go present myself to Rhames, and Bear had to go his own way. There was no sense in putting it off. I moved toward the road but Bear raced by, beating me to the parking lot. When I caught up to him, he was staring out toward Cormorant and barking wildly.

A dust cloud rose in the desert across the road. I squinted into the sunny glare and saw that it was centered around a black Ford pickup that was racing in our direction. It was one I'd know anywhere, one that only a single person would be driving.

Quarles.

I didn't even think. I grabbed Bear's collar and ran.

6

Quarles threw open the door of his truck and stepped out.

"Where've you been?"

"I was looking for the dog," I said. "I thought he was somewhere behind the store and —"

"I tell you to do a thing, you do it and come back. You don't make me wait. You don't take your time."

"I'm sorry," I said. "I thought I could find him, but I guess he —"

Quarles's open hand slammed into my jaw, nearly knocking me down.

"Don't lie to me. Supply truck radioed about some kid playing with a mutt." Quarles reached for the dogcatcher he kept in a metal sleeve on the side of the truck. "Useless. Like always, if I want something done, it's on me."

"Look," I said, jogging to keep up with him. "I found him. Okay? But he was too fast. I almost had him, but then he ran off and I couldn't get him. He's just one dog. Little too. We should get back for afternoon prayers."

Quarles ignored me and checked each storefront. I hoped he would get frustrated by the time he reached the supermarket, but when he got there, he went in the front door. I followed him, barely breathing, as he moved up and down the aisles. When his back was to me, I looked into the corner where a short hall led down to two bathroom doors. Both were closed.

Five minutes, I thought, staring back at the hall. *Just be quiet for five more minutes.*

Quarles finished going through the rows and headed toward the register.

"I told you, he's not —"

A high-pitched whine came from the back hall. Quarles froze, his hand tense on the shaft of the dogcatcher.

No. "Wait. Quarles . . ."

By the time Quarles reached the hallway, Bear's claws were scraping against the thin wooden door. His free hand fell to the bludgeon on his belt.

"He's not worth it."

He turned and stabbed the tip of the lead club into my chest.

"I'm rid of you soon," he said in a deadly rumble. "So what you do isn't my concern anymore. But you're going to help me take this one. Make my life harder and I'll tell Monroe what you've done."

A sick feeling was growing in my gut, but I somehow managed to nod. Quarles forced the bludgeon into my hands.

"If he gives me a problem, put him down."

Quarles moved to the door. I wanted to tell him to stop, wanted to beg him, but a bad word from him to Monroe could hurt me, hurt James. I just stood there, stupid and small, as he reached for the door handle. When he opened it, Bear was sitting in the center of the room, ears up, tongue hanging out of his mouth.

"This mutt is what you were keeping from me?"

He reached for Bear's collar, but there was a growl and then Quarles reared back with a yelp. Bear darted through his legs and into the store. When Quarles staggered out of the bathroom, one hand was dripping blood onto the tile floor.

"No stray bites me," he said as he drew a black .38.

I backed out of the hall, keeping between Quarles and Bear, the club in my hand. Quarles thumbed the hammer back and leveled the gun at my chest.

"I can kill you too, boy. Nobody'd question me. Now move away."

I was rooted in place, couldn't move if I wanted to. Quarles made a disgusted sound and pushed past me. As soon as he did, something in me unlocked. I twisted around and swung for his wrist, shattering it with the club. Quarles dropped to his knees with a scream, sending the gun skidding across the linoleum. I stepped back, amazed at what I had done. Quarles looked at me with blood-shot eyes.

"Quarles, wait. I didn't mean to —"

"I should thank you," he said, drawing himself up. "Gives me the reason to do what I've wanted to do since I met you."

Quarles lurched forward, grabbing my collar and swinging me into one of the floor displays. My bad arm hit the shelf, and the pain sent me to the floor. The club skittered away from me.

I tried to get up, but Quarles drove his fist into my stomach, knocking the wind out of me. He lifted his hand again, and Bear jumped at him with a snarl, digging his teeth into the man's calf and thrashing wildly. Quarles kicked him into a far wall and then scooped up the club. Bear cowered, ears back, eyes wide, as Quarles came for him.

My hand hit a hot piece of metal as I scrambled away. Quarles's revolver. I grabbed it just as Quarles was raising the club over Bear's skull.

He was starting to swing when I lifted the gun and pulled the trigger.

7

I sat with my back wedged into a corner, ears ringing, my hand cramping around the handle of the revolver. Time seemed to distort around me, speeding past, then slowing to a crawl.

There was a shuffling sound beside me. Bear had come around Quarles, and we were sitting shoulder to shoulder. He shifted his weight from paw to paw with an urgent whine.

Quarles was facedown with three bullet wounds in his back, one high and two low. Each one was a spot of black ringed by a circle of dark red. A pool of blood, the thickness of motor oil, had spread out underneath him, a misshapen circle stretching from his waist to his head.

I heaved violently, vomiting up acidic bile. After it passed, I stayed there on my knees, my stomach muscles clenching. I breathed deep until they stilled, then turned to the door. Quarles's truck sat across the parking lot, a black splotch against the tan desert. How long had it been sitting there now? Minutes? Hours? I imagined the dogs going mad for food back in their kennels. How long until someone noticed? How long before they came looking?

I forced myself up onto legs as shaky as a fawn's, then took a few steps before squatting down by the dead man's shoulders. His face was turned toward me and his eyes were open wide, staring blankly. Their blue centers were surrounded by a maze of burst blood vessels.

I grabbed the edge of Quarles's coat in my one good hand and threw myself toward the back hall. His body skidded a few inches, but the effort forced me to my knees, panting. There were at least five more feet between him and the narrow bathroom door.

Bear stood by the door, watching me, his front paws tapping anxiously against the tile.

I dug my heels into the floor and I pulled again, grunting, until his body moved. I got him another few inches, rested, and did it again and again until we were at the edge of the bathroom. I dropped his coat and collapsed against the wall.

Bear scurried across the store, giving the slick of blood a wide berth. He sat before me, making an impatient huffing sound. Somehow I got up again and pulled until I got Quarles into the bathroom.

His body ended up curled around the base of the filthy toilet, chin on his chest, arms limp at his sides. Looking down at him, numbness spread through me, and I felt like I was seeing him from high above. I suddenly realized how little I knew about him. Did he have a wife? Children?

I staggered out of the bathroom and shut the door.

Bear stayed close as I covered Quarles's blood with whatever trash I could find. If someone was searching the store, they would figure out what happened pretty quick, but it might at least buy me some time.

But time to do what?

I didn't breathe at the Cormorant checkpoint. My hand gripped the steering wheel as two sentries looked over the truck in front of me. I checked the rearview. Bear was lying on his side in one of the back cages. When I looked forward, one of the sentries was waving me up.

He took my tech operator's dispensation papers and studied them. His sleek M4 hung on his chest, one hand never more than a few inches from the grip and trigger.

"This is Quarles's rig?" he asked, looking down the length of the truck.

"Yes, sir," I said. "He's gone after a pack we found. He wanted me to drop this dog back in the kennels and come back for him tonight."

"No one in or out until after prayers and supper."

"Yes, sir," I said. "No problem."

He waved me on and I pulled the truck through the gate and up to the kennel. It was fully dark by the time I parked and got Bear out of his cage. Inside the kennel, the dogs were barking wildly, starved for the supper no one had given them. Bear shied away, trembling. He wouldn't move, so I had to lift him awkwardly onto my shoulder with one hand and carry him down the aisle.

"It won't be for long," I said. "Promise."

The other dogs threw themselves against the bars of their cages and snarled at the intruder in their midst. When I finally got Bear into a cage, he pressed himself up against the bars and whined.

"I'll be back," I said, reaching my fingers through the bars to scratch his ear.

Bear retreated to the far corner of his cage and cringed away from the other dogs. I hated leaving him there, but what could I do?

I left the kennel and then climbed the hill into camp just as the last of the crowds were moving into the Lighthouse. I caught sight of James at the rear of the pack and yanked him out of line.

"Cal? What are you —"

I put one finger to my lips and pulled him away, keeping us to the shadows as we made our way down to the barracks. Once we were inside, I lit a single lantern and shut the door.

"What are you doing?"

I took James's backpack out of our footlocker and pushed it into his chest. "Fill it."

"Why? Cal, what's going on?"

"We have to go," I said, turning my back to him and filling my pack with clothes, camping gear, maps.

"Go where? What are you — Why do you have blood on your clothes?"

I was leaning over my bunk, the straps of the backpack tight in my hand. Looking down, I saw that my pants, from cuffs to knee, were stained with Quarles's blood.

"There was an accident," I said quietly, my back still to James. "With Quarles."

"Is he dead?"

The words stuck in my throat but I didn't need to say anything. James could see. I pulled him down onto the bunk beside me.

"We need to leave," I said. "Now."

"Leave? What are you —"

"Quarles's truck is out by the kennels. I told the sentries I'd be driving out again tonight to look for a pack of strays."

"Where would we even go?"

"I don't know. West maybe, cross into California. We'll figure it out."

"But —"

"If they find him, I'm dead."

James went quiet, staring down at the concrete floor. The walls of the barracks ticked as the building settled into the desert night.

"James?"

"We'll go to Monroe together," he said slowly. "We'll explain it to him. He was just about to make us both citizens. He'll —"

"It was a lie. He's going to keep you as his valet and send me away with Rhames to be a soldier."

James looked up at me, his eyes sharp like he was searching out a lie. When he didn't find one, his face went dark, shadowed in flickering lantern light.

"Remember when we used to talk about escaping?" I said. "We put it aside for too long, James. This is our chance. We have to take it. Are you listening to me? We need to —"

"I'll get Milo," he said. "He can get into the storage sheds and draw us some supplies."

"There's no time for that."

"We need food," he said. "And a tent. I'll grab him on the way out of Lighthouse and meet you at the kennels."

"James."

"He won't talk," James said. "Don't worry. I'll be fast and we'll be gone before anybody knows what happened."

James rolled up off the cot and slung the pack from his shoulder.

"Everything is going to work out for the best," he said. "You'll see."

Looking up at him, I felt a surge of astonishment. For years I thought he was the weak one, the sickly one. Turns out I didn't know my brother at all.

I nodded and James slipped out of the barracks. I changed out of my uniform and into Path-issued boots, jeans, and a denim jacket. I threaded a sheathed knife onto my belt, then finished packing. I could feel the minutes ticking by double time.

I reached behind my back until I felt the warm end of Quarles's gun. I pulled it out and snapped the chamber open. One round left. The thought of having to use it again made me sick, but it would be stupid to leave it behind. If someone got in our way, we couldn't stop. I closed the chamber and tucked the gun into the small of my back. The last thing I did before I left was stuff my bloody clothes beneath my mattress.

Outside, bells began to chime. I slipped out of the barracks, one eye on the crowds exiting the Lighthouse.

I felt an unfamiliar buzz of hope as I moved into the shadows and ran toward the kennel.

The kennel was quiet when I got there, but it didn't last long. As soon as I stepped inside, the dogs began to stalk their cages, low growls in their throats. We had to move fast. Once they saw that dinner wasn't coming, every ear in camp would turn to the sound of their barking.

Bear met me at his gate with a whine. "See?" I said, scratching his snout. "Told ya I'd come back."

I threw open the bolt to his cage and led him past the cages in the back of the truck and into the passenger seat.

"No more cages for you, okay?"

By the time I got back to the kennel, the dogs had started to bark. The only thing that would keep them from an all-out revolt was food.

I grabbed the scraps bucket, but before I could give out the first taste, I heard footsteps behind me. I turned with a start. It was only James silhouetted in the dim glow of an open door.

"Where's your stuff?"

"Left it by the truck."

"Great," I said, dropping the bucket onto the cement floor. Someone would come by the next day and feed them. They weren't my problem anymore. "Milo come through?"

"Yeah, he was perfect."

"Good. Come on, let's get out of here before these dogs bust their cages."

James grabbed my sleeve and held me back. "Cal, wait. Maybe there's another way."

"I told you. If they catch me —"

"I know, but listen, the two of us? Running in an old pickup truck? And we don't even know where we're going? They'll find us. You know they will. We should just go talk to Monroe."

I took him by the shoulders to calm him down. "You just have to hang in there a little while longer. We can talk more in the truck. Now, come on."

I started to go but stopped dead before I made it three steps. Two soldiers had appeared in the shadows, blocking the exit.

"Cal . . ."

I eased back slowly, drawing James along with me.

"Go on," I whispered, trying to keep my voice low and steady. "Out the back door. Head for the truck."

Two more soldiers stepped into the doorway behind us. The growls from the pens grew louder, sawing at the air. One hand disappeared behind my back and found the butt of the revolver.

"Get ready to run," I said.

"You have to talk to them, Cal."

I turned to James and found him staring at me through the gloom. "James?"

He took a step toward me. "I told them it was an accident," he said. "Captain Monroe knows what Quarles is like. All you have to do is come with us and talk to him about it. We'll get you back on Path."

"They'll kill me!"

James took another step and I grabbed him, whipping Quarles's revolver out from behind my back at the same time. The soldiers rushed forward, sweeping the rifles from their shoulders and clicking off the safeties.

"Wait!" James pleaded with the soldiers. "It's okay. Cal, just give me the gun and we can talk. They're surrounding the kennel. There's nowhere to go."

I looked up above me and backed up slow into a dark corner, keeping James close. The soldiers eased in, stepping into the main aisle as they converged. Behind me, the snarls of the dogs moved from cage to cage like rolls of thunder.

"When did they get to you?" I said, edging backward. I could feel the far wall get closer. "Huh?"

"Just put the gun down. They'll listen to you."

My back hit the wall. Two chains rattled above me.

"I don't think so."

"Cal —"

I grabbed one of the chains and gave a sharp tug. The cage doors flew open and dozens of half-starved animals burst into the aisle. The soldiers tried to back away but the dogs were faster. There was a scream as one man went down and then the others began firing their weapons wildly. Rounds crashed into the cages and the walls. A few animals howled pitifully and fell.

I clamped both arms around James and ran for the back door. Reinforcements were already coming in from across the camp. I pushed James into the truck's passenger seat with Bear and slammed the door. The sentries at the main gate were moving into position. I pulled James's seat belt over him and Bear and cranked the engine. Shots crackled behind us, slamming into the cages in back. I hit the gas.

"Cal, this is crazy. You have to stop!"

"Put your head down!"

Rounds pinged off the side of the truck as the sentries began firing. When it became clear that I wasn't stopping, they fired a few more rounds, then dodged out of the way.

There was a squeal of metal as we hit the gate and tore it from its moorings. I kept my foot hard on the gas, and we were through, dragging pieces of torn steel behind us. The highway west was only minutes away.

"This isn't going to work," James said. He was pressed into the passenger-side corner, Bear in his lap. "Seriously, how do you see this ending? We can't —"

Rotating red and blue lights appeared in the rearview mirror, followed by wailing sirens. Military Police. My stomach tightened.

"Cal?"

The lights grew brighter as they gained on us, filling the inside of the truck. The exit onto the highway was just ahead.

"You can't outrun them," James said. "We're in the middle of nowhere, so it's not like you can lose them. What happens when they get a chopper in the air?"

"They're not sending a chopper after two kids in a stolen truck."

"PULL OVER!" an MP announced over his loudspeaker. "YOU ARE UNDER ARREST."

I swerved at the last second and took the highway exit. The MP overshot it, but as I accelerated down the ramp and onto an empty two-lane road, I heard his brakes squeal. It was only seconds before the MP's lights emerged in the rearview again. The truck's engine revved as the speedometer climbed past seventy, then eighty. It hit ninety and the truck began to shake. Still, the MP drew closer.

"Even if we made it to the border," James said calmly, "no one will let us across. Monroe will listen to you, Cal. I promise."

"When did you do it?" I asked. "When did you trade Mom and Dad for him?"

"I didn't," James said. "I grew up. That's all."

The panic that had been fueling me began to drain away, replaced by a buzzing numbness. My foot eased off the gas and the truck slowed. Eighty-five. Eighty. The MP cruiser was moving alongside us now, its bumper approaching my door.

"It's okay," James said soothingly. "We'll go back home and everything will be just like it was."

Just the sound of that word in his mouth, *home*, and something inside of me went molten. I glanced out the side window. The cruiser had pulled even and was moving ahead.

"Hold on to Bear," I said.

"What? Cal —"

I jerked the wheel, hurling us into the side of the cruiser. There was a shriek as metal hit metal and then a split second of weightlessness before the seat belt yanked me back. James's screams, mixed with the glass and steel crash. Everything was lit by the red and blue of the police lights until they winked out and everything went dark.

We ended up sideways in the middle of the road. The windshield was a spiderweb of fractures, and smoke poured out of the hood. James was slumped in his seat, dead pale with his arms clapped around Bear.

The cruiser was twenty feet down the road, flipped upside down at the end of a trail of shattered glass and torn metal. The windows were smashed and I couldn't see anyone moving inside.

"James? Are you okay?"

He moaned. I pushed open my door, but my legs were useless. I collapsed the second they hit asphalt. I lay facedown, every nerve in my body buzzing at once. *No time*, I thought, nearly delirious. *Got to move.* Glass crunched under my palm as I forced myself up. I kept one eye on the cruiser as I came around the front of the truck, like it was a monster that could come to life any second.

Bear was as dazed as James, whimpering and shaking as I lifted him out of the truck. I checked him for injuries but found only cuts and scrapes. I set him down by the side of the road, then undid James's seat belt. He fell into my arms and I eased him down beside Bear and grabbed our backpacks. I got mine on and staggered out into the roadway.

"Come on," I said, draping the backpack over James's shoulders. "We have to go."

"No," he mumbled, nodding listlessly toward the wrecked MP cruiser. "We have to stay. Have to help them."

I stared at the cruiser. There was still no movement inside. No sound.

"They're fine," I said. "Let's go. Bear, come on."

James tried to pull away from me but he was too weak. I threw my arm around his shoulder and drew him away from the side of the road. Bear trailed along behind us as we moved into the desert.

I dragged James along until the flat land fell away and we found ourselves at the crest of a ravine. There was a narrow trail heading down into it, but it was impossible to see how far it went or if it would even support our weight. I looked around for another option and found none. I pulled a single chemical glow stick out of my pack and cracked it. Any light was risky, but taking the trail blind was sure to be suicide.

I headed down first, stepping slowly into the chem stick's pale green glow. James came next, with Bear sniffing along behind us. Now that the shock of the crash had passed, every step sent waves of pain through my body. The bones in my wrist felt like they were grinding together. Soon, exhaustion began to nip at every muscle, settling over my thoughts like a fog. The dark of the chasm yawned beside us as the trail grew more and more narrow. We had to find someplace to rest, and fast.

It was an hour or more before I let James sink to the rocky floor and then sat down beside him, struggling to catch my breath and wishing away every stabbing pain throughout my body. When I could summon the strength to move again, I cracked another glow stick and looked around.

We were on a small shelf of rock just wide enough for the three of us. Bear sat panting, eyes shining eerily in the chemical green. The gash on his side was still sealed, but he yanked one of his front paws away with a yelp when I tried to look at it. He tucked it close to his body and licked at it.

James was beside me, bent in half over his knees, with his back to me.

"James?" He didn't turn, so I reached for his shoulder. "Listen to me. I —"

He fell into the light and I saw that his mouth was open wide and he was gasping soundlessly, tears streaking the sides of his face. Both hands were clasped over his chest, clawing at his lungs.

I dropped the light and tore through my pack, nerves screaming as I searched through clothes and useless gear. I found the inhaler, dropped it, grabbed it again. James started to thrash in the middle of the trail, pounding at the dirt with one fist, his face streaked with panic. I pulled him to me and set the inhaler to his lips, but one hand flew up and knocked it away.

"Don't need," he insisted in a tortured rattle. "Don't . . . need . . ."

"Yes, you do. Now take it before you pass out."

I forced the inhaler into his mouth and clamped his jaw shut around it. I triggered a blast of medicine into him and then another.

I watched as he struggled, and timed the next blast for the tiny intake he could manage. With each puff from the inhaler, I felt the rigid muscles in James's back yield. The wheeze faded and James settled into a halting, staticky breath. His arms were limp, and even in the green glow, I could see the palor of his skin and the sheen of cold sweat all over him. I dropped the inhaler and wiped the sweat from his forehead.

"You're okay," I whispered. "You're going to be okay."

Bear appeared in the dark, sniffing at him with great concern. James managed to lift one weak hand and pat his side. He took a shaky breath, then pulled himself into the deeper shadows on the opposite side of the platform. Bear followed, standing halfway between the two of us. He looked over his shoulder at me.

"Look," I said to James's back. "You need time to adjust. Okay? Once we get away from them, you'll see."

I stopped at the faint sound of James's voice.

"James? I can't hear you. What are you saying?"

I moved closer until I was at his back. I put my hand on his shoulder and turned him around.

". . . consecrate my life to the Glorious Path. I am the light in the darkness. The hand offering guidance to those who have gone astray. I am the rod that falls upon the backs of the defiant. . . ."

My hand fell from his shoulder as I backed away. The glow of the chem stick faded and I was left there in the deep dark with nothing but the sound of my brother praying.

8

I spread our map out on the ground the next morning and bent over it.

Path states were bordered in gold, Fed in blue. I used a pencil to sketch out the western and eastern fronts. The closest Federal territory was California, but that was a pipe dream. California was a major prize for the Path, second only to the new Federal capital in Philadelphia. Fighting along the border had been intense for years. James was right; we could never cross there.

I moved my finger over the map to Nevada and Oregon, which, with California, made up the Federal-controlled land in the region. Nevada was a slightly better bet, but it was still westward, the wrong direction, and the word for the last few weeks was that Idaho was probably going to fall any day. If we were in Nevada when that happened, it'd close off our only route back to New York. We'd be trapped on the West Coast until the end of the war — forever if the Path came out on top.

The only possibility left was Wyoming, which seemed insane. Between us and Wyoming were more than eight hundred miles of

Path lands in Arizona and Utah. On top of that, Salt Lake City sat too close to the Utah–Wyoming border and was among one of the Path's major strongholds. Two scruffy-looking kids and a dog trying to walk anywhere near that city would be in jail before they took two steps.

I kicked the map away and sat back against a rock. It couldn't have been more than eight o'clock in the morning and the sun was already intense. I wiped a film of sweat from my forehead and reached for our canteen but stopped before taking a drink. It was almost a thousand miles to Fed territory and we had one canteen and a handful of food. I set the water back down.

James was at the end of the trail, knees hugged to his chest, watching without expression as Bear splashed about in a thin stream of water. James and I hadn't said a word to each other since we'd woken up at dawn.

I rummaged in my pack and threw an MRE down to him.

"You should eat," I said. "We'll leave as soon as it gets dark."

"Leave for where?"

I grabbed my own breakfast and ripped it open. Beef stew. "Home."

"You think you're going to get all the way to New York? Cal —"

"We just have to get across the border," I said. "Once we explain that we're captures, the Feds will help us from there. And the Path isn't going to get bent out of shape searching for two escaped novices. We'll travel at night. We'll be careful."

"You can't run away from this."

"Run away from what?"

"You *killed* someone."

It was like a punch in the gut. I flexed the sore muscles of my right hand, still able to feel the kick of the gun.

"You know the kind of person Quarles was."

"And you made sure he never had the chance to become anything better."

I glared across our camp. "And how many people has the Path killed, James?"

"It's a war. It's different."

"You learn a lot about war sitting in camp and fetching Monroe's coffee?"

"As much as you did mucking out a dog kennel."

I threw the half-eaten MRE into the dirt and stormed down the trail.

"You want to know how I really got that medicine for you?" I asked, holding up my cast. "How I got this? It was a little deal I worked out with your buddy Monroe. Your medicine in exchange for Rhames going at me with a baseball bat so I'd look pathetic enough to draw some Feds out of their base. I was right there, James. I listened while they gave them the Choice, while they murdered men, women, and children."

"That's not true!" James said. "Anyone who refuses the Path is taken to a camp until the end of the war. After the war —"

"I was there! I was right there. What did they *do* to you?"

"They didn't do anything to me! I made a choice."

"Then make another one. Get your things together. As soon as it's dark, we leave."

"I'm not going."

"I swear to God, I will tie you up and drag you home if I have to."

James pressed his wrists together and thrust them toward me. "Do it."

"James —"

"I am on a Glorious Path," he spat at me, his voice quickly finding the rhythm of a first-year novice prayer. "I will not turn from it even if it means my death. I will not succumb to the temptations of the lost and the wicked. I will be their beacon instead."

He stood there, hands out, daring me. I went back and rooted through my backpack until I found a length of rope. Bear ran up from the stream, growing increasingly distressed as I bound James's wrists, yanking the knot tight enough to make him gasp.

"We leave when the sun goes down."

I left James, snatching the map off the ground and flattening it in front of me. I searched the map's blocks of gold and blue for a way out. Salt Lake City sat like a citadel near the southern edge of the Wyoming border, but north of that, the border looked nearly empty. A plan started to snap together — head north, skirting west to avoid Salt Lake City, then head east to cross the border. It was a tough route, but as long as we stayed away from the hornet's nest of SLC, maybe we had a chance.

I sat back and breathed deep, trying to calm the thud of a head-ache that was pounding just behind my eyes. Once it calmed, I drew my finger across the map, past Wyoming and South Dakota and Iowa, all the way to New York and Ithaca.

I closed my eyes, seeing it all as it was — the lake, the trees, the cobalt-blue walls of our house — going over each image like they were the words of a prayer.

After the sun had been down for more than an hour, I threw on my backpack and went down to the stream. James and Bear were nowhere to be found.

"James?" I called as loudly as I dared. Nothing. "Bear?"

I cracked another chem light and held it up. A shuffling sound came from somewhere beyond its reach. I crept toward it as silently as I could until I came around a pillar of rock and saw him.

James was on his knees in the dirt, his back to me, his bound hands in front of him. His forehead was pressed into Bear's neck and his entire body was shaking. At first I thought he was having another attack, but then I heard his voice.

"I just want to go home."

He said it over and over, quiet, but so strained it was like the words were slicing his throat on their way out.

"I just want to go home. I just want to go home. I just want to go home."

Bear grew anxious, dancing back and forth and then setting his front paws on James's legs with a whine. James flung his hands over Bear's head, drawing him in as he cried. Soon Bear went still and then James did too.

A rock shifted as I took a step, and James turned toward the sound. When he saw me, he left Bear and slowly crossed into the circle of green light. James put his bound hands out in front of him.

"You said you'd be dragging me."

Bear whimpered at his feet, staring up at me. I seized the ropes and flung James out onto the path ahead of me. He stumbled, nearly pitching into the dirt before righting himself and continuing on without a word. Bear shied back with a growl.

"What? You want to stay?"

Bear barked once, an angry yap, but then I took his collar and hurried him along too. As we climbed, the deep blue sky shaded to black. By the time we were topside, the stars were out, circling a full moon. The land was quiet and flat, vastly dark. Bear dashed out into the night to explore. I found the Big Dipper and traced a line from it to the North Star.

Beside me, James began to pray.

It was like a knot tightening inside me. I remembered the nights I stood in the dark by his bunk trying to quiet him as he sobbed. We'd just been taken by the Path and he'd gone days without food, surviving on nothing but the few drops of water I was able to force into him. How many of those nights had I lain below him in the bunk, sleepless, terrified that I'd wake to find my brother dead of grief?

Listening to him pray, some dark part of me wished I had. I felt sick even as I thought it, but at that moment, even his absence seemed more welcome than standing beside this stranger.

"We should go if we're going," James said when he finished his prayer.

I slipped my knife out of its sheath and cut his bonds with a single slash. James looked up at me, confused, as the ropes fell to the ground. I shoved his pack into his chest.

"Go home."

James was motionless for a few seconds and then he drew the pack toward him.

"Maybe we don't have to go back to Cormorant," he said, tempering the edge in his voice. "Beacon Quan told me about this place in Oklahoma called Foley. It's a real Path town, way behind the lines. Just a few farms and a small Lighthouse. Maybe we could —"

"The highway we came in on is that way. Leave now and you'll be in your bunk before morning."

James started to protest, but whatever fight he had in him seemed to evaporate. "What do you want me to tell Monroe?"

"Tell him whatever you want," I snapped. And then, "Tell him . . . tell him I had a gun and I tried to force you to come with me but you managed to escape. Say I'm heading west to California."

James nodded. I dug through my own pack and held out the asthma inhalers.

"Here."

"I don't need them."

"Don't be —"

"I don't have asthma."

"Then what was that last night?"

James kicked the sand at his feet and then looked up at me. His eyes were gray in the moonlight. "A lack of faith."

"James . . ."

"I should go."

Bear trotted out of the dark, tail wagging. He ran to James, who dropped down beside him and gave him a scratch under his chin.

"Take care of him," he said.

James slipped his backpack on and started away. Bear followed for a few steps and then stopped to look back at me, confused. He barked toward James, but my brother had already begun to melt into the darkness.

I wanted to call out to him, stop him, but I knew it was useless. Even if I found the right thing to say, even if he walked by my side for the next thousand miles, the truth was I lost my brother years ago. I stood there until the dark overtook him, and the whisper of his footsteps faded away to nothing.

"Come on, Bear," I said, and then I put my back to all of it and headed north.

• • •

Bear and I walked until we fell from exhaustion.

We were at the edge of a cliff. The moonlit desert spread out below us, huge and blank. Bear went to work on his paws, licking at the pads and digging out small stones and grit. I put an MRE down in front of him, then tore open one of my own. It tasted as bland as sawdust, but I forced down every bite. As I reached for our canteen, something rustled behind me. I whipped around, thinking I'd see James coming out of the dark, but there was nothing but desert brush blowing in the wind.

I imagined him back at Cormorant, safe in his bunk, but then all the things that could have gone wrong struck me. He could have gotten lost, or hurt or —

I slammed the door on the thought. James got what he wanted. There was no reason to dwell on it. I poured Bear some water, then dug through my pack, searching for something to fight the chill that numbed my fingers and toes. I found two sweaters and slipped one on over my T-shirt and tucked the other tight around Bear. I thrust my bare hand into my pocket and lay out alongside Bear to share warmth.

I closed my eyes, desperate for sleep, but nothing inside of me would go still. James haunted me no matter how hard I tried to push him away.

I remembered one Sunday night when Dad set up our "bunk beds" — what he called two hammocks hung in the backyard garden, one above and one below. That night it was a reward for me and James behaving when we took Grandma Betty to church. Or James behaving, really. I was simply half asleep, observing the homily through half-closed eyes. James sat up tall in the pew, listening with his whole body. Even then I thought he was simply playing an expert-level game of "Good Son."

That night I lay in the top bunk mashing buttons on my PlayStation, with James below me. Mom and Dad and Grandma Betty were inside the house, just visible through the living room window. Dad was playing a new song for them. His voice mixed effortlessly with the jangle of his guitar and the tinkling of Mom's and Grandma's wineglasses.

> *"Moonlight girl,*
> *Why'd you leave me so soon?*
> *I'm rambling and I'm ragged and I'm running on fumes.*
> *Moonlight road,*
> *Why don't you lead me on home?"*

Eventually they went to bed and shut out the lights, leaving me and James alone in the dark. The creaking sway of the hammocks' ropes against the maple tree made me think of the rigging of a sailing ship. I closed my eyes and imagined us as sailors at sea, crashing through the waves.

"Why doesn't it all just fall apart?"

I had thought James was asleep until his voice rose up from the bottom bunk.

"Why doesn't what fall apart?"

There was a long pause and I leaned over the bunk. James seemed to be staring past me and the tree branches and the wisps of clouds to the stars.

"Everything," he said.

I sat up in the desert, clamping my arms around my middle and leaning over my knees. It felt like there was an immense weight pressing down on me from all sides. Something touched my jacket, and I turned with a start.

Bear had his front paws perched on my shoulder. He was very still, examining me closely, his tan-dotted brows drawn together. He let out a breathy woof and I pulled him to my chest, inhaling the warm smell of him. My breath quaked in my throat as it went down. I let Bear go and he fell into my lap, drawing his legs beneath him. I tucked the sweater back over him and sat there with my palm on his side.

I looked up at the stars. Among them, the moon was full and white. A ghostly snatch of music swirled around me.

"Moonlight road," I sang, hearing the chords in my head. "Why don't you lead me on home?"

Bear twitched and shuffled. I ran my hand over the gloss of his coat and pulled him in tight. I looked over my shoulder again, out at the miles of darkness stretching to the south.

He's where he belongs, I thought, and heard a door fall closed in my mind. I turned back to Bear and sang to him until he fell asleep.

PART TWO

9

I woke at dawn to find a mile-long line of vehicles parked beneath the cliff we had camped on.

Turned out that our hill overlooked a northbound highway that was now filled with a mix of Path and conscripted civilian trucks. The convoy was bookended by heavily armed Humvees and led by a minesweeper that had come to a stop and was surrounded by a small company of soldiers.

All along the line, drivers had left their cabs to lean over their engines or pace impatiently along the highway shoulder. Bear stretched out beside me, watching the trucks with his ears at attention.

"Supply convoy," I said. "If we're lucky, it'll run right along the western front to the Utah border. Maybe farther."

Bear looked at me quizzically.

"You feeling lucky?"

Bear huffed impatiently and thumped the ground with his paws.

"Yeah, me neither. Come on."

Bear followed as I crept down a narrow trail. Rocks and slick patches of dusty sand slipped underneath my feet. A night of rest had blunted the knifelike throb of my injuries, but just barely. Bear seemed better off, though, navigating each obstacle like he was born on a mountain. I had to keep a hold on his collar the whole way down, afraid that if either of us hurried, we'd be seen and it would be game over.

We crouched behind a low outcropping of rock at the foot of the cliff. A silver-and-red eighteen-wheeler sat directly across from us. Its driver was circling his rig nervously, eager to go, and watchful. No help there. Ahead of him sat five more civvy trucks. Their cargo doors were open, but they were surrounded by groups of drivers talking and waiting for the signal to move.

Bear and I kept low and close to the cliff face as we went down the line of trucks, studying each one in turn. We came to the second to the last, a beleaguered-looking blue-and-white tractor-trailer. The driver stood at the back by his open cargo door, pulling out and restowing pallets of bread and boxes of dry goods.

There was a radio squawk from the cab of the truck, and the driver ran around to get it, leaving the cargo door hanging open. The driver in the truck behind him was nowhere to be seen, and the Humvees at the rear of the convoy were empty. It was our chance. I pulled at Bear's collar and we both sprinted toward the highway.

When we reached the rear of the truck, I scooped Bear up and tossed him into the cargo hold. I climbed up after him and he circled my legs, panting and pawing at me as I pushed us back to the far end of the trailer. I sat us down behind a set of shelving units that ran floor to ceiling down the truck. The driver's door slammed again. Bear surged forward but I grabbed him, holding him back into my chest with my cast. I had to clasp my other hand over his muzzle to keep him quiet.

Footsteps came down the asphalt on the other side of the truck's wall. Bear tried to squirm away and I petted him slowly across his back to calm him.

"Shhh," I breathed into his ear. "Shhh."

The footsteps paused at the back of the truck, and I listened with every cell in my body, heart thumping. Boots shifted against sandy asphalt and then he climbed up into the trailer. I held Bear tight, but he managed to wiggle his muzzle out of my hand and loose one sharp bark.

"Rup!"

My heart seized as it resounded off the close metal walls in the truck.

"Hello?"

Bear squirmed as I wedged us back into the corner, my mind spinning uselessly, searching for a plan. The man started moving again. I needed time, and there was only one thing that might get it for me. I let go of Bear and he jumped into the aisle and ran to the driver.

"Rup! Rup rup!"

"Well, hello. How did you get up here?"

Bear's tag jangled as the man wrestled with him. I felt the butt of Quarles's revolver sticking into my back, but I knew pulling it was out of the question. With so many soldiers around, the driver would know that shooting was an empty threat. Still, I dropped my hand beside it just in case while I tried to come up with a story.

"Somebody else back here?"

Bear's paws scrabbled against the wooden deck, with the driver's boots echoing behind him. Next thing I knew, Bear was piling into my lap, and I was looking up into the face of the truck driver.

His dark eyes were set deep within brown skin. He wore an untucked western shirt and worn boots. A chewed-up pencil was tucked behind one ear. We both froze a moment and then he looked out the back of the truck. I gripped the revolver, sure he was going to call for help, but then he slowly lowered himself to my level.

"Got a name, kid?" he asked.

I hesitated, my mouth dry as the desert floor. Had the Cormorant MPs released my name?

"Henry," I said, just to be safe.

"Henry," he repeated with a scant grin that might have said he didn't believe me and didn't particularly care. "My name's Grey. Grey Solomon. When's the last time you ate, kid?"

"When did I —"

Grey pulled a paper-wrapped package off a shelf and tossed it to me. "You're as skinny as a leaf. Here."

Bear dove for the package, shoving his nose inside and pawing at the wrapper. Grey laughed and hauled him off.

"Take it easy," he said. "Here. One for you too."

He threw another onto the floor. Bear jumped off my lap and buried his face in it, snorting as he devoured a small loaf of bread.

Grey turned back to me. "It's okay," he said. "Go ahead."

My stomach groaned at the idea of food. I opened the package and ate slowly.

"Don't know what it is," Grey said. "But the thought of somebody not eating just doesn't sit right with me. You're a runner, I guess."

"A runner?"

"You a novice running from the Path?"

Everything about Grey said citizen to me, but there wasn't the blaze of a fanatic in his eyes, just a kind of amused weariness. Still, it was best to be careful.

"No, sir," I said, keeping my voice small. "I'm a citizen. Farmhand on a ranch down south."

I moved forward, just enough so that my bruised face fell into the light. I set my cast on one bent knee, wincing as I did it.

"Who did this to you?"

"No one. I'm —"

"Son . . ."

"Our beacon," I admitted, quickly formulating a story. "He was . . . doing some things he shouldn't have been. Figured out I knew about it."

"And you saw a way to escape."

"Yes, sir."

Bear finished his bread and returned to Grey to beg for more. Grey pulled him close and scratched at his side.

"Where you headed?"

"Utah," I said. "North of Salt Lake City. I have a few relatives up there."

Grey considered a moment. Bear yipped as a driver behind us cranked his engine to life.

"Look," I said, getting to my feet, "I don't want to cause anybody trouble. I'll take Bear and go. You can —"

Grey stopped me with a hand to my chest. I could see his mind turning fast as he stared out the back of the truck. More engines started up ahead and behind. The convoy was getting ready to move. The truck behind us blew his horn, and Grey waved him down.

"Okay, kid, you just stay here and I'll —"

"Yo! Mr. Solomon! Time to go!"

Three Path soldiers jumped up into the truck. The leader stopped cold the second he saw me. He was bald and sinewy in desert-tan fatigues. A subtle nod from him sent the other two to opposite sides of the truck. Everyone's hands were on their weapons. Bear jumped forward, eager to meet his new friends, but I held him back by his collar.

"Who do we have here, Mr. Solomon?"

I was about to jump in, but Grey beat me to it.

"Mr. Vasquez! This here is my sister's boy," Grey said, as smooth as could be. "Adopted. He lost his folks in a Fed bombing raid. He was *supposed* to join us back in Yuma."

"I'm sorry, Uncle Grey."

Grey turned to me. "And you brought that damn dog."

"He just followed me!"

Grey rolled his eyes, then dug through a box on one of the shelves. "Look, fellas," he said with a smile. "He missed the convoy and just now got caught up. I told his mom I'd try to get him back on Path and if I don't, *my* mom is going to have my hide. You understand."

Grey lifted his hand from the box and held three big bars of chocolate out to the men.

"He won't cause any more trouble. I promise."

Vasquez ignored him, staying sharp, his eyes moving from me and Bear to Grey and back, his index finger tapping his trigger guard.

"Your pack," he said to me. "Take it off and kick it over."

I slipped out of my backpack and tossed it between us. Vasquez took a knee and tore through it, scattering my clothes around the truck. The revolver in my back felt like it was on fire. What if they wanted to pat me down? There was nothing behind the soldiers but highway and desert. Even if I managed to run, there was nowhere to go.

"Satisfied, Mr. Vasquez?"

Vasquez looked up over my things, eyeing me hard before turning back to Grey.

"Like you said, Mr. Solomon, he's your responsibility. He causes any trouble, he's mine. Got it?"

"I do. Yes, sir. No worries here."

Vasquez took the chocolates from Grey. Both of us nearly jumped when Vasquez's comm squawked on his shoulder.

"Wanderer One, this is lead. We're alpha charlie and on the move in five."

Vasquez took the mic off his shoulder. "Understood. Wanderer One out." He looked at me like he was memorizing my face, then signaled to the other two. They lowered their weapons, and the three of them jumped off the back of the truck. Neither of us moved until we heard the soldiers' boots pass the side of the truck and disappear down the line.

Once they were gone, Grey looked down at me and Bear so hard it was like he was trying to see straight through us. He didn't need to say a word. He was praying we were worth it.

10

"That's not the first time you've done that."

Grey didn't take his eyes off the road. "First time I've done what?"

"Lied to somebody like Vasquez."

Grey flicked his headlights on. We had been driving for hours and were now somewhere in Utah. The Californian front sat out in the darkness to our west.

"I think he's calling me a liar, Mr. Bear." The dog made a pleased snuffle as Grey rubbed his ears. "Mr. Bear says it takes one to know one, *Henry*."

My mind spun for a denial, but if Grey planned on turning me over to Vasquez, he would have done it by now.

"When'd you know?"

"Pretty much right away," Grey said. "You're slick, I'll give you that, but not half as much as you think. So what's the story? You a capture?"

I nodded. "About six years ago."

"Why run now?"

"Commander decided I should be helping give people the Choice."

Grey downshifted as we came up a steep rise. "He the one who did the work on your face?"

"One of his men, yeah."

"And now you're trying to get to . . ."

"New York."

Grey started to say something but pulled it back and shook his head.

"What?"

Grey glanced over at me. "Look, things may not be perfect here, but over in the Fed . . . I mean, do you even have any idea what the world was like before Hill?" Grey held up his hand before I could say a word. "Course you don't. What are you? Twelve?"

"I'm fifteen."

"Whatever. Back then, we were smack-dab in the middle of three wars and a depression that was getting ready to celebrate its tenth birthday. And you think anybody was trying to do anything about it? Heck no. Before Hill came along, politicians and their buddies were raking in billions while regular folks starved in the streets. And that's *still* the way it is in President Burke's Fed. I bet there are folks over there right now who are so rich they barely even know there's a war going on and wouldn't care if they did."

The cab lit up red as brake lights flared in front of us.

"Ah, man. Not this again."

Grey's air brakes squealed as he brought us to a shaking stop in the middle of the road. Bear stood up to peer out the window as we sat there, engine rumbling. This had happened throughout the day. Scouts at the front would see something and the whole convoy would stop, waiting for the bomb team to check the road for IEDs.

Every time it happened, tension settled over the convoy like a fog. Grey tapped the fingers of one hand on the big steering wheel, while the other lay ready on his gearshift. I could feel the entire convoy leaning forward and waiting. Fingers on triggers. Muscles taut.

"They always find them?" I asked.

"Last run I did, a troop carrier ran smack into one of those new ones the Brits are sending over. A bloodier mess you've never seen. Twenty men torn to shreds."

"The British are helping the Feds?"

"It's all hush-hush since Hill promised any foreign country caught interfering is getting a nuke for their trouble, but yeah, they're helping. Just can't be too obvious about it."

A trio of soldiers trudged up from their places in the rear of the convoy. I sank into my seat until they passed us by. Outside, the darkness lit up from artillery fire at the front. Tremors moved through the ground and up into our bones. Bear dug himself into my side with a whine and I stroked his side until he calmed.

"You think he'll win?" I asked.

"Don't think anything," Grey said. "I know."

"How?"

"You ever heard Hill speak?"

"I've read speeches."

Grey scoffed. "Not the same. Not by a mile. I was at a rally out east, near the front, and he made this surprise visit to see the boys. . . ."

Grey was quiet for a moment, reaching over to scratch Bear's head, while he puzzled something out.

"You know how you read in history books about people like George Washington and Alexander the Great, and you get to thinking that's the only place folks like that live? In books. Well, I saw Nathan Hill standing not one mile from the front and I'm here to tell you, he's one of them. He talked to those boys for hours and when he was done, it was like . . ." Grey's eyes shone as he remembered. "It was like all their lives they had been living on dust, and someone finally gave them a drink of water. Mark my words, the minute California falls, this whole thing is as good as over." Grey laughed a little to himself. "So I guess it won't matter where you end up, huh?"

Static came through the radio mounted over our heads. Bear woofed at it, and Grey reached up and switched it off, leaving just the rumble of engines around us in the dark.

"So if you're such a true believer, why do you help people like me?"

Grey shrugged.

"You've done it before, right?"

Grey glanced up at me and then went back to petting Bear. "Hill and the beacons," he said slowly. "They're smarter men than me. I know that. But I don't like giving folks the Choice. Simple as that. People ought to come to the Path on their own. Give 'em the chance and they will."

Grey reached across the cab to smooth down a curled piece of tape on the dash. It was holding up a picture of a pretty, fine-boned woman with a heart-shaped face and springy curls.

"I don't know," he said. "Maybe I also just got a feeling for people who aren't where they want to be."

Grey tapped his fingertip against the dash, then sprang up suddenly, like he was snapping himself awake.

"Man, we cannot be stopping this long." Grey snatched the radio and keyed the mic. "Patel. This is Solomon. I can feel those Fed drones circling, my friend. What is it? Private Weims spot another weaponized tumbleweed up there?"

The radio crackled with static. A few seconds later a heavily accented voice came back. "Nope. It's a roadblock this time, Sol."

"A roadblock?" Grey said, then lifted the transmitter again. "What are they looking for, Patel?"

Static filled the cab as Grey waited. Bear sat up, suddenly alert. The air in the cab seemed heavier now. I put my hand on Bear's shoulder and held on tight.

"Yo, Mr. Patel!"

"Sorry. Just through it now," Patel said. "They're looking for a kid, Sol. A kid and a dog."

11

Both of us sat mute until the convoy moved again, this time at a painful crawl. I was holding Bear down in my lap, but he was anxious and shaky, trying to throw me off.

"How many until they hit us?" I asked.

"We're tenth in line," he said. "But Vasquez is third. Soon as he hears what they're looking for . . ."

"Can we run?" I asked. "It's dark. Maybe —"

"No. They'll see." Grey pulled aside a set of curtains behind us that led to a cramped room filled with a blanket and pillows. "There's a cutout panel at the bottom of the sleeping quarters. It leads outside to the space between the cab and the trailer."

"What about Bear? They'll hear him. I can't —"

"I'll hold on to him. Once we're through the roadblock, I'll slow down enough for you to run and I'll let Bear out too."

I started to go, but Grey held me back.

"Listen," he said. "There's a man named Wade who lives in a little speck of a town called Bride Creek. Runs the post office, so he's got a truck and a tech dispensation. He's helped runners like you cross over into Wyoming before. I haven't heard anything from him in a few years, but he's a good man."

Grey pushed a map into my hand. There was a small town circled in northwest Utah.

"I'm heading east, Grey. I can't —"

"There's a lot of desert between here and Wyoming, and a lot of Path. If you're smart, you'll go west and take the ride."

Brake lights went out ahead of us and we moved up another space.

"What are you going to do?"

"See if I'm as slick as I like to think I am. Now go!"

My eyes met Bear's as I sank into the back. He was shuffling from paw to paw and whining, nearly frantic. I took his shoulder and squeezed, trying to pass him all the reassurance I could.

I grabbed my pack and dug to the bottom of the compartment. Once I found the outline of a panel, I pushed it open and was hit with a blast of desert air mixed with the stink of diesel. The truck shook as Grey hit the gas and moved one step closer.

I dropped my pack on the other side, then wriggled through, finding myself on the steel platform where the cab coupled to the trailer. I closed the panel behind me and crouched low.

"Cut your engine!" someone called from up ahead.

There was a pause, and then Grey powered down. Heavy footsteps approached the truck. When they got closer, four of them peeled off and began a search down either side of the truck. Flashlights knifed through the darkness. I dropped off the platform and hid behind one of the big tires just underneath the cab. Beams of light glinted off the steel where I had been hiding just seconds earlier.

"Mr. Solomon! Step down out of the cab, please."

The driver's-side door clicked open, and there was a bark from Bear as he followed Grey out.

"Move to the side of the road, please."

I watched from around the edge of the tire as soldiers escorted Grey toward the shoulder. Once there, headlights from the truck behind us slammed into him, making him stand out starkly against the night. He was surrounded by five soldiers, including Vasquez. Bear had moved away from the group and was sniffing along the front of the truck.

"What's up, fellas?" Grey asked brightly.

Good, I thought. *Keep cool, Grey.*

"Where's your nephew, Mr. Solomon?"

It was Vasquez. I stopped breathing in the pause that followed.

"Look, guys . . ."

"Why'd you lie to us, Grey?"

Grey swallowed hard. "I know I shouldn't have," he said, looking them each square in the eye. "But he seemed harmless, you know? I mean, you saw him. Ninety pounds soaking wet and busted up all to hell. He gave me a line about trying to see some relatives, and I wanted to give him a break. I should have been straight with you."

"Where is he now?"

"He got twitchy a few miles back and bailed."

"Leaving you the mutt?"

"Said the dog slowed him down. Asked me to keep him. I know. I should have figured something was up and given you guys a call. I'm sure if you backtrack a little, you can find him. He was only —"

"He tell you he was a murderer?"

A pulse of fear struck me in the chest. Grey said nothing.

"Killed a kennel master back at Cormorant," Vasquez said. "Shot him in the back three times and stuffed him in a toilet. Worked for the man for three years. You got anything to say to that?"

I lifted myself into a crouch, muscles straining, ready to run.

"Grey?"

"I don't know anything about that," Grey said. "I fell off my Path, boys. I swear I did, but that's all. I repent. I honestly do."

"We can forgive you, Grey, but only if you tell us where he is. Right now."

The side of the road was just feet away; after that, there was nothing but black. If I ran straight and hard, maybe they'd lose me.

"I told you, he —"

"Where was he headed?"

When Grey didn't respond, I turned back. The guards hadn't picked up on it, but he was looking beneath the truck, right at me, his eyes bright with terror. The blood in my veins turned to stone. Grey turned back to Vasquez.

"I don't know, sir."

Vasquez looked to one of the other soldiers, who nodded.

"Fine," Vasquez said. "That's fine."

He pulled his sidearm and shot Grey in the chest.

12

I hugged my knees to my chest, trying to stifle the scream that was rising in the back of my throat. I wanted to close my eyes, wanted to look away, but I couldn't do it. I couldn't move.

Two soldiers stuffed Grey into a black body bag and then dragged him off. A slick of blood gleamed in the headlights. Down the road, Bear was barking a percussive stream, his claws digging into the roadway, teeth bared. A soldier turned and unleashed a volley of gunfire that hit the road and sent Bear fleeing into the darkness.

There was the slam of a door and then Grey's engine came to life above me, snapping me out of my trance. I grabbed my pack and darted out from under the truck just as the big tires began to turn.

I sprinted across the road and into the dark, half blind, every other step sending me crashing to the ground. Pain sang through my wrist, my back, my side. Each time, I forced myself up and kept going, running to a drumbeat of images that pounded through my head: Grey standing in the glare of his headlights, his eyes on me, Vasquez lifting his weapon, Grey falling. Over and over: Grey falling, like a suit of clothes suddenly empty.

One word and I could have saved him. The truth of it was like a dull blade, gouging into me. I crumpled to my knees in the dirt, gasping, lungs shredded. The taillights of the convoy had disappeared down the road, leaving me surrounded by darkness. I saw myself stepping out from under Grey's truck and saving him again and again. It was like some part of me was trying to convince myself that I had actually done it.

Claws scraped my side. I recoiled to find Bear beside me, ears back, eyes wide with fear. I shoved him away and got to my feet, staggering deeper into the desert. Bear returned a second later and I hurled a clump of dirt at his feet.

"You can't follow me anymore. You have to go!"

Bear growled and started forward again but I kicked up a shower of sand, forcing him back.

"Go, you stupid dog. Just get away!"

Bear shadowed me as I took off again, alternating between angry barks and a pained whimpering that cut into me almost as keenly as the image of Grey falling. Every time he got close, though, I whipped around, stomping at the ground between us and ordering him off. Each time he'd look up at me bewildered and hurt, but I persisted until the chime of his tags and the padding of his paws grew distant. Soon it was swallowed up in the thick of the night. Gone.

I pressed on alone, an ache clamping down through the center of me. Someone would find him, I told myself. And even if they didn't, he was better off without me.

The temperature dropped fast as the night deepened. Pinprick needles of wind tore through my clothes. Images of Grey dogged me, and soon they were joined by others — Quarles and Connery and Dr. Franks. Even James. Because wasn't he just as dead as the rest of them? I saw that day six years ago when the Path officers led us from our aunt and uncle's car. They were taken one way and us the other. When they put the Choice to me and James, I didn't hesitate. I killed us both and didn't even know it.

I tried to drive it all away, tried to tell myself that I wasn't to blame. Grey could have sold me out, but he decided not to. *Each man walks his own Path*, I thought, sickened to feel Monroe's words in my head.

Exhausted, I collapsed again, onto my knees and then my back. The sky above me was choked with stars. I listened for Bear, expecting that any second I would hear the clink of his tags coming out of the dark. But there was only a low moan of wind and the distant tread of the war out on the front.

After the Path had taken us, we were loaded into the back of a truck. James and I sat trembling side by side with the other captures, while a beacon patiently explained what our new lives would hold. He said we had been given an opportunity to find a new life and a new purpose. He told us that the way would be hard and painful and most of all uncertain, because a man never knew what he would find when he looked deep inside himself. The only promise he could make us, he said, was that our Paths would inevitably lead us to one of two things — what we desired or what we deserved.

The moon arced over the vast emptiness of the desert and my body grew slowly numb in the cold.

I thought I finally knew where mine had been leading me.

I didn't expect to see the dawn but I guess the desert wasn't done with me. I woke the next morning to the sun beating against the land. Shards of glass seemed to lie in my bones and muscles. I forced myself up with a groan, making my head spin and my vision collapse to a dark tunnel. I breathed deep until it passed, then I looked around, squinting from the glare.

I expected to see a field of sand, but instead there was a plain as flat as glass and blazing white, like I was sitting in a field of snow. I thought it was a trick of the heat until I lifted my hand from the desert floor. White flakes crumbled from my fingertips and fell away like ash. I brought my fingers to my lips and touched them to my tongue.

Salt. Not snow. Salt. I was in the middle of a salt flat that stretched nearly to the horizon, the crystals glittering, broken only by a range of bare mountains in the far distance. There was no cactus or brush as far as I could see. I might as well have been on the surface of the moon.

I turned toward a metallic chime and found Bear sitting tall amid the white, watching me, his tags gleaming in the sun. As soon as he saw me looking, he turned away like I was beneath his notice.

"I told you to go," I said. My throat felt coated in sand, the spiny granules shredding my flesh as I spoke. How long had it been since I'd had water? Twelve hours? More?

I searched for my backpack and found it a few feet behind me. The second I had it in my lap, my heart fell. It was empty. At some point during my flight from the Path, the zipper had come open and all of my supplies — food, water, Grey's map — were now scattered between where I sat and a highway that was lost somewhere in the distance. I reached around behind my back and wasn't at all surprised to find the revolver gone as well.

I threw the pack away with what little strength I could muster, then looked out at the barren plain around me. I wondered if Grey would still have saved me if he knew how pointless his sacrifice would be.

There was a rustle as Bear crossed the salt field. He stuck his nose into my side and I reached out to push him away. When my hand brushed his side, everything inside of me went still. I took his collar and drew him back. His fur was wet. I moved my hands over his ears and paws and found them all covered by a thin film of water.

"Where'd you find it? Where'd you find the water?"

Bear jumped back with a growl, confused at first, but then he wheeled around and flew out across the desert. I somehow found the energy to chase after him, stumbling and weaving, and after a few minutes, the salt beneath my feet disappeared and we were back on hardpacked sand. A few ancient-looking shrubs appeared. They were little more than gnarled trunks and spindly branches, but they meant that water had to be somewhere nearby.

Bear disappeared over a hill, and when I came down the other side, I saw a circle of reeds and grasses rising around an oasis no bigger than a manhole cover. Bear dropped to his belly and lapped at the water.

There was a scummy haze of algae clinging to the edges of the pond, and tiny bugs flitting over its surface, but I was too thirsty to care. I cupped one palm awkwardly and filled it with the dark water. When that was too slow, I simply leaned over the edge and slurped the water up. Together, Bear and I nearly drained the pond. When he began chewing on the thin grasses around the water, I followed suit, pulling up handfuls of the bitter roots. My stomach tried to rebel but I forced them down. When I had eaten and drunk all I could manage, I fell into a heap beside Bear.

The water and food lifted some of the fog that had settled around me. I looked across the span of sand and sky. Mountains rose in the west, and to the east a few outcroppings of cacti reached up toward the sun. I studied their curves and the tan horizon behind.

The roadblock had forced Grey to drop us early so I could only guess where we were. I was sure that Bride Creek was still to our northwest, but how far was impossible to say. As close as sixty miles? As far as a hundred? More? And all of that through solid desert. The closest city was almost certainly Salt Lake City. In all likelihood it was just out of sight to our east, possibly as few as thirty or forty miles distant. Of course, being close didn't change the fact that landing in a Path jail meant my death just as surely as starving in the desert.

But what if I'm smart? I wondered. *Move at night, fast and quiet. Could I slip through the cracks and cross the border?*

Bear squirmed onto his back, rubbing himself against the torn reeds with his feet in the air. I could still hear his bark as it echoed through the back of Grey's truck. How was I supposed to sneak through the stronghold of Salt Lake City with him by my side?

And there's more too, I thought, recalling the voice on Grey's radio as we waited at the roadblock. *They're looking for a kid. A kid and a dog.*

Bear had settled down to a nap by the side of the pond. He huffed and mumbled in his sleep, one paw twitching as he dreamed. I moved closer, laying my hand along his side. His fur was warm and smooth. His ears, velvety. I drew my hand along the lines of his ribs as he breathed gently in and out.

I knew what I had to do. The night before, I was half mad and blundering through the dark. If I was careful and if I moved fast, he wouldn't find me this time. I'd be miles away before he even realized I was gone. Thinking of it, my breath went short, but the idea that

Bear could make it all the way to New York with me was a little kid's fantasy. He had survived on his own in a desert before he came across me and could do it again. The fact that he had found this oasis proved that.

I stroked his back and he shifted in his sleep. "Maybe you'll find somebody better."

I drew my hand away and stood over him, fixing my eyes on the eastern horizon. Out beyond Salt Lake City, beyond deserts and mountains, Ithaca lay waiting.

But before I could move, my thoughts drifted back to Grey, the memory of him like the edge of a bruise. I saw him standing on the side of the road, then flinched when I heard the clap of the shot. Why had he done it? That was the question that clung to me. He could have saved himself so easily. A single word and he would have been the one headed home instead of me. Instead he chose to die for someone he barely knew. *Why?* I didn't think I'd ever understand, but the fact of it was there, stark as the desert around me.

I looked down at Bear, suddenly seeing him as clearly in the future as I saw Grey in the past. Hours from now he would shake off sleep to find himself alone, wondering why I had abandoned him when he had never abandoned me. And where would I be then? Across the border and safe in Wyoming? Would Bear's memory sting as keenly as the memory of Grey?

I knelt down beside Bear and gently nudged him awake. His eyes opened with a great yawn and he batted at me with his paw. I placed my hand on his side and looked west.

"Come on," I said. "It's time to go."

13

We staggered into Bride Creek just after sundown five days later, half starved and aching from the road. The town itself was nothing but a few weathered buildings set back from a road that wound up into the hills. Still, it felt like there were a thousand eyes on us, watching every step. I kept us off the road, creeping through a drainage ditch, freezing at every sound.

The post office was a white box at the end of a dirt road. A gravel driveway led away from it to a ranch house not much bigger than the office. Its windows were dark and a gate hung open in front of it, turning lazily with a squeak that seemed massive out in the emptiness.

I wanted to go up and start pounding on the door, but we had to be careful. Knock on the wrong door at the wrong time and we were through.

There was a field of knee-high brush on the other side of the road from the house. I patted Bear's side and he followed, head low from exhaustion, limping on his right paw.

Bear crept off into the brush to hunt while I struggled to stay awake and watch the house. Every joint in my body felt like it was filled with rust. I pulled a handful of sandy grass from my jacket pocket and chewed on it. It was gritty and bitter, but days of constant hunger helped me force it down.

For the last five days, Bear and I had rested through the heat of the day and walked at night. Two nights through the desert. Two nights more along a razor-straight and abandoned rail line. We spent the final night climbing a single-lane road into the mountains. When Bear managed to find more pockets of marshy water, we drank all we could and then devoured reeds and grasses and tiny translucent things that scuttled through the muck. At first my stomach growled incessantly, but eventually that muted to an empty gnawing.

I walked in a kind of mindless trudge, memories and old songs floating through my head, there and then gone again. It was as if some long-buried clockwork forced my legs to keep pumping. Whenever I felt certain I was about to fall, I would reach out for Bear, holding him close until some bit of resolve passed between us and we would set off again. In the last miles, I kept Ithaca at the front of my mind every second, like a lantern I was striving to grasp. How Bear kept going and where he found the strength in that tiny half-starved body, I'll never know.

I was about to nod off when a pair of headlights appeared up the road. A small pickup truck emerged from the dark and turned into the driveway. It was covered in dents and rusty bruises. POSTAL SERVICE was clearly emblazoned down one side.

The lights winked out and there was a squeak of hinges. A tall man with shaggy hair emerged. He stuffed his keys into his jeans pocket, then reached into the back of the truck for a pair of turkeys and what looked like a 20 gauge shotgun. He hung the shotgun from his shoulder and then made his way across the yard and to the house, game in hand. Once inside, lantern light illuminated the thin white curtains. The man's silhouette moved back and forth in a front room.

Bear returned with a field mouse in his teeth and settled down to eat it. He paid me no mind as I moved out of the grass and into a ditch, watching for any movement on the road.

A light came on at the side of the house. I dropped low and circled the house until I stood alongside it and peeked in. The man was sitting at a table in a small candlelit kitchen, looking down at a yellow mug. His face was deeply lined and thin, framed in long gray hair and a scraggly beard. He spooned some sugar into his mug, then stirred and sipped. In the center of the table was a plain-looking cake dusted with sugar and cinnamon. My stomach growled, urging me to the front door, but I stopped when a girl appeared in the hallway.

She was maybe ten years old with curly auburn hair, wearing a blue top with red swallows embroidered at the neck. She wiped the sleep out of her eyes, and the man snatched her up under her arms and lifted her into the air. Even through the closed window I could hear the trill of her laugh. He pulled her close and nuzzled her neck, eliciting even more laughs, and then dropped her down into a chair at the table.

I watched as he cut her a piece of the cake and pulled a jar of milk out of an icebox. When she was done with her cake, the man had her clean up the dishes. Then he poured himself another cup of coffee, blew out the candles, and together they vanished into another room.

Bear pushed his snout into my shoulder when I returned to our hiding place but I elbowed him away. I stared at the house, trying to tell myself that the girl didn't matter, that I could still march up to Wade's door and demand a ride to the border. But even as the thought formed, I knew I couldn't do it. Grey said he hadn't heard from Wade in years and it was clear why — choosing to risk his own life for people like me was one thing, but risking hers would have been unthinkable. If the Path found out that Wade had helped me, they would kill him for sure. But what would happen to her? Would she be made a companion? Something worse?

I looked for an alternative as the lights in the house winked out one by one. Once they were gone, the white body of the old pickup truck glowed faintly in the moonlight.

Something snapped into place. Maybe I didn't need Wade at all.

I slipped back across the road, avoiding the driveway for the soft grass in the yard. My heart beat in my throat as I stood on their front porch and reached for the doorknob, hoping that, like any good Path citizen, Wade saw no need to lock his door. There was a soft click and I eased it open an inch at a time. The inside of the house was lit in dim shades of gray moonlight. I stood in the doorway until my eyes adjusted and then I crept inside.

I moved down the hall, muscles tight as iron, stepping carefully so none of the wood slats in the floor would send up an alarm. There were two bedroom doors, but which was Wade's and which was the girl's? I took a guess and pushed one open. Inside, a cool night wind streamed in through gauzy curtains to where the girl lay on her side beneath the sheets. A rustic-looking desk sat under the window, covered with papers, pencils, and books. A stuffed bear sat in the corner. The girl turned over, sending a jolt through me, though she didn't wake.

I drew her door closed behind me and kept going. The last door opened onto a larger bedroom where Wade slept beneath an ornate gun rack. There was a hunting rifle, but I didn't see the 20 gauge.

My heart was thrumming in my ears as I searched the room. His nightstand was empty except for a lamp and a book. The dresser top was barren. My nerves buzzed. How long had I been in the house now? Ten minutes? An hour? Either seemed possible and either was too long. I was pushing my luck. Bear and I had made it this far on our own; maybe . . .

But then I saw it. Just below the open window was a pile of discarded clothes. Boots, a shirt, a pair of jeans. I checked that Wade was still asleep and then I made my way across the room. When I lifted the jeans, there was a faint metallic clink and I knew I had found what I was looking for. I slid my hand into the front pocket, and Wade's truck keys spilled into my hand.

"Stand up and raise your hands."

My world collapsed to a single dark point. I stood slowly, the keys dangling from my hand. Wade sat up in bed, the 20 gauge steadied on one knee, pointed straight at my chest.

"Grey Solomon sent me," I managed to say, my voice trembling.

"Don't know anyone named Grey."

"I'm not Path."

Wade kept the shotgun trained on my chest as he went to the window. He turned from me just long enough to draw the curtains back and scan the grounds outside.

"He told me you used to help people like me," I said. "But I didn't want to get you and your girl involved."

"So you figured you'd just steal my truck."

"I was going to get myself to the Wyoming border and then leave it somewhere it would be found easy."

Wade closed the curtains and returned to the bed. I took a step forward, but stopped when the barrel of the shotgun rose again.

"So you're a capture, then."

I nodded.

"Where from?"

"Cormorant. In Arizona."

"And Grey Solomon brought you here."

"Most of the way. There was a roadblock and I bailed out."

"Grey doing okay these days?"

I flinched and tried to hide it. "He's fine," I said, my voice husky. "He sends his regards."

Wade studied the wrinkles on the bedsheets in front of him. Close up he looked hawkish and severe, with a sharp nose and piercing eyes. His gray hair hung in untidy waves around his head.

"Got any supplies on you?" he asked. "Food? Water?"

"No, sir."

Wade looked me up and down, then sighed deeply and slid out of the bed.

"Well, come on. Guess you can add stealing a pack and some food to your story if you get nabbed."

Wade dressed in the dark before leading me out quietly past his daughter's room. He lit an oil lamp in the entryway and carried it to a door at the edge of the kitchen. Wade nudged it open, revealing a rickety flight of stairs that led down to a dirt-floor basement. It was lined with steel shelves full of supplies.

"Have at it," he said, standing at the doorway. "But I hope you like Spam."

I hurried down the stairs, eager to be on my way and out of Wade's life as soon as possible. I was halfway to the floor when I heard the basement door slam behind me.

I turned back and found Wade looming at the top of the stairs, his back to the door, his shotgun aimed at my head.

"On your knees," he said. "Do it."

I rushed him, hoping to catch him off balance and make it through the door, but days on the road made me too slow. Wade grabbed a fistful of my jacket and threw me down the stairs. I hit the dirt with a shock and my vision grayed out. I could feel myself slipping away, but I thought of Bear out there alone and I reached up and grabbed hold of the nearest stair, feeling myself sink even as I climbed. Wade's boot pressed into my back, pinning me to the floor.

"Please . . ." I said in a thready mumble. "I was just trying to . . ."

There was a rattle of chains and I felt a steel cuff locking onto my ankle. Wade pulled me off the steps, then dropped down by my shoulder.

"What are you doing?" I asked.

"Some Path folk I know will be stopping by tomorrow. Gonna have to turn you over to them, son."

"No," I said. "You can let me go. I won't say anything. I swear. They'll never know I was here."

"Sorry, son," Wade said as he climbed the stairs. "I'll leave you a lantern to see, and you've got enough slack to get to the food and water on those shelves. Looks like you could use both."

"They'll kill me."

Wade stopped. He gripped the barrel of the shotgun and stared at his feet, his back to me.

"I'll put in as good a word for you as I can," he said in a near whisper. "They're fair people. They'll listen."

Wade moved a single lantern onto the top step and then started out the door. The sound of Bear's barking came from somewhere outside.

"Wade. Wait!"

He closed the door and threw the lock home. I made another stab at getting up, but I was too weak. The chain tangled my feet and I went down again. A door upstairs opened and closed shut again. Bear's barking became louder and more hysterical — then there was a yelp and he went silent. I scrambled to my feet.

"Bear!"

Seconds later the basement door flew open and Wade dragged Bear down by his collar. He said nothing, just dropped Bear in front of me and then went back up the stairs, locking the door behind him.

I pulled against the chain until I could reach Bear. He was lying on the bottom step, looking up at me with a dazed expression. I pulled him into my lap, forcing him to stay still while I ran my hands over his body. My heart raced, but there was nothing. No blood. No broken bones. I let him go and he squirmed out of my lap to explore the basement.

I stared at the door, trying to control the rage building up inside me. I jerked hard on the chain around my ankle, but the other end was padlocked to one of the steel shelves. My head swam from the exertion. I breathed deep and slow until it cleared and then I made myself search the rest of the room for anything I could use. Nothing. Dirt floor. Concrete walls. No tools. No windows. Only one door and a lantern that I couldn't reach.

I fell back into the dirt, staring at the door. It seemed impossible that we could have come so far for this. End of the line. I heaved at the chain in frustration and hissed in pain as the steel cuff bit into my ankle.

Bear barked behind me and I turned. His front paws were up on the shelves, scrabbling at the stacks of food that sat there. Crackers, beans, tuna, cases of water. Trapped or not, we were both still starving. I grabbed anything with a pull-top lid and tossed it into a pile on the floor. We ate four cans of tuna between us, along with handfuls of saltines. I filled the empty cans with water and let Bear drink.

There was a rattle as the lock at the top of the stairs was thrown. I sat there, struggling for some kind of plan but feeling myself crumple under my own bone-deep weariness. I reached for one of the bottles of water and my hand brushed an aluminum lid. I hissed and yanked it back. A thin trickle of blood ran down one finger and into my palm. I held the lid up into the light and ran my thumb along its keen edge.

Footsteps thudded above us. Bear growled and the short hairs at his back and neck raised. I slipped the sharp bit of metal under my leg and waited. The door creaked open. I expected to see Wade, shotgun in hand, but instead it was the girl.

She stood in the doorway, barefoot in pink-and-gray pajamas. She lingered there, her hand on the doorknob, looking down at us. Bear whined, but I stilled him with a hand on his back and drew him toward me. She took the lantern and closed the door just enough so that only a sliver of light escaped.

"I heard your dog barking," she said. "My name's Ellie." She descended another stair and stopped. "Can I . . . ?"

Bear made a breathy sound of anticipation as her foot hit the dirt floor. He stretched forward onto his belly, ears at attention, back end shaking. I kept my eye on the door as she approached, that infinitesimal streak of black. Freedom.

My hand dropped down by my leg, my fingertips resting on the jagged piece of metal. Ellie knelt in front of Bear, just out of my reach.

"Is he friendly?"

I drew my finger along the metal lip of the can. "Yes."

Ellie edged forward, but Bear was faster. He belly-crawled over to her and buried his head in her lap, sniffing at her until she giggled and fell back onto the bottom stair, delighted. Ellie rubbed at his head and his ears and scratched his muzzle when he forced it into her hand. Bear flipped over onto his back and kicked at the air, with his tongue hanging out. As I watched them play, something sank inside me. My hand fell from the can's lid. This girl wouldn't be my ticket out.

"What's his name?"

"Bear," I said.

"Does he do tricks?"

I took a cracker out of a nearby package and held it over Bear's head. He popped up onto his back legs and pawed at the air. Ellie laughed and clapped and I dropped the cracker into Bear's mouth. When he was done, he shoved his face into Ellie's lap, searching for more.

"He can catch a stick if you throw it to him."

Ellie looked up. "Really?"

I frowned, studying the walls of the dank basement. "Course there's not really enough room in here to show you. If —"

"I can't unlock you," she said. "Sorry."

Ellie went back to wrestling with Bear, and whatever strength I had left me. Every pointless mile Bear and I had walked stung.

"Why does he have you locked up anyway?" she asked. "Are you running from the soldiers too?"

I nodded slowly.

"I'm supposed to hide down here when they come," she said casually as she petted Bear. "So they don't see me."

"Why doesn't your dad want the soldiers to see you?"

Bear huffed as Ellie stroked his side. "Wade's not my dad," she said.

"No? Who is?"

Ellie looked back to the door, suddenly wary. "Maybe I should —"

"Do you want to give Bear a cracker?"

I held the box out toward her. Ellie's eyes locked on it but she hesitated. It wasn't until Bear yipped and clawed at the box that she grabbed it out of my hand. I inched closer as she fed a cracker to Bear in pieces, a look of intense concentration on her face.

"How about your mom?" I asked, trying a different tack. "Where is she?"

"Mom got sick when I was little," she said.

"Oh. I'm sorry."

"I only remember her a little bit."

"It's been a long time since I've seen my mom too."

Ellie glanced over at me as Bear ate out of her hand. I checked the door and moved a little closer. Ellie finished feeding Bear. He lay at her feet, staring up at her as she stroked his head. Bits and pieces clicked together in my head. I decided to take a leap.

"I was taken away from my mom and dad by the soldiers when I was around your age," I said. "I was trying to get home again, but Wade is going to give me back to them. To the soldiers."

"I told you. I can't —"

"I know," I said. "I just thought that, after they take me, they'll probably bring me to a base nearby, right? Maybe I can try to find your dad for you."

Her hand went still on Bear's side.

"Your real dad's a soldier," I said. "Isn't he?"

Ellie said nothing.

"What's his name?" I asked. "Do you know?"

She nodded, eyes still locked on Bear. "Wade doesn't think I do. But I heard my mom say it once."

"Maybe if you tell me, then I can find him for you. He'd probably like to know you're doing okay. "

"I'm not supposed to talk about him."

"Why not?"

Ellie took one of Bear's front paws, but he snapped it away and then they wrestled back and forth for it. They played for a while, until Bear's lids went heavy and he fell asleep sprawled out in front of her.

She stroked him as he slept and slowly began to talk.

The basement door opened again early the next morning.

This time Wade was there, towering in the door frame with a rising sun behind him and the shotgun by his side. Bear growled as Wade came heavily down the stairs, but I held him back. Wade took a seat on the bottom step, the shotgun across his knees. His eyes were dark and lidded, like he hadn't slept.

"Anything you want before they come?" he asked. "Any message you want me to get to your folks or anything?"

I shook my head, and Wade started to go.

"What are you doing this for?" I asked. "Money?"

Wade stopped where he was, his back half to me. He looked up into the house and shook his head.

"Then what?"

"Goodwill," he said. There was gravel in his voice along with a hint of what sounded like real regret. "These days you need just about all you can get. I don't mean you any . . . Things just are what they are. Like I said, I'll vouch for you as best I can. Tell 'em you were repentant. Whatever. I just thought, I don't know, maybe we could get some kind of story together before they come. Ease your way a bit."

"Will they take me to Salt Lake City?"

"I suspect they will. Yeah."

"Camp Eagle?"

Wade raised an eyebrow. "Why? You know folks there? Could help if you do."

"Don't know anyone," I said. "But there's someone I'm looking forward to meeting."

"Who?"

"Jeff Sinclair." Wade didn't move an inch. The old walls of the house settled around us, ticking like a clock.

"He's a colonel there," I said. "Or was. Maybe he's higher up now."

"Don't know the man."

"Really? I'd think you would, since you've been hiding his daughter from him for the last five years."

"I don't know what —"

"Ellie's mom was a woman named Larissa Kenning," I said, sick of playing games. "She was a companion at Camp Eagle. From what Ellie said, I'm guessing Colonel Sinclair took a liking to her. Want to hear what else I'm guessing?"

Wade said nothing.

"I'm guessing she got pregnant, which isn't exactly something that can happen to a companion of the Path, especially if it's by an officer. If Sinclair found out about it, he would have had the problem taken care of, so I'm guesing that Larissa ran. Eventually she found her way here to you, but she died not long after — Ellie didn't really know how, just said she was sick."

"Cancer," Wade said in that raw voice. "Hit her when Ellie was five."

"And you've been taking care of her since then," I said. "That's why you have to turn in people like me, isn't it? Got to look like the perfect citizen."

Wade had gone dead pale, his hand limp on the stair rail.

"Sinclair even know she exists?"

Wade shook his head. I stood up in the middle of the basement.

"Then this should be easy for you," I said. "A one-way trip to the Wyoming border guarantees he never will."

Wade looked at me for the first time since I'd mentioned Sinclair's name, staring a fire across the basement.

"Doesn't matter to you that she'd end up a companion just like her mom?"

"Like you said, things are what they are."

Behind Wade, the crack of sunlight had grown brighter along the edge of the door.

"We don't have much time."

"No," Wade said. "I guess we don't."

Wade climbed to the top of the stairs and shut the door with a dull clap. All the air seemed to vanish from the room. Bear began to growl.

"Wade . . ."

I stumbled backward as he came down the stairs, shotgun in hand.

"You don't want to do this," I said, my heart racing and my hands up, trying to ward off the shotgun that was now rising toward my chest. "I'm just asking you to help me like you helped people before. Like you helped Ellie."

Wade jammed the barrel into my chest and pushed me down to my knees.

"And then what do I do?" he asked. "Sit around waiting for the day you need to trade Ellie's name for something else?"

"I won't. Wade, listen to me —"

"Get up," he said. "Turn and face the wall."

"How will you explain it to her, Wade? She knows I'm here. You think she wants to grow up with a murderer?"

"She won't know a damn —"

"What are you doing?!"

Ellie was standing in the open door at the top of the stairs. When Wade turned, I eased back to the steel shelf I was chained to. Bear ran to join me, cowering at my feet.

"Go to your room, Ellie."

"No!"

I began to draw the slack chain toward me, gathering it into a heavy loop.

"He's just trying to get home," she cried as she came down the basement stairs.

"He's a liar, Ellie! Now get upstairs."

"I won't!"

"Then I'll drag you up there myself."

I swung the length of chain the second Wade started to move, knocking the shotgun to the floor. Wade scrambled for it, but I grabbed it first. I jumped back, training it on him, balancing the barrel across my cast.

"Unlock me," I said. "And then I'll —"

The blast of a car horn sounded outside. No one in the basement moved. The horn went again, followed by two car doors opening and slamming shut. Boots crunched across the gravel. Wade swallowed hard, his face a sheen of sweat. The Path officers called Wade's name and banged on the front door.

"Tell them you came downstairs to check on me," I said. "But when you got here, I was gone."

"They'll search the house," Wade said.

"Mr. Wade!" a voice called.

"Keep them talking out front. I'll go out back until they're gone. Once they are, you get us to Wyoming and we're done."

"I'll give you the keys to the truck," he said. "You can go your —"

I dug the shotgun's barrel into Wade's chest.

"You will drive me yourself. And if we're caught, I talk."

The soldiers pounded on the door, harder now. Wade nodded and I backed off.

"Go."

Wade moved toward the stairs, stopping to take Ellie's arm.

"She stays with me until it's done," I said. "Give her the key to the padlock and leave."

Wade swallowed his protest and handed her the keys. The soldiers knocked again and Wade was gone, up the stairs and out the basement door. Seconds later I heard the front door open and Wade's voice greeting the soldiers.

I lowered the shotgun and waved Ellie over. She kneeled down beside me to undo the lock on my ankle. Bear stayed away, deep in a corner, watching her. The lock popped and the chain fell from my ankle.

"Would you really have told?"

Ellie looked up at me wide-eyed. She cringed when I grabbed her by the arm and pushed her toward the stairs.

"Let's not find out."

I waited until dark and then led Wade into the driveway at gunpoint. The night was still, but I couldn't shake the feeling of eyes watching us from behind every tree and blade of grass.

Wade threw one of his packs into the bed of the truck. When he was done, I waved him over to the driver's-side door. He stood there, keys in hand, staring up at the dark house.

"Move."

Wade pulled the door open and slid into the driver's seat. I slammed it shut, then helped Bear up on the other side. Wade's hands were limp on the steering wheel, his big frame sunken.

Bear gave an anxious woof at a squeak of hinges across the yard. I looked up to find Ellie in the light of the half-open door. She was barefoot in jeans, her arms crossed over a red sweater. The house was bright and warm behind her.

"Start the truck," I said.

Wade nodded feebly, then threw his shoulder forward. The key turned and the truck grumbled to life. He looked up at Ellie one last time. The way he looked at her, it was like he was trying to will every bit of himself out across the yard and by her side. Without thinking,

I pulled Bear down and held him close, his back against my leg. Wade grabbed the gearshift and started to pull.

"Wait."

Wade turned to me. My stomach churned as I looked up at Ellie. Wade started to say something, but I stopped him before he could.

"Give me till morning," I said. "Then report the truck stolen. I'll leave it near the border. Somewhere easy to see."

"I don't under—"

"Just tell me how to get to the border."

Wade gave patient directions, which highway to take and when to leave it for a few off-the-map dirt roads that avoided checkpoints. When he was done, I told him to go, but he didn't move. He sat there in the driver's seat, looking out the windshield.

"What happens if they stop you?"

"If I find out you had anything to do with it, I start talking. If not . . . then it's on me."

"Listen, son, I wish things were —"

"The longer we sit here talking, the better the chance someone sees us."

Wade put his shoulder to the door and stepped onto the gravel. Ellie came farther out onto the porch, backlit in the lantern light from inside. I could see her trembling.

"It scares me sometimes," Wade said. "The things I'd do to keep her safe. Maybe one day you'll understand."

Wade shut the door, and the driveway crackled under his boots as he rejoined Ellie on the porch. She was crying when he put his arm around her and led her back inside. The door closed behind them.

I moved Bear into my lap and slid in behind the wheel, leaving the shotgun on the passenger seat. The gearshift clicked into reverse and I backed slowly out of the driveway and onto the road.

I sat there, engine idling, looking back at the house. It was like an island glowing in the dark. I let go of the steering wheel and drew Bear up to my chest, hugging him tight with my eyes closed. He draped his head over my shoulder, breathing in short puffs that warmed my back. In that moment, the boundary between us felt as thin as a wisp of smoke.

14

We stole through winding back roads, watchful, headlights out wherever we could, following Wade's instructions to the letter. A few times we saw Path vehicles, but we managed to pull off and go quiet in the dark. Every muscle in my body hummed, tight as steel, until they passed us.

We drove until just before dawn, when exhaustion forced me to find a place to pull off the road and hide the truck. We ate as much of Wade's food as we could and then slept through the day. Bear snored with his head in the palm of my hand, heavy and warm. When night fell, we set out again.

An hour into the second leg of our trip, we came around a turn in the road, and I could see a line of lights miles out on the roadway. A checkpoint. This was it. Wyoming lay on the other side. I put the truck in reverse and hid it behind the bend in the road. Bear looked up at me when I cut the engine.

"We'll have to go on foot again if we want to cross. You up for it?"

Bear curled around and began to chew at his paw. I tried to take a look but he snatched away with a throaty growl. I looked out the window, imagining the hard miles lying out there in the dark.

"As soon as we're across the border, we'll find a place to lay up for a while," I said, rubbing his ears. "Okay? And once we're home, it's feather beds and steak dinners. I promise."

Bear stood up and stretched, which I decided to take as an okay. I opened the door slow, sure a rusted hinge would be as good as a thunderclap out here in the middle of nowhere. Bear clambered out, his metal tags tinkling when he hit the ground. I knelt down beside him.

"Better do something about that too, I guess."

I undid his collar and stuffed it in my pocket. Free of it, Bear shook himself out vigorously, then sniffed his way across the road. I collected the bag Wade had packed for us, then stopped and looked back in the cab. Wade's shotgun lay on the seat, black as a snake. I didn't know what was coming, but I could still feel the kick of Quarles's revolver. I hated the hot violence of the thing. I shut the door and left it behind.

I led us about a mile north of the roadway and then turned east, moving as fast as I could while staying low and quiet. Bear moved along beside me, his dark coat making him nearly invisible. As soon as we were within sight of the checkpoint, I hit the ground, and Bear followed suit. The blockade consisted of two Humvees on each side of the road. I belly-crawled to get a better look.

There were two soldiers currently outside manning the gate, one facing out to Fed territory, the other watching the Path side. I was pretty sure there were more soldiers than the ones I was seeing, probably doing patrols out on either side of their position. The only thing to do was get as far from the roadway as possible and cross where the land went rocky and uneven.

I crawled to Bear and together we headed north. Once we were a couple miles from the road, I stopped and listened. Not a sound. I turned east, heading toward the border. A half mile or less and we'd be in Fed land. Not home free, but a good sight closer. I felt a racing excitement build in my chest. No more Path, no more running, no more —

Footsteps sounded in the dark.

Bear turned toward them but I pulled him to the ground and clamped a hand over his muzzle. The footsteps grew louder until I saw the faint outline of a sentry making his way down the line toward the roadway. He was about thirty feet from us and closing fast. If we kept still, I thought there was a good chance he'd walk right by.

The sentry moved to within twenty feet of us, then ten. Then five. I could hear his breathing and the crunch of his boots on the sand. Bear struggled in my arms. I cursed myself for removing his collar. I tried to hold him down but with only one good hand I couldn't stop him as he wriggled himself free and shot away.

The guard reacted immediately, lifting his weapon and turning in our direction. I wanted to scream at Bear to stop, but a single word from me and we'd both be dead.

"Who's there?"

The sentry barely got the words out before Bear leapt up at him, panting and wagging his tail.

"Hey, fella, what are you doing out here?"

And just like that, the guard was down on one knee, with Bear jumping all over him. I dropped my head into the dirt.

"Anybody else out here with you?"

It would be only seconds before the sentry stopped being distracted by Bear and started searching. The guard post was out of sight, two or more miles away. A low hill stood between us and them.

"Yeah," I said, easing up off the ground with my hands up. "I'm with him."

The guard pushed Bear away and snapped his rifle up in my direction.

"Whoa!" I said, keeping my voice down as much as I could. "Wait a second. No harm here. Just me. I'm unarmed."

"On your knees," he ordered.

I did as I was told, careful to keep my hands up where he could see them. Bear left the sentry's side and bounded over to me, looking up at me with a panting grin like he couldn't believe his luck finding us a new playmate. I swore that if we lived through this, the first thing I was doing was buying him a leash.

"What are you doing out here?"

"Camping," I said. "Me and my dad, we're back that way a few miles. Bear here ran off and I was just looking for him."

"Ain't a very smart place to be camping, kid."

"I know," I said, forcing a nervous laugh. "Me and Dad, we were never outdoorsy or anything. But Hill says men of the Path should be resourceful and self-sufficient in all weathers and landscapes. We're trying to do our part. Didn't mean to cause any problems. Honest."

The soldier tipped the barrel of his weapon up. "Okay, hands behind your back."

"But I said —"

"I don't care what you said. We've got reports of an escapee traveling with a dog."

"Escapee? No, I told you I'm just —"

The sentry placed the cold O of his weapon's barrel squarely on my forehead. Bear growled, low and deadly sounding.

116

"Hands behind your back," he repeated. "And if the dog jumps, he's getting one in the chest."

"Okay. Okay." I slowly lowered my hands, pausing only to draw one down Bear's back. "Shhh. It's okay. We're fine. Okay?"

Bear glanced at me and then the sentry. His growl eased.

"We're all fine."

I put my hands behind my back as the guard slid around me. He pulled out a zip tie and I winced as he bound my right wrist tight to my cast. Once he was done, the sentry reached for his radio. This was it. If he called us in, we were as good as dead. I slipped one foot underneath me, ready to push off, but the sentry stood motionless in front of me, his hand on the mic, poised to key the transmitter. What was he doing?

The sentry dropped the radio and then sank to his knees, his arms raised over his head. A dark figure appeared behind him, a rifle in his hands, the barrel pressed into the back of the sentry's skull.

"Let's take it easy," the sentry said. "I've got backup just down the line. Way more than you can handle, so just —"

Before he could finish, the man smashed his rifle's stock into the back of the sentry's head, just under his helmet. The sentry collapsed in front of me, and Bear barked wildly as four more soldiers appeared out of the darkness.

"Mark, shut that dog up," someone whispered. "Now."

The one with the rifle advanced on Bear and I threw myself at him, slamming my chest into his side and knocking him face-first to the ground. His knife shot away into the dark and then Bear was after him, snarling.

A gun barrel dug into my temple. "Call him off. Now."

"Bear, get back."

Bear turned, his lips revealing a row of sharp teeth.

"It's okay," I said, and nodded him away. Bear looked up at the soldiers beside me and backed off with a growl.

"Who are you? What are you doing here?"

It was a woman's voice. No. Not a woman. A girl. Were these Fed soldiers?

"I . . . I'm camping," I said. "With my father. Whatever you're doing is none of my business. Just cut me loose and let me go. You'll never see me again."

The collapsed soldier's radio squawked and a voice emerged, full of static. "Wolf Three, this is Den. We heard something up your way. Confirm contact. Over."

There was a pause and then the barrel fell away from my temple, allowing me to turn and see my captors. There were four of them, but they weren't soldiers. It was three boys and a girl. All about my age. The girl carried a sawed-off shotgun. All the boys were looking to her as the radio sounded again.

"Wolf Three, this is Den. Confirm contact. Over."

"I know what to say," I said. "Cut me loose and I'll talk to them."

The girl looked down at me, uncertain.

"If someone doesn't answer, they're coming here in force and we're all dead."

She glanced to the boy with the rifle and he took the radio off the soldier's belt and held it up to my mouth.

"Cut me loose or I say nothing."

The girl's glare didn't waver and neither did mine.

"Wolf Three, this is Den. We are in motion. Over."

There was the distant sound of engines coming to life down the line, and the girl nodded at one of her friends, who disappeared behind me. When the zip tie binding my hands popped, I grabbed for the radio, but her friend held it back.

"Say the wrong thing," the girl said as she leveled her shotgun at Bear's head. "And you watch the dog go down before you do."

I snatched the radio away from him. "Den, this is Wolf Three," I said, deepening my voice and hoping the connection was bad enough to make it indistinguishable from their comrade's. "I am alpha charlie. Repeat. Alpha charlie. Came across a stray dog, but the mutt ran off. All is on Path now. No need for assistance. Over."

There was a deadly pause when we all held our breath. The engine-revving sound stopped.

"Wolf Three, this is Den. Understood."

I dropped the radio in the dirt and fell to my hands and knees, panting, my heart thrumming in my ears.

"Okay, people," the girl with the shotgun said. "The plan hasn't changed. Take him and the dog and move."

"You don't need me," I said. "I called them off. Let me —"

The shotgun rose to my forehead. "You go where I say you go. Now call the dog to you and move."

Bear and I were pushed deeper into the Path side of the border until we came to a trench that had been dug into the sand. We dropped behind it. Bear stayed close to me, the tension in the air having cured his natural friendliness.

"Carlos," the girl in charge said. The boy named Carlos slung his weapon and disappeared into the night.

None of them were in uniform, just ragged-looking hiking gear and scavenged weapons. The girl was an inch or so taller than me, with a square jaw and arms that were covered in rangy cords of muscle.

"Look," I said. "Whatever you're doing, you don't need me to —"

"I don't know you," the girl said. "So if you think I'm going to let you and your mutt wander around in the middle of my operation, you're crazy. If you're good, we let you go when we're done. It's either that or you take a short walk out into the desert with Hector here."

Hector was tall with a shaved head and massive shoulders. He stood behind her, grinning, one hand balanced on a hunting knife that hung from his belt. I let my head fall against the berm behind me, cursing under my breath. The girl reached her hand back and one of the boys handed her a pair of binoculars. She lifted them and looked out toward the road.

"Hitting the checkpoint is useless," I said. "They'll just have a new crew here by the morning."

The girl said nothing, continuing her scan. I turned onto my stomach and looked over the berm. The lights of the checkpoint were about a mile to our east. The road cut across the desert right in front of us.

"Something else is coming, isn't it?"

Her eyes flicked over to me and I knew I was right.

"A supply truck?"

"Look, just keep quiet, and when we're done you're free to go, okay?"

I scanned the landscape again, counting off soldiers and vehicles. A plan started to form. "That promise isn't going to do me much good when you're all dead."

She dropped the binoculars to glare at me. "You remember that short walk I mentioned?"

I scooted closer to her through the dirt. "I'm guessing from the way you're set up, you figure on sending these guys to flanking positions on either side of the checkpoint and then hitting them all at once when the supply truck is stopped. With that plan, you'll last about two minutes."

"We have the element of surprise."

"Which is what will buy you the two minutes. I've been living with a Path special forces unit for six years. Trust me. You can't take them all on at once; that's what they expect you to do."

Carlos reappeared and crouched on the other side of her. "Target's five miles out, Nat."

Nat nodded and he melted into the dark. She examined the terrain a moment, gnawing on her bottom lip, and then turned to me.

"And so what *don't* they expect?"

I locked eyes with her. "If I help, you take me with you back to Fed territory and then help me get transport east."

"You're not in a great position to make a deal."

"Fine, stick to your plan. I'll wait here while you all get killed."

"Nat," Carlos said. "Time to move."

Nat's eyes narrowed on me, sharp as spikes. "Deal. Now tell me your idea."

Nat listened, and once I was done, she waved everyone in. The three heavily armed boys gathered around her.

"We all know how important this is," she said, speaking slow and calm and looking her men in the eye just like I had seen Path commanders do before an operation. "Our friends are counting on us, but we gotta remember that this isn't hero time. This is working-together-and-doing-our-job time."

Each boy nodded solemnly.

"Now," she continued, glancing over at me. "We've got a little change in plan. . . ."

•   •   •

Minutes later I was kneeling in the middle of the highway with Bear at my side and Nat's prone body lying in front of us. I had pulled Wade's truck nose down in a ditch around the bend in the highway, out of sight of the checkpoint. We were lit in the yellow blinking hazard lights.

"You ready?" I asked.

"I don't know," Nat said. "I'm suddenly wishing I had taken drama class instead of metal shop. You sure this is going to work?"

I shrugged. "They say no plan —"

"— survives contact with the enemy. Yeah, I've heard that one too."

Nat peered down the road, then tucked a length of hair behind her ear.

"So you were really living with Path special forces? And now you're a runner?"

"Name's Cal," I said. "The dog's Bear."

"You named your dog Bear?"

"Yeah, he —"

Two lights appeared in the western dark. Nat sucked in a breath and held it. I leaned over her, my hands on her arms, my face close to hers. Her eyes were closed. Bear whined and I rubbed his head to calm him down.

The supply truck strained up a hill and then its lights were filling the roadway around us. I had the sick feeling of being a spider in a web. Part of me hoped they'd swerve around us and keep going.

"Almost here," I whispered in Nat's ear.

"Showtime."

The truck was a three-axled monster with a boxy cab. There were two shadowy forms inside. There was no going back now, so all I could do was hope there wasn't extra security hiding in the rear of the truck. When it was less than fifty feet out, I jumped up and started waving my arms over my head. Bear ran to my side, keeping up a steady stream of barking.

The truck didn't slow. Thirty feet. Then twenty. What if they had been told to not stop for any reason? My heart pulsed, but then their air brakes squealed and they came to a halt just a few feet ahead of us. Engine rumbling. Headlights beating down at us. There was a pause and then the doors opened and boots hit the ground. Nat was right. It was showtime.

"Thank God!" I exclaimed. "Thank God you stopped. Please help us. I don't know what's wrong with her!"

Two soldiers rushed into the pool of light; one had a sleek MP5 rifle and the other was toting a black shotgun. As soon as he saw them, Bear ran up and began prancing around their feet and barking eagerly. For once his instincts were perfect. If he had been a bigger dog, they might have already been shooting, but the last thing the soldiers expected was his tiny whirling excitement. They looked from him to us and back again.

"Back," one of the soldiers said. "Get back."

"Bear! Come here! It's okay. He's harmless."

Bear backed off with a yip but stayed between us and the soldiers, dancing around, his claws clicking on the asphalt.

"What are you doing here?"

"We were camping with our dad," I said as Bear spun. "He said we had to get on Path, but we wanted to go home, so we took the truck, but then she just collapsed on the way back. I don't know what happened. Please help us!"

"Take the dog and step back from the girl," the soldier said. "Now!"

I took Bear by his shoulders and pulled him away. "Just help her. Please. Come on, Bear."

The lead soldier slid his MP5 around behind him. "Keep an eye on the boy, Turner," he said as he knelt by Nat's body. Turner put the shotgun on me as his partner eased closer to Nat.

"I don't know what it is," I said. "She won't wake up. She's had seizures before. Maybe —"

Nat began to whisper, rolling her head back and forth. "I'm sorry . . . I don't . . . the truck just . . . Dad . . ."

The lead soldier leaned in to hear her better and that's when Nat started moving. One hand grabbed his wrist while the other swept Carlos's handgun out from beneath her. The soldier jerked back, and Nat used the momentum to get both of them standing. She turned his arm behind him, then jammed the gun into his side. Turner pivoted to get a bead on her, but Nat swung her man's body between them as a shield.

"Put it down or he's dead!" she ordered. "Do it now!"

Turner hesitated and that was my chance. I sped in on his blind side and ripped the gun out of his hand.

"Okay," the leader said, his hands up. "Let's all just take it easy here. You gotta know this ain't gonna happen, girl. There is an entire outpost right ahead of you. Taking our rig isn't going to do you a bit of good."

"Thanks for the advice," Nat said, stripping his MP5 off over his head. "Now, on your bellies on the side of the road. Move."

Nat got them down and I pulled out a handful of plastic zip cuffs I had taken off the first sentry. I bound their hands behind them and stepped away. Nat pressed her pistol into the leader's skull, but I batted the weapon away before she could fire, earning me a deadly look.

"There's no need," I said. "Let's go."

Nat climbed up into the driver's side while Bear and I took the passenger seat. She handed me the shotgun.

"Ready?" she asked.

"Get down, Bear."

Once he was safely in the wheel well, I leaned out the window and fired three blasts into the sky. Boom. Boom. Boom. The shock of it sent a painful jolt through my wrist. Bear yelped at my feet, pushing himself farther into the darkness. Nat angled the MP5 out her window and peeled off a stream of fire. I grabbed the radio mic off the dash and keyed the channel open.

"Den, we are under attack. Repeat — we are under attack."

I nodded to Nat and she put the truck in gear, accelerating around the corner and onto the straightaway.

One of the Path Humvees had abandoned the checkpoint and was racing toward us. I found myself wishing they'd stop and turn back, but it was too late. There was a flash from the side of the road as Hector fired his RPG. The smoke trail streaked toward the side of the vehicle, but at the last second the driver gunned the engine and swerved. The rocket slammed into the dirt on the other side of the road and went up in a cloud of fire and sand. The Humvee kept coming. The turret gunner was in his place, hands on his weapon.

"What do we do?"

"Keep going," I said, trying to control the panic in my voice. "As far as they know, we're on their side."

Nat laid on the gas, but in the next second I was proved wrong. The gunner in the Humvee leaned into his turret and squeezed off a stream of fire from his .50 cal. The rounds ricocheted off the roadway, chiming against the hood and shattering a headlight. Nat's side-view mirror exploded in a shower of glass and metal. She clapped a hand on her shoulder with a gasp but urged the truck faster.

The gunner let go another salvo. This time he walked his fire over to us, tearing up the roadway before a string of bullets tore into a corner of our engine block. There was a screech of twisting metal and then I braced myself as the truck went into a spin, pinwheeling down the highway until our back end smashed into the side of the Humvee. The mass of the truck sent the Humvee skidding off the road and we all came to a dead stop. There was broken glass everywhere, and smoke was pouring out of our truck's ruined engine.

I ducked to check on Bear and found him cowering but unhurt. By the time I was back up, Nat was already diving out of the truck.

"Nat!"

I grabbed the shotgun and followed her. The Humvee was half on the road, half in a ditch. The gunner was slumped over his weapon, unconscious. Nat had her rifle up and was stalking toward the vehicle.

"What are you doing? Nat, let's go!"

The driver's-side door flew open and a soldier leapt out, his side-arm out and zeroing in on Nat. I lifted my shotgun, but before I could even get it leveled, Nat squeezed off three rounds. They hit the soldier in the chest and he crumpled onto the road.

There was a clatter as Nat's rifle hit the asphalt. She stumbled backward and to the ground, her legs sprawled out in front of her.

She had gone chalk pale, mouth open, her eyes fixed on the dead soldier bleeding out into the road. He was young. Nineteen or twenty with the broad features and blond hair of a farm boy.

An explosion down the road rocked the ground beneath us. The checkpoint was now engulfed in flames. Black figures circled it, spraying the remaining Humvee with gunfire.

"Nat," I said, my voice shaking along with the rest of me. "We have to go. Someone must have gotten a com out in the middle of all of this. More will be on the way."

Nat didn't respond, didn't move. She just stared at the boy. His eyes were glassy, lifeless. I dropped the shotgun and grabbed Nat, turning her toward me and shaking her hard by her shoulders.

"We have to move. Now!"

Nat pushed me away and rolled over onto her hands. Her back heaved and she vomited into the roadway. When she was done I helped her up and we went around the truck to get Bear. He jumped into my arms, shaking, and I held him tight.

"Come on," I said to Nat. "We'll meet up with the others and walk across the border."

Nat was bent over her knees. She shook her head. "No, we need what's in the truck."

"Nat —"

"I'm not doing all of this for nothing!"

Down the road, Carlos and the others were already on their way back to us. The fire raged behind them, lighting up the sky for nearly a mile. Even if no one got a signal out, the Path was going to see the fire and send help. We didn't have much time and certainly couldn't afford to walk out.

"Start unloading," I said. "Fast."

I left Bear with Nat and ran into the dark toward Wade's truck. When I got there, the hazards were still going, flashing yellow in the ditch. I got in and cranked the engine, but then it was like my brain locked down. I sat there, my hands on the wheel, the engine idling. My fingers were ice-cold. I kept seeing that dead soldier's eyes, blank as a doll's.

The world outside the truck was spinning madly, a flickering show of darkness and flames. I closed my eyes and breathed deep, but it did nothing. I bit down hard on the side of my lip, and the world snapped back into focus. I spit blood out onto the road and got moving.

By the time I got back, a fire had started in the supply truck's engine. Flames overwhelmed the front of it, but Nat and the others had the cargo laid out on the road. Cardboard boxes and wooden crates were stacked four feet high. I brought Wade's truck to a halt and they packed all they could into its bed.

"Move over," Nat said. "I know the way."

I shifted over to the passenger side. Nat let Bear in, then got behind the wheel. He was shaking badly, his tail between his legs. I pulled him close to me and he curled up, burying his face in my leg. Nat made sure Carlos and the others were in the bed and then drove away.

She slowed to navigate through the wreck at the checkpoint. Flames tore through the last remaining Humvee, putting off intense heat and billowing smoke. Its charred black skeleton was clearly visible inside, along with other dark shapes I made myself look away from. I tried to tell myself that the people inside were Path, that they would have killed us if they could have, but it didn't seem to matter. My stomach roiled.

I turned to Nat to tell her we had to go but her eyes were blank and locked on the burning vehicle.

"Nat?"

I touched her shoulder and she snapped out of it with a gasp. Nat steered delicately around the wreck and then stepped hard on the gas, hurtling us down the highway as fast as she could.

No one said a word for the rest of the trip.

15

Nat pulled Wade's truck into the parking lot of a sprawling building and slid out of the cab. I was frozen in my seat, astonished, staring at the banner by the front doors.

WAYLON HIGH SCHOOL. HOME OF THE WYOMING WILDCATS.

"We did it, I whispered into Bear's ear, my hand clutching his back. "We're out."

"Cal!" Nat called. "Let's move it!"

Bear leapt out of the seat, and I followed him. Nat grunted as she grabbed the truck's back gate. Her arm was slick with blood from her shoulder to her elbow. I went to help, but she pushed my hand away. The gate fell and the three boys jumped out. One of them switched on a big flashlight and drew it around the truck's bed.

I expected weapons, but what I saw was box after box marked as carrying medical supplies: bandages, surgical instruments, drugs, antibiotics — an entire hospital's worth crammed into one truck.

Nat straightened up and squared her shoulders. "We did it, guys," she announced. "Everything we needed. Good job. Now let's get this stuff unloaded and to the people who need it."

"Then we sit and wait for the party they're going to throw us," Hector said. "Right, Nat?"

Nat smiled, but it seemed forced. "Yeah, right," she said. "Bet my dad'll give us the keys to the city."

They loaded their arms with boxes and began ferrying them across the parking lot and up to the school's front doors. I winced as Nat dropped a box into my arms and pushed me into the school. Bear stayed close through a maze of locker-lined halls until we came to a crowded gymnasium.

The air in the gym was dense with the stench of blood and decay. The floor was packed with rows of steel-frame cots. Medics in stained smocks tried to minister to the men, women, and children who filled them, but there were too many wounded. Some of the inhabitants were still, but others were thrashing and moaning. Every few moments, there was a scream that burrowed into my spine. Bear whimpered and pressed his body into my leg.

"Drone strike," Carlos said quietly beside me. "Right in the middle of town. Path mostly ignores us out here, but every now and then, they like to make sure we know they're still around."

"Enough chatter, 'Los," Nat said. "Let's get this stuff where it needs to be."

"You got it, boss." Carlos and the others fell to it immediately, ducking out of the gym and jogging toward the truck. Nat set her boxes down and waved over one of the medics.

"Truck's out in the lot," she said. "Send everyone you can spare."

"But your arm," the medic said. "You're —"

"I'm fine," Nat said. "Go."

The medic withdrew, pointing everyone in sight out the door and into the parking lot. The few who stayed behind tore into the boxes as they were delivered and then sprinted across the room, delivering what was inside to the patients.

When I turned back, Nat was gone, mixed in with the rest of the citizens of Waylon. If there was a time for me to disappear, it was probably right then. The Path would almost certainly retaliate for her strike, and I needed to be long gone before that happened.

I scanned the room for Nat, wanting to at least thank her for helping to get us out. I found her sitting beside a cot a couple rows away, leaning over someone's body. I took a step forward but stopped when I saw that she was crying.

Bear kept going, though, dodging through the rows of cots and piling into Nat's side. He thrust his head underneath her arm and I expected her to push him away, but she wrapped her arms around him instead.

The boy in the cot next to Nat was unconscious. A partially bandaged burn, red and crusted black, ran from his chest to his forehead on his right side. From the way the blankets fell over him, I could tell he was missing his right leg and most of his right arm.

Nat kept her arm around Bear as she talked quietly to the boy on the cot. She ran her fingertips along his good arm and then set her hand in his, bending his limp fingers around it so it was like a seed curled up in soil. When a medic appeared with an IV stand, Nat jerked her hand away. She wiped her tears and moved into the aisle as he ran a line into the boy's arm.

Bear looked back at me, and I nodded him ahead. He followed Nat across the gym and through one of the back doors.

I looked to the door as medics and civilians raced in and out. Sitting on a table nearby, there was a stack of sterile dressings and a suture kit. I grabbed them and crossed the gym toward the back door.

I found Nat in an empty science lab, leaning against a large marble-topped workstation, Bear on his side in front of her. When I pushed the door open, Nat whipped around, sniffing and wiping her eyes with the back of her hand.

"Sorry," I said, my voice overloud in the little room. "I can get Bear and go if you —"

"No," she said. "It's fine. I mean, if you don't mind. He can stay."

I let the door close behind me and stepped inside, squinting at the harshness of the fluorescent lights. Nat looked different now that the aura of command that surrounded her at the checkpoint had evaporated. She seemed younger. Smaller too. She sat quietly examining one of Bear's paws, pushing him away if he tried to protest.

"His pads are cracked," she said. "And he's skinny."

"We've come a long way, I guess."

Nat placed a hand over his still-too-prominent ribs. "Gotta look after your troops."

"He's fine," I said, but when Bear crossed the room to meet me, I couldn't help but notice he was limping. She was right. He was clearly favoring one of his front paws, wincing when the other hit the tile.

Just hang in there, I thought. *We're almost home.*

I swung the pack off my shoulder and cracked open one of Wade's cans of tuna. I set it down in front of Bear and he devoured it.

"I thought you might need this," I said, holding up the bandages. "For your arm."

"I'm fine," she said. "Thanks."

"Gotta look after yourself too."

Nat glared at me but yanked up her blood-soaked sleeve. I cleaned the wound with antiseptic and a length of the bandage, then opened the suture kit and selected a threaded needle.

"What are you doing with that?"

"You need stitches."

"I'll wait for a medic."

"They're busy," I said, and hooked the needle into her arm.

"Ow!"

"Sorry." I slipped the needle in and out of her skin, remembering our survival instructor's admonitions to keep the stitches small and tight.

"Your friends in the Path teach you that?"

"They're not my friends." I said. "*Your* friends in the Fed teach you how to assault a supply truck?"

"My mom did."

I looked up to see if she was joking.

"Oh, right," Nat said. "You Path guys prefer your women in veils instead of body armor."

"I'm not Path," I said.

"Maybe, but you sure looked surprised when you figured out it was me who was in charge tonight."

There was a teasing glint in Nat's eye.

"Well . . . maybe a little," I said. "This is going to sting."

I finished the suture, then pulled to make sure the edges of the wound were tight together. Nat hissed as I did it.

"Sorry."

I tied off and unrolled the bandages. Bear left his dinner to lie down between us, presenting his belly to be rubbed. Nat obliged.

"I learned everything from my mom," she said as I began to wrap her arm. "She was in the Army since I was little. Became a ranger as soon as they started taking women. Most of my friends were playing with dolls while I was learning how to strip an AR-15."

"She out east now?"

Nat shook her head. "Her unit got hit by a Path drone a few months ago."

"Oh. I'm sorry. I —"

"Forget it," Nat said. "Everybody's got a story, right?"

Neither of us spoke as I finished wrapping her arm. The building was silent, just the distant sound of bodies moving in other rooms, and the rise and fall of Nat's breath. I had the awkward realization that I hadn't been alone in a room with a girl since I was nine years old.

I quickly packed up the suture kit, then looked over my shoulder at one of the science lab's windows. It was still dark, but it couldn't be much longer until sunup. I thought about all those vehicles sitting outside and all the miles me and Bear still had to go.

"I thought I'd feel good about it."

I turned back. Nat's hand had gone still on Bear's side and she was staring at the tile floor.

"I mean, they were Path," she said. "Right? And we needed the medicine. But when I think about it, when I see that guy lying there I —" Nat cut herself off, overcome. "He didn't look much older than Steve."

"That's your friend?" I asked. "The one who got hurt in the strike?"

She nodded. "He hasn't been conscious much since the attack. And when he is, he's in so much pain that it's like . . ." Nat faltered, searching for the right words. "It's like he's right there, alive, in front of me, but at the same time . . ."

"It's not him."

Nat's pale brown eyes met mine. She nodded, then looked away. Her jaw clenched as she gritted her teeth, determined not to cry in front of me.

"I think all you can do is try to push it away," I said. "Move on."

"Move on to what?" Nat demanded.

"I just —"

"I don't want to move on," she said. "I want to find the part of me that makes killing them hard and rip it out."

"No, you don't."

"Yeah," she said, eyes blazing, "I do."

"Natalie!"

The door to the science lab banged open and a man in a brown police uniform came storming in. Before either of us could say a word, he grabbed me by the arm and slammed me into the lip of the table.

"Hey! What are you —"

Bear started barking as the man yanked my elbows behind me. Steel cuffs closed on my arms, just above where my cast ended.

"What are you doing?" Nat said. "Dad, answer me!"

"The guys told me he's Path, Nat. He's going to jail."

"He's a runner," Nat said. "And he helped us."

"Helped you do something you had no business doing!" Nat's father pulled me off the table and moved me between him and his daughter, his big hands clamped on my arms.

"You and your friends could have been killed."

"But we weren't!"

"And it's a miracle! If your mom was here —"

"She'd be proud of me!"

Nat stood with her chin thrust out, her face reddening with anger.

"We will talk about this in the morning," her father said. "For now I want you home. And if you so much as set a foot outside the front door, *one foot*, I swear you will end up in a cell beside his. Now go."

"He doesn't belong in jail," Nat insisted.

"And how do you know that, Natalie? How do you know that some kid you just met isn't a spy? How do you know the Path isn't going to come running when they hear their post was overrun? You think they're going to let that go?"

Nat looked away from her father and stared at the floor.

"Yeah, you might have helped save some of these people, but what if what you did helps put a hundred more in their position? Or a thousand? You think Steve would have wanted you to make that trade?"

"You don't know what he'd want," Nat hissed.

"Pretty sure he'd want you to think a minute before you nearly get yourself killed," he said. "Now get home."

Nat's father yanked at my arm, leading me and Bear through the gym and outside, where he pushed me up against a police cruiser. Wade's truck sat two rows down. If I had just taken Bear and walked out when I had the chance. . . .

"Gonna tranq that dog if you can't keep him calm."

"Bear," I said, pulling out of the man's grip and kneeling beside him. "Take it easy, pal. It's fine. We'll get this worked out and then we'll be on our way. Okay?"

Bear whimpered and pushed his muzzle into my cheek.

"I've got a kennel back at the station for our dogs," Nat's father said, his voice softening somewhat. "We can keep him there until we get you sorted out. He'll be fed and watered, just like you."

A police van pulled up behind us, and another deputy hopped out. He threw open the back door and waited. Bear whined and I leaned into his ear.

"I won't let anything happen to you," I whispered. "I swear. Now go."

Bear didn't resist when the deputy led him into the van. Once they were away, Nat's father opened his door and pushed me into the back. He slammed the door and started the engine.

I looked out the window and saw that Nat and her friends had gathered on the sidewalk. Nat watched, arms crossed angrily over her chest as her father took me away.

16

Nat's father and I wound through the streets of Waylon on the way to the police station. I was in the back, leaning painfully against my side to keep from crushing my bound arms.

Most every house we passed was dark, with windows and doors boarded up. The cruiser's headlights caught scarred and crumbling buildings and lots full of ashes. In places, it looked like entire neighborhoods had been flattened.

"Admiring your people's handiwork?"

"They're not my people," I said. "Let me talk to the Feds and I'll explain."

"Oh, don't worry," he said. "I'm pretty sure some intelligence folks will be very eager for a chat."

He pulled the car around a low brick building and parked next to the van that had taken Bear away. Once he hauled me out, we made our way through three locked doors and into the jail. There, cops milled about amid a near-constant screech of radio traffic. Fluorescent lights pounded down on white tile. My eyes ached from the glare. How did these people stand it?

Nat's father led me to a cell and popped off my cuffs before shoving me inside. The steel door slammed shut.

"This is how it's going to be," he said. "You're Army property now, not ours, so don't expect to see a lawyer or a judge. My guess is they'll come pick you up sometime tomorrow for questioning." He leaned against the cell, crossing his arms. " 'Course, since they don't really share any of that intelligence with us, if you have something worthwhile to say right here and now, I'm sure we could work something out."

"I don't know anything," I said. "I was taken by the Path six years ago and I'm trying to get home. That's all."

"Suit yourself," he said. "Someone will bring you supper."

He unlocked the outer door and started to open it.

"She was amazing."

Nat's father stopped at the doorway.

"The Path didn't stand a chance against her," I said. "You should be proud."

Nat's father turned his head slightly toward me, said nothing, then walked out the door. It closed with a boom, and I was alone.

I lay on the bunk staring at the bars. The adrenaline charge that had kept me going for hours was gone and I felt weak and empty. I told myself that the Feds would listen, that once I explained the last six years, they'd help get us back home. They had to.

I closed my eyes and slipped a hand into my pocket. Bear's collar sat at the bottom, twisted into a ball. I drew it into my fist and held on tight.

•   •   •

A few hours later, there was a buzz and the door that led back to the cells opened, silhouetting two guards and a prisoner.

"Sorry about this, kid," one of the guards said.

"No problem."

Nat stepped inside the cell next to mine and flopped down on the cot. I looked at her through the bars, stunned.

Nat shrugged. "I took one step out of the house."

"Your dad threw you in jail?"

"He's trying to make a point," she said. "He'll let me out tomorrow when he remembers that the Feds haven't sent us any medical aid in three months."

"I don't understand," I said. "The Feds can't send medicine? They can't help?"

"Ha! Help the white trash of Waylon, Wyoming? Please, they have to save their pennies in case some trillionaire's son gets the sniffles. You want some advice now that you're back home in the Fed? Get rich. Fast. 'Cause, I tell you, if you're far enough from the front and have a little money, this whole war is something you see on TV."

I could barely process the idea. In the Path, citizens gave the war effort everything they had, and in return they were given everything they needed. I had no love for Nathan Hill, but he'd never abandon his own people like that.

"Oh, hey. I swiped this for you."

Nat handed me something through the bars and I raised it into the light. Black paper and silver foil. I tore it open and the smell of chocolate hit me like a wave. I nearly laughed out loud.

"I haven't had one of these in six years."

"Seriously? Well, it's no steak dinner but think of it as a thanks, I guess."

I traced my fingers over the logo pressed into the chocolate and then over the bumps on the other side. Almonds. My favorite. I snapped the bar in two and handed half to Nat.

"Thanks," she said, and bit off a corner.

I chewed slow, drawing the chocolate over my tongue, savoring it until it dissolved. I suddenly remembered the smell of fallen leaves and chimney smoke.

"After my brother and I went trick-or-treating, we'd trade candy and I made it my goal to get every one of these he had."

"Did it work?"

I laughed. "He was easy," I said. "He loved Nerds. You know? The fruit things?"

"Right."

"So I pretended that I did too — in fact, I loved them so much he was going to have to trade me two or three chocolate bars to get just one box. Worked every time. Sucker."

"I always looked for those caramel things. The ones on a stick?"

"A Sugar Daddy."

"Right," Nat said. "A Sugar Daddy. Every cavity I ever had as a kid can be directly traced back to a Sugar Daddy. So where's your brother now? Still at home?"

I felt a twinge and forced an image of James out of my head. "Still at Cormorant."

"Why?"

"He's Path now."

There was a distant buzz as another cell block opened somewhere in the building. Nat turned on her side and drew herself up to the bars.

"I didn't just happen to get thrown in jail," she said. "I stepped outside for a reason. Two reasons actually. First, Carlos knows a guy who can get us fake IDs that say we're eighteen. We're going to get them, then head to a recruiting station in Casper to enlist."

"Why are you telling me —"

"Because you're coming with us."

"No, I'm going home. Your dad is calling the Feds. Once they get here I'm going to talk to them and —"

"Whoa," Nat said, holding up her hand. "Hold on a second. Do you think they're going to *help* you?"

I stared at her through the bars.

"You've been living with the Path. You worked for them."

"They made me work for them. I ran away."

"After *six years*," Nat said. "They've converted half the country, Cal. Do you think our government is just going to take your word that you're on our side now? Once the MPs finish questioning you, they'll put you in jail for treason."

"No, that's not —"

"If you're going to live here, you're going to have to seriously get up to speed. But look, don't worry, I can talk to my dad. Once he's cooled off, he'll listen to me and then he'll go talk to the sheriff. He won't let the MPs take you. And I know you're trying to get home, but you know the Path. You lived with them. We could use you. I mean, if you want your brother back one day, if you want to stop them from taking anybody else, you have to fight." Nat had risen to her knees and was grasping the bars.

If I say no to her, I thought, *I'm never getting out of here.*

"Yeah," I said. "Okay. Let's do it."

"Perfect! I'll talk to my dad tomorrow morning. Once you're out we'll —"

There was a buzz and the door to our cell block swung open. Two silhouettes stood in the doorway. Keys jangled as they approached with loose-limbed staggering gaits. I could smell beer from ten feet away.

"What's this?" I whispered through the bars.

Nat moved from the cot onto the floor. "The other reason I got myself thrown in jail."

A flashlight snapped on, blinding me.

"Not much to him," one of the men said. "Is there?"

"There's enough, I guess," said the other, earning himself a laugh.

"Hey, guys!" Nat yelled from her cell, startling the two. "It's me! Nat!"

The flashlight beam slid from me to her. I grabbed the blanket off the cot and took the opportunity to slip into a dark corner.

"Nat," one of them said, surprised and trying to steady his slur of a voice. "I didn't know you were here."

"Karl brought me in for pissing Dad off."

"Oh, well, we were just —"

"Save it, Limon," Nat said. "You came here for a game of bounce the Pather off the wall. Right?"

"We —"

"Relax," Nat said. "Dad was going to let me go in the morning anyway, so how about you guys give me a little early release and then you can stay and have your fun. Seriously, something I don't see is something I don't have to tell my dad about. And if I don't tell him, he doesn't tell Sheriff Jeffords."

The officer with the light laughed. Limon leaned in close to the bars, drunkenly grinning, his pale moon face just inches from Nat's.

"Who do you think sent us, Nat?"

Nat said nothing and Limon laughed, clearly pleased to have stunned her. He turned away, but Nat grabbed his sleeve before he could go.

"He helped me, Limon," she said, dropping her sarcastic lilt. "Jenny is in that gym too, right? She's going to get antibiotics because of him."

Limon tore away from her. "My wife wouldn't be in there in the first place if it wasn't for Pathers like him."

"He's not —"

"Enough talking," the other officer said. "Let's do it and report back."

"But he doesn't know anything!"

Limon unlocked my cell door, then made way for the officer with the light. As soon as he stepped inside, I sprang out of the corner and threw the blanket into the air between us. It hit the officer in the face, blinding him for the second it took me to dodge around him. I pivoted toward the still-open cell block door and it was almost within reach when something slammed into my back, knocking me to the ground.

He turned me over with his boot, then stood over me, grinning, a black baton in his hand. He kicked the cell block door closed with a dull boom. "Get him up."

"Limon!" Nat called out from her cell. "Stop it!"

The other officer hauled me into the cell and put my back against the wall. Limon strutted in behind him, slapping the baton in his palm.

"Guess this is where your path gets you, kid. So unless you can tell me the Path's plans for this region . . ."

"I don't know anything. Honest. I'm just a —"

He pistoned the tip of his baton into my gut. Pain exploded through me and I started to crumple, but the other officer held me up to the wall.

"Okay, let's try another one. What are the locations of Path safe houses along the border?"

"I told you! I don't —"

The baton struck again, this time a stinging blow to the side of my arm.

"Limon, stop!" Nat yelled.

"What are the codes for incoming Path bombing runs?"

Before I could say anything, the baton slammed into my side, pinging off a rib. The pain was electric. I bit down on a scream, knowing that it would only get his blood racing faster. Limon pinned me to the wall with the baton, the tip of it grinding into my shoulder. He leaned in close.

"Now," he said. "I want to know the numbers of Path forces on the other side of the border."

"A hundred," I said weakly, feeling unconsciousness tug at me.

"What?"

"A thousand," I breathed. "A thousand men. And artillery. A Stryker brigade."

Limon took my chin in his hand and turned my face up to his, examining me with watery, bloodshot eyes.

"Your friends murdered twelve of my buddies, kid. Damn near killed my wife. So if you think I've even begun hurting you, you're mistaken."

"I don't know anything."

Limon glanced at his partner. "Well, too bad for you, I guess."

He stepped back and raised the baton over his head.

"Limon, no!"

He let it fall, but before it could strike, there was an explosion just outside the station. The floor of the jail shook violently, sending us all to our knees. Limon scrambled for the baton, but I kicked it into a corner and made for the door. The other officer grabbed my ankle and pulled me back just as the cell block door flew open.

"Natalie!"

Nat's father stormed in, grabbing at the keys on his belt.

"Dad! You have to help Cal!"

Nat's father stopped short when he saw the jumble of bodies in my cell. He reached into the cell and yanked Limon out by his arm. "What are you two doing? Get to your stations."

He shoved Limon out the cell block door and then came back for the other one. Sirens were going off outside now, whooping shrieks that reverberated off the walls and steel bars.

"Get to your vehicles and sober up," he said as he tossed the second officer out of the cell. "We've got Path incoming."

The floor shuddered with another explosion. I struggled up onto the cot to catch my breath, my body vibrating from the beating Limon gave me. My cell slammed shut.

"Dad! What's going on?"

There was a rattle of keys and a door opened. "Mayor gave the order to evacuate."

"What about Cal? You can't just leave him here!"

"He's a prisoner! Now come on!"

Nat's father had them halfway to the cell block door when the biggest explosion yet sent Nat crashing into his back. They both hit the ground. Nat was up first, digging for something on her father's belt. The next thing I knew, my cell door was being thrown open. I started to run, but Nat pushed me back. There was a clatter of steel as she fumbled with something between us. Cold metal slapped against my wrist.

"What are you doing?"

Nat's father appeared at the cell door. "Natalie, we don't have time for this. We have to go right —"

Nat stepped to the side and her father stared openmouthed at the handcuffs that now secured my wrist to his daughter's. Nat tore another key off the ring she'd stolen from him and threw it down the drain of the sink behind us.

"Sorry, Dad," she said. "Looks like it's both of us or none."

The three of us ran through the police station. It was packed with a torrent of officers tearing up and down the hall, and the noise from outside was nearly deafening now. Emergency sirens wailed all around us.

"Is it drones?" Nat asked.

"Not this time. Manned bombers and ground troops on the way."

The crowd parted and the front door of the station appeared before us. I stopped dead.

"Bear," I said. "Where is he?"

"No time!" Nat's father said. "We have to go now. There are trucks waiting outside."

Nat turned, darting down a hallway, dragging me with her by our cuffs. Her father yelled after us, but then he was on our heels as we ran down the cell block.

"Here!" Natalie threw herself against a door and we found ourselves in the midst of a kennel full of furiously barking dogs in cages.

"Bear!"

"At the end," Nat's father said. "Last row!"

Nat and I ran for it as her father started opening cages to free the other dogs. Bear was cowering at the back of his cage, too terrified to bark. I got the gate open and he jumped into my arms.

"Okay, buddy, let's get out of here."

I pinned Bear to my chest with my cast and we all ran back out into the station and toward the front door. Outside, vehicles were already pulling away. Another officer appeared to lead the police dogs into a van as Nat's father led us to a parking lot where one police cruiser still remained. I barely had time to push Bear into the backseat before Nat's father was gunning the engine and pulling out. We left the station and tore through the town of Waylon.

The Path's bombing run seemed to have subsided, leaving a ruined town in its wake. Everywhere we looked, there were fires. The frames of houses trembled within coronas of flame, and scores of trees burned, throwing off showers of sparks in the kicked-up winds. All around us, people were fleeing however they could. Cars careened through the streets, mixing with families on foot, loaded down with their possessions. Injured and dead lay on the sidewalks, some wept over, some abandoned. Nat's father ignored them all, weaving through the streets, trying to avoid craters that pitted the roadway.

"Where are we going?" Nat shouted, but her father ignored her. He steered us around a traffic jam, half of the car on the road, half on the shoulder. We shot across a grass divider and onto a service road, where he shut off his headlights and sirens and pushed the speedometer to seventy.

Bear trembled in my lap. A blur of trees passed outside our window and then switched to a high steel fence. I leaned forward and saw the outline of a control tower and a few small private planes and helicopters.

"Get off the road!" I shouted, grabbing at the bars between us.

"What?"

"Get off the road now!"

"Why?"

I pointed out ahead. "Because of that!"

The entrance to the airport appeared in front of us. Parked outside were three Path Humvees and ten or fifteen soldiers. Nat's father jerked the steering wheel and the car fell off the roadway and down an embankment.

"If there's an airport, it's the first thing the Path seizes," I said as we bounced over the field. "They'll have the place surrounded in an hour."

Nat's father cursed, then conferred with someone on the radio. We ended up on a dirt road, eventually meeting up with a small convoy of evacuees deep in the woods and out of sight of the Path. There were police and civilian vehicles as well as a single yellow school bus. All of them were parked with their lights out just off the roadway. Nat's dad pulled over and got out of the car, leaving us inside with the engine running.

He joined a crowd of men, including Limon and his buddy, who were gathered around an older man consulting in low tones. All of them were armed, but I didn't see anything heavier than AR-15s and shotguns. Dozens of terrified civilians surrounded the officers. They were a mix of young and old, men, women, and children. Entire families bunched together.

"This is because of me," Nat said, staring darkly out of the window. "This is for what happened at the checkpoint."

"You don't know that," I said. "They've hit the town before."

"Not like this." I started to speak again but Nat cut me off. "Tell me what happens next."

"Once they have control of the town, they'll gather everyone together and give them the Choice."

"And my guess is the people who refuse to join up don't really go to cozy little concentration camps to wait out the war."

The windows of the yellow school bus were full of the faces of children, most of them younger than us. I thought of a little boy holding a toy out to me in the middle of the California desert, his relieved family smiling behind him.

"No," I said. "They don't."

Ahead of us, the sheriff was arranging the armed men into teams, pairing them off and pointing them toward vehicles.

My God, I thought. *He's going to try to take the airfield.*

The door was locked and there was no catch or door handle on the inside, so I threw my shoulder against the window, making a racket until Nat's father noticed and returned to the cruiser.

"You can't do this," I said as he pulled us out of the car. "All you're going to do is get yourselves killed."

He grabbed the cuffs attaching me and Nat and worked a key into them. "We don't have a choice."

"You do," I said. "Surrender. Say you make a choice for the Path. All of you. They'll take you, but no one has to die. It's the only way."

He popped the cuffs off of us and then stared down at me. "Son, these people murdered my wife and tonight they put my town to the torch, killing God knows how many people in the process. Every person here will fight them until we don't have breath left in our bodies. Anybody who'd do different is a coward."

He waved another cop over.

"Get them on the bus," he said. "Now. We move out in five."

"Dad!" Nat shouted. She tried to go after him, but the other deputy held her back and started herding us toward the bus. Bear was on him immediately, jumping up and digging his paws into the man's leg. When the deputy turned to swat Bear away, Nat twisted out of his grip and sprinted back to her father's cruiser. I followed, jumping into the passenger seat as she slammed the driver's-side door shut.

"Nat, what are you —"

She threw the car into reverse and took off, barely giving me time to close my door. She sped out of the field and onto the roadway. I looked back at Bear barking after us.

"Whatever you're planning isn't going to work," I said. "We need to get your Dad to —"

"What?" Nat said. "He's not going to surrender, Cal. This is my fault. I'm not just letting it happen."

"What are you going to do?"

"I think you've got a little less than three minutes to figure that out."

Nat gripped the steering wheel as the road to the airport vanished beneath us. Up ahead the tree cover thinned and the airport's perimeter fence appeared. Nat reached over and opened a compartment under the dash.

"See what we have to work with."

I rooted around inside, pushing aside papers and pens until my fingers hit steel. I pulled out another pair of handcuffs and a gray case that sat beside them. I dropped the cuffs in my lap and opened the case.

"Pull over."

"Cal, we don't have time to —"

"Just do it."

Nat cut her speed and moved us off to the side of the road. The airport entrance was just visible a couple miles down the road. I lifted the taser out of its case and held it up between us.

"Okay," I said, suddenly calm. "Here's what we do."

17

The .50 cal gunner on one of the Humvees fired a warning volley and I brought the cruiser to a halt in the middle of the road. There were three Humvees sitting in the revolving blue· and red of our dome lights, one dead center in front of the airport entrance, with the other two on either side. Four soldiers stood in the space between them, three with weapons pointed at us, and the other, a compact man with a steel-gray crew cut, watching grimly.

"He'll be the one in charge," I said, keeping my eyes forward, not looking at Nat slumped in the passenger seat beside me. "You sure you're ready for this?"

"I just hope my dad is paying attention back there."

"Yeah. Me too." I swallowed a lump in my throat and stepped out of the car slow, careful to keep my hands where the soldiers could see them. No one reacted, so I went around to the passenger side and pulled the handle. Nat rolled out of the seat, her hands cuffed in front of her. I took her arm roughly and pushed her out ahead of me as I approached the checkpoint.

"Not a place you want to be right now, son," the sergeant

announced. "Got no quarrel with kids, but if you don't want to get your-self shot, you better get in that car and drive back the way you came."

"You're here because of a raid on an outpost on Route 84," I said. "Five soldiers killed, two Humvees and a supply truck destroyed."

There was a brief pause. "You seem well informed," the sergeant said.

I shoved Nat onto her knees in the gravel.

"This is the one who led the raid. Her mom was a Fed ranger. She got some of her buddies to help out."

"And who am I to thank for this out-of-the-blue bit of good fortune?" he asked, his tone as dry as dust.

"Call sign's Bloodhound," I said. "I report to Captain Monroe, commander of Cormorant Base just outside Yuma, Arizona. I was detached about a month ago to infiltrate Fed territories. Ended up here on a fluke."

"You'll forgive me if I find it a little hard to believe that someone who looks like they should be in day care is working special ops for Cormorant."

"Uh, yeah," I said. "That's kind of the idea, Sarge. Look, you want her or not?"

The sergeant's eyes flicked over to two of his subordinates.

"Cuff them both; we'll figure it out later."

"Wait!" I cried. "I told you, I'm with Cormorant special —"

The closest soldier reached for Nat, just as she scooped up a handful of gravel and tossed it in his eyes. When his hands went up, Nat was on him, throwing her bound hands over his head and pull-ing him back. He gagged as his Adam's apple was trapped beneath the cuff's short metal chain. The second soldier moved forward with his weapon up, but Nat dropped low behind her captive, fouling his shot.

"I will wring his neck right here!" she screamed as the man choked. "I swear, you people will not —"

I jammed the taser into the small of her back and hit the trigger. There was the snap of electricity and Nat convulsed, making an awful retching sound as she hit the ground. I dropped to my knees and pulled her hands from around the soldier's throat. The second soldier was completely frozen, staring down at me over his rifle.

"Give me a hand!" I bellowed. "She got the brunt of it, but he's out too. Let's go!"

We got Nat up and started dragging her back to the checkpoint.

"Throw her in the back of Two," the sergeant said, pointing us to a driverless Humvvee with a gunner standing up in the turret. "And you, the next time you end up with a prisoner, you cuff their hands *behind* their back, not in front. Now move it."

"Yes, sir!"

We brought Nat to one of the Humvees and threw her into a heap at the turret gunner's feet. When the soldier went to rejoin his team, I followed Nat inside and slammed the door.

"Hey," the gunner called. "What's going on down —"

I shoved the taser into this side. There was a flash of blue and he dropped into the rear of the Humvee, unconscious. I grabbed Nat and pulled her up.

"You okay?"

"Fine," she said, groggy but shaking it off.

It didn't take them long to notice something was wrong. By the time I got to the driver's seat, machine gun bursts lit up all around us, pinging off the Humvee's armor. Nat kicked the gunner out of the

Humvee and took his place. A second later the .50 cal was sweeping the area, sending the Path scattering. The thunder of the thing was unreal, punishing.

"Cal!" Nat screamed between bursts. "To the right!"

I looked out the side window. The other gunner was rotating our way. I fumbled at the Humvees's controls before getting it into reverse and jamming my foot on the gas. We escaped a volley of fire but crashed into the gate behind us. Nat's next shot sent the gunner ducking back into his rig. After that she shredded the other Humvee's engine.

I tried to get us moving forward, but there was a metallic grinding sound behind us. We were hung up on the steel fence. Sitting ducks. I gritted my teeth and stood on the gas, but the wheels just spun. Gunfire was erupting all around us now.

Nat turned toward her father's cruiser, sending a stream of fire into its back end until the car exploded with a lung-battering *woomf*. The Path soldiers fled from the column of flames. Black smoke fouled the air.

"Helicopters are coming in!" Nat cried from behind me.

I gave up trying to go forward and put the Humvee in reverse, crashing through the gate. Once we were through, I got us turned around and we sped toward the runway. We had given Nat's dad a chance; all I could hope was that he'd made use of it. We had our own problems to deal with.

Two Black Hawk helicopters had started their descent into the airport's floodlights. Nat opened up with her gun, and the Black Hawks' engines surged as their pilots aborted. Our reprieve wouldn't last long, though. They'd find somewhere safer to land and offload their crew of Marines.

The airfield came into view. It was small, just a control tower and two runways filled with a few helicopters and private planes.

There was a blast behind us and I turned to see a fleet of civvy vehicles and police cruisers coming through the wreckage of the burning blockade. Mixed in with them was the last of the Path Humvees with a civilian up in the turret. The school bus was bringing up the rear. They made it. I pulled our Humvee to a stop at the edge of the runway. Seconds later, their vehicles were swarming around us.

Nat's dad jumped out of the lead car and ran toward us, Bear close at his heels. "Natalie!"

Nat dropped down out of the turret just as he ran up. "Dad, wait! I had to —"

Her father's knees went weak as he threw his arms around her, nearly dragging them down. Nat stiffened at first but then fell into it, clasping her arms around his back and pressing her cheek into his chest.

"I can't believe you did that," he said, his voice thick. "I can't believe you just did that. Are you okay?"

"I'm fine," she said. "It's okay. I'm fine."

"So help me God, girl, you are getting in that helicopter this second and getting the hell out of here. You got me?"

"Yes, sir."

"Okay, both of you, go!" he said, running off to organize the teams that were prepping the aircraft. "I've got work to do."

Bear's paws hit my calf and I grabbed him up into my arms. I didn't realize until then how much I was shaking. I held him close, taking a second to breathe in the grassy smell of him.

"Okay, pal," I said. "Let's get out of here."

The three of us ran across the tarmac to a waiting helicopter that had CHANNEL 9 TRAFFIC TEAM emblazoned on the side. The pilot was doing his preflight as we piled into the rear seats, Bear dancing at our feet.

"Never had a dog in here," the pilot said. "Better get strapped in and hold on to him. Word is I'm taking off as soon as this bird is ready."

"What happened to the injured?" Nat called up to him. "The ones at the school?"

"Don't know," the pilot said, shouting over the blades that had just begun to turn. "Plan was to load everyone that could be moved onto trucks and head east but it's pretty chaotic down there. Now strap in and put on the headsets if you want to talk."

Nat put on the headset and drew her harness over her shoulders. When she was done, she stared out the side window, her hands in a tense fidget in her lap. I pulled my headset down and adjusted the mic in front of my mouth.

"He's okay," I said. "They got Steve out and he's going to be okay."

Nat said nothing. There was a roar of engines as the first plane took off, with three more queued up behind it. Across the tarmac, another helicopter took to the air. I prayed the Path would see them for what they were, civilian evacuees, and let them go.

When the last plane took off, Nat's father pulled in his perimeter force and stood on the tarmac, directing them to waiting choppers. Already I could see Black Hawks touching down at distant corners of the airport. Black-uniformed soldiers poured out of their sides and started toward us.

"Okay!" our pilot called. "I think the welcome wagon is here. Time to go."

"What about my dad?"

"It's okay — he's with Billy."

The pilot pointed to where a deputy was forcing Nat's father into another chopper across from us. Their doors slammed and their blades started to turn.

The helicopter's engine revved and I felt us lift into the air. Bear whined and I pulled him underneath my harness. The other choppers made it off the ground, and soon we were all up over the dark tree line. For a disorienting moment I thought an early dawn was creeping over the horizon, but as we climbed higher, it became clear that it was the town of Waylon burning out of control.

"Oh my God . . ." Nat breathed.

The pilot flew us in an arc north of the town to avoid the wind-blown clouds of smoke from burning trees. Inside Waylon the streets were black seams, marking the boundaries between grids of burning buildings. Hundreds of vehicles were lined up on the roadways out of town, but they stopped dead a few miles out. The Path had already set up checkpoints. Right now those unlucky enough to be stopped were being taken from their cars and massed into orderly groups for the beacons. I looked for signs that the Fed Army had arrived but found nothing. The town had been left to die.

Our trio of helicopters pulled away from Waylon, but the destruction didn't stop. The sun came up, bloody and dim, through clouds of black smoke that rose from town after burning town. The Path may have come for Waylon, but they clearly weren't stopping there. Nat stared down at the scene below, unblinking.

The pilot's voice came through the static of our headsets. "Nat?" he said, turning back to us. "Hold on, I've got your dad. Billy, go ahead."

One of the other helicopters rose beside us, a reddish dawn gleaming off its silver side. I could just make out Nat's father through her window.

"Are you two okay?" he asked over the radio.

"We're fine," Nat shouted into the mic. "What happened to the hospital? Did they get away?"

There was a pause and a burst of static.

"Dad?"

"Honey, we don't know. We can't seem to raise anyone down there."

"Have the Feds come?" I asked.

"Word is there will be reinforcements, but no one knows when. Sounds like there are battles going on everywhere now."

"Where are we going?"

"We think we can make it into South Dakota. We haven't heard anything about —"

His voice cut out and the line went from static to hurried voices all talking over each other.

"Dad?"

"— we have to turn, we —"

There were heavy booms below us. Our helicopter shuddered and pitched left.

"What's going on?" I shouted up to the pilot, but he was too busy with his controls to respond. The helicopter next to us wavered, dropping out of sight before surging up again.

"Dad!"

A string of explosions thundered and then Nat's father's voice returned in our headsets.

"Don't worry — we're just going to climb to get away from this," he said. He pressed closer to his window, one hand on the glass. "This will all be over soon and then we'll —"

There was a roar behind us. "Up!" someone cried. "Up! Pull up!"

Nat's father turned to us, his wide face framed in sandy hair, his big hand pressed against the glass like he was reaching out to her.

"Dad!"

Nat threw herself against the glass as the helicopter next to us erupted in a wall of fire.

18

The shock wave sent our chopper reeling, until the pilot somehow righted us again. Warning sirens screamed through the cabin, and the air was thick with smoke streaming in through gashes in the windshield. The smooth turn of the rotors above now sounded labored, straining, then slacking, over and over.

Nat was sitting limp in her chair, the shaking of the helicopter rocking her like a doll. I grabbed her chin and turned her to me. Her eyes were wide and there was a smear of blood on her forehead.

"Are you hurt? Nat?"

She tore away from me and drew her knees up to her chest, hugging them close and letting herself fall onto the side of the chopper. Bear was cowering on the floor beneath me but he looked unharmed, so I popped my harness and leaned forward into the cockpit.

The pilot was wrestling with controls that jerked and shimmied in his hands. Dials were spinning wildly.

"Can I help?" I screamed over the blare of the sirens, but it was like I wasn't there. I pushed myself farther forward and saw that the dash directly in front of the pilot was covered in a dark slick of blood.

Windows were smashed, and there was a long gash on his left side. Blood covered his hands and was pooling in his lap.

The air shuddered with explosions all around us.

"Strap in!" the pilot yelled.

Once back in my seat, I dragged Bear up into my lap, pulling the harness over both of us and fastening it tight. He struggled and whined, but I just pressed harder. The ride grew wilder by the second as the pilot struggled to keep us in the air as long as he could, constantly pulling us up out of sudden plunges while the helicopter pitched from side to side. The world outside the window spun madly and the smoke inside the cabin grew thicker, choking me and burning my eyes. The warning sirens screamed on and on.

I spared a look at Nat and she was terrifyingly still, huddled up like a child, not lifting her face from between her knees.

"We're going in!"

The engines strained one last time and then a sea of green came at us from below. I grabbed Bear and held on as we went belly first into a stand of trees. Everything in the cabin pitched forward, loose bits hitting the windshield like bullets and smashing the glass. The belt around my waist cut into my middle and I screamed out in pain. Bear howled but I refused to let him go.

The helicopter tumbled onto its side, momentum carrying it through the trees, their limbs slamming into the helicopter's steel hide over and over, sending body-rattling booms through the space around us. Glass shattered and metal tore. Nat began to scream, long and high. The still-turning rotors snapped as they tried to cut through the assault of trees.

When we finally came to rest, I lay over Bear's body, panting, arms aching, but too terrified to move. He was still, but his heart thudded heavy against my thighs. There were a few metallic groans as the helicopter settled into place and then it was astonishingly quiet. Even the distant booms of the war were wiped away.

Every muscle in my body burned as I sat up. Nat was breathing but unconscious. A gash dripped blood down one arm. The window next to me was shattered by a heavy bough. What remained of the window was splattered with blood. I let go of Bear and touched my cheek. My fingers came back stained bright red.

I unhooked the belt around my waist and eased Bear over between me and Nat. He went to her, his small legs unsteady, sniffing at her neck and her torn arm. I grabbed the edge of the front seats and pulled myself forward into the cockpit.

The pilot was unconscious, hands at his sides, slumped against the harness across his chest.

"Hey," I said, unnerved by the sound of my own voice breaking through the silence. I pushed at his shoulder. "We gotta get out of here."

He didn't move, so I dragged myself up farther into the passenger seat.

"Hey."

I turned his head toward me and that's when I saw a shard of glass as big as my hand buried more than an inch into his throat. Blood, thick and black, covered his chest. I don't know how long I sat there staring at him. I didn't seem to be able to move until Bear's whine turned me around.

His paws were up on the helicopter's door, scrabbling to get out. I looked into the sky behind us, and even though it was clear now, we couldn't afford to wait around. We had to move. Nat was still unconscious, so I reached over her to force her door open. Bear jumped out

first, stumbling when he hit the ground but quickly righting himself. I followed, crawling over Nat, then leaning back in to undo her
harness.

She moaned. Her head, bloody from a spray of glass, lolled to one
side. Her eyes opened, surveying the damage around her.

"Can you move?"

Nat looked at me but said nothing. Twin sonic booms split the
silence above the tree line as two fighters streaked past. I dug one
arm behind Nat's back and the other beneath her knees. A knife of
pain shot through my busted wrist, but I lifted her up and out of the
helicopter anyway, easing her weight onto my chest.

I got us away from the helicopter, then set Nat down at the base
of a hill. The forest seemed to stretch out endlessly on all sides. Were
we in Wyoming still? South Dakota? I squinted up into the sky, hoping to orient myself off the sun, but a blanket of gray clouds were
in the way. Without knowing north from south or east from west, I
could walk us right into the Path and not have any idea until it was
too late.

Nat stirred, drawing her knees up to her chest and hugging them
close. She started to cry, her chest convulsing. I moved toward her
but she shied away, hiding her face.

Gravel tumbled down the side of the hill we were on. I looked up
to see Bear nearly at the top. Maybe if I got up higher, I could get
some idea of where we were.

"I'll be right back," I said. Nat didn't move.

I dug my fingers into the trunk of a tree and pulled myself up.
Once I made it to my feet, my body wavered like smoke in a breeze,
so I held on and waited for it to pass. I moved from tree to tree,
grasping branches to hold myself steady. Every injury, old and new,

gnawed at me as I climbed. Eventually the shock of the pain faded, leaving just an endless and dark exhaustion. It was as if there was a hole in the center of me and I was slowly draining away. My head reeled, and bursts of lights seemed to dance with shadows in my field of vision.

Whenever I felt like I had nothing left, I looked back at Nat. She grew smaller behind me, a single body nearly lost amid the rock and elms. If I didn't find us a way out, we were done. The peak of the hill drew closer by inches. Bear sat at the top, his dark body outlined in the gray sky.

At the top of the hill was a rocky platform studded with scrub pines that held a commanding view of the land below. I slid down the side of a tree and sat beside Bear.

Below, for as far as I could see, was an unbroken expanse of trees, rising and falling as they climbed hills and fell into valleys, like a mossy blanket laid over the earth. I turned in every direction and that's all there was, wilderness stretching out to the horizon. I imagined we could have sat where we were a million years in the past and seen the exact same view. I searched for the sun to try to at least find our bearing but the sky was still too overcast.

Even if we mustered the will to walk a hundred miles, we might discover we were going in the wrong direction the entire time. Instead of finding civilization, we would only end up deeper and deeper in the gradually darkening woods, more and more alone.

I thought of Nat lying below and told my legs to move, to walk anywhere, in any direction, but the commands grew cold somewhere along the way. I fell back into the dirt and watched as night enclosed us.

· •   •   •

I was lying in the dirt, barely conscious, when I heard the footsteps.

I tried to open my eyes, tried to move, but it was as if I had been lashed to the forest floor, half in and half out of a dream. Bear growled low beside me.

A hand grasped my shoulder. "Hey. You okay?"

It was a man's voice. I opened my eyes, but my vision swirled and it was like I was seeing him from very far away. All I could make out was brown hair shining in a flashlight's beam. Wind blew in the trees around us and a sleepy warmth moved through me.

"James?" I said, my voice a woozy drawl.

Another voice came up the hill. "Someone else down here."

Thunder shook the earth somewhere far away. "There's a storm," I said. "We have to go in now. We have to . . ."

There was a blast of radio static and then another voice. "Pick them up. We'll take them with us."

It was another man's voice, deep and strong from somewhere nearby. I opened my eyes and saw a tall man with dark skin.

"Grey?"

I struggled weakly as hands dug beneath me and lifted me up. Bear barked, but the sound of it was distant and dreamlike. My consciousness slipped away as they bore me off. I swayed in their hands, drifting back and forth as though I was on the deck of some great sailing ship.

19

I woke with a gasp, feeling like I had been buried alive.

I thrashed and twisted, until a great weight fell off my chest and I could breathe again.

When my eyes adjusted to the dark, I was able to make out the dim contours of a room. It was large and nearly empty. Across from me, there was the outline of a closed door, its gaps letting in enough light to fill the room with gray and black shadows. Next to the door was a large cabinet. I saw no other doors or windows.

My muscles ached as I sat up, finding myself in the center of an enormous bed. The weight I felt on my chest was a blanket with down filling, heavy as lead. My clothes were gone and had been replaced with nothing but a pair of soft boxers.

"Bear?" I called. "Nat?"

My body protested as I slid off the bed. The soles of my feet hit the ground and I almost drew them back in shock when they sunk into a thick pile of soft carpeting. Where was I?

I stood up and limped across the room to the door. I grabbed the handle and turned. Locked. In the half-light, I could make out a small table and lamp sitting beside the bed. I made my way back and fumbled underneath the shade until I found the switch and clicked it on. The light stabbed at my eyes, but when they adjusted, I found a tall glass of water, beaded with sweat, beside the lamp. Icy rivulets coursed down my cheeks as I drank. I set the empty glass down, panting.

The bed was nearly seven feet long, covered in a thick gold-and-tan blanket with sheets the color of cream beneath. I searched the drawer on the nightstand and the ones in the dresser, but they all came up empty.

The lamplight revealed a second door on the other side of the room. It led into a bathroom filled with glittering chrome fixtures. I stood in front of the mirror that sat above the white sink. The blood and sweat-caked dirt had been washed off of me, replaced with a faint scent of lavender. Adhesive bandages closed my wounds. Even my cast had been scrubbed clean of dirt and blood. Why would someone go to all the trouble to wash and heal me only to lock me up?

I scrambled for options, but anything I came up with seemed ludicrous. Bust down the door and escape? Even at my best, it was unlikely. Make a racket until my captors finally had to come for me? Maybe, but what then? Attack them and make a run for it, hoping I found Bear and Nat along the way? Ridiculous. I was wracked with cuts and bruises and my muscles screamed at nearly every move I made. There would be no daring escape. All I could do was wait.

I looked down at the floor's marble tile. Of course that didn't have to mean I was helpless.

I brought the water glass to the bathroom and wrapped it in a thick towel that hung by the shower. I set the bundle on the tile floor and stomped on it so that the glass shattered with a muffled crunch. A mix of shards remained. I picked through them, taking the largest and sharpest piece I could find. The rest went into the empty cabinet under the sink. The towel went neatly on the rack.

I returned to the bed, tucking the glass shard underneath the mattress where I could get at it quickly. Once it was set, I cut the light and drew the heavy blanket over me. Exhausted as I was, sleep didn't come easy. I was plagued with thoughts of Bear and Nat. Were they somewhere nearby, alone and afraid?

I saw Nat's father's face pressed against the window of the helicopter just before the flash that took them down. What must Nat be going through right now? I hated that there was nothing I could do but wait.

I draped my hand over the side of the bed so my fingers rested by the edge of the shattered glass.

Wait and be ready.

I woke again to the sound of automatic-weapons fire.

It was coming from somewhere inside the building. A jet streaked overhead and then another, the roar of their engines followed by the dragonfly hum of helicopter rotors. I slipped the glass shard out from under the mattress and rolled out of bed. Maybe I could use the dresser to break down the door and then —

The door to the room was open.

"RPG!"

I flinched as the noise from an explosion rocked the house. A barrage of machine-gun fire answered, followed by a scream.

I moved to the door in a crouch. On the other side there was a hallway of sunlit hardwood beneath yellow walls. There were more voices now. Two different ones at least, talking back and forth. There was another explosion, but this time there was something off about the sound of it, something flat and distant.

"Awesome!"

I clung to the dull end of the glass shard and stepped into the hallway. The polished wood was warm beneath my feet. I crept along it, past framed paintings that hung beneath pinpoint floodlights.

"Whoa!"

"Got it! You suck! You! Suck!"

The hall opened up into a sunken den. There was a black couch against one wall facing a TV screen that was at least two feet high and three across. On the screen, three burly soldiers moved down a street that was hemmed in by crumbling skyscrapers, shooting at adversaries that leapt out of alleys and fired from smashed-in windows.

"Use your grenade launcher."

"Dude, I only have like two left."

Two guys sat in the center of the couch facing the TV, video game controllers in their hands. They were both thin and tan in shorts and T-shirts, one guy with shaggy brown curls, the other blond. A coffee table in front of them was cluttered with game cases, magazines, and piles of junk food. The room trembled as an in-game F-18 thundered across the screen.

"Oh my God, would you two idiots turn that down?!" A black-haired girl appeared from an adjoining kitchen, a paperback book open in one hand. "For real, I can barely hear myself —"

Her book hit the floor with a smack the moment she saw me.

"What, Kate?" the blond gamer shouted. "I can't hear —"

He turned to Kate, then followed her gaze to me. My fingers tensed on the glass in my hand.

"Uh . . . hey, man," he said, elbowing his shaggy-haired friend in the side. "How, uh, how are you?"

On the screen the soldiers had paused in the middle of the street, their barrel chests panting.

"Where am I?"

The blond kid popped off the couch and jogged over to the steps.

"Hey, no worries, man," he said, extending his hand as he came up the stairs. "I'm Reese. We'll —"

I caught him off balance, throwing my shoulder into his side and slamming him against the wall. The girl screamed when I pressed my cast into his throat and raised the shard of glass.

"Are you Path or Fed?"

"What?"

"Path or Fed?!" I shouted, keeping my eyes locked on his. "Where are my friends?"

"Take it easy. We can —"

Reese tried to move forward and I pushed him back again, wincing as my cast hit his throat. The tip of the glass touched his cheekbone.

"Dude, seriously, we're just trying to help you. Okay? I swear."

"Then why'd you lock me up?"

Kate piped up from behind me. "Because you were acting like this!"

I glanced at her, leaving my cast and the glass right where they were.

"Sergeant Mitchell and his guys found you and brought you back here," she said. "But you went crazy, like you were going to kill us. You even broke Christos's nose."

She nodded over toward Shaggy, who had a white bandage plastered over the bridge of his nose. Red and blue bruises radiated from it.

"So we shoved a couple Valium down your throat and locked you up. Figured after you got some sleep you'd be, I don't know, thankful or something. You know? For saving your life? That's why we left the door open this morning."

"Where's Nat?" I asked. "And my dog?"

"The girl's in the bedroom next to yours," Reese said, voice shaking, eyes on the jagged tip of the glass. "The dog was acting like he needed to pee, so the others took him out. I think they went down to the lake. He's fine. We fed him and everything."

The bitter taste of adrenaline filled my mouth. I swallowed it and stepped away from Reese, keeping my eye on him in case he decided to try to take advantage and come at me.

"Okay!" Christos exclaimed after a pause. "We've made some serious progress, folks!"

"Christos," Kate warned.

"What? Reese isn't going to have his throat cut. I think that's an achievement. Others may disagree, but I'm all for it."

"Who are you people?" I asked. "What are you doing here?"

"Uh, just, you know," Reese said. "Playing video games."

"I don't think that's what he means, Reese," Kate said. "Why don't we take things one step at a time? We made some burgers a while ago for lunch. Are you hungry? Do you want something to eat?"

My stomach rumbled but I ignored it. "I want to see Nat."

"She's that way," Christos said, pointing down the way I had come. "Last room on the right."

"There a key?"

"We didn't lock her room," Kate said.

"Why not?"

Reese and Christos looked to Kate.

"She hasn't moved since we found you guys," she said. "She won't eat. Hasn't said a word. She just lies in bed crying."

There was no response when I knocked on Nat's door.

"Nat?" I said. "It's me. Cal."

I opened the door into another room just like the one I had woken up in. The light from the hall spread across a small form curled up into a ball on the bed. Part of me thought I should just close the door and leave her be, that she'd come out when she was ready. But then I stepped inside and closed the door behind me.

"Nat?"

I sat down on the edge of the bed. Her back was to me and I hesitated a moment before reaching out and touching her shoulder.

"Hey."

When she didn't respond, I moved closer. Her eyes were open, staring blankly at the dark wall in front of her. She was still in her clothes from the day before, a sweat- and blood-stained T-shirt and jeans. They had wiped the blood and dirt off her face and bandaged up the deeper cuts, but I couldn't be sure she wasn't hurt worse, somewhere I couldn't see.

"Are you injured?" I asked. "Natalie?"

She was motionless for a long time, and then she moved her head slowly from side to side.

"Do you want something to eat?"

Again she shook her head.

"Water?"

Nat's eyes shut and her body seized as if she had been hit with an electric shock. Her knees rose up tighter to her chest. She looked like she was trying to disappear.

I drew away, but before my feet could hit the floor, Nat's fingers had encircled my wrist. She was still facing away from me, curled up like a seedpod, one arm reaching back. I eased back onto the bed and drew my legs up, lying just behind her. There was only a thin border of darkness between us.

"I think I'm going crazy," she said. Her voice sounded like it was coming from a hundred miles away.

"You're not going crazy."

"I just keep seeing it. Over and over."

I lifted a hand to smooth her hair along her forehead, which was damp despite the air-conditioned chill in the room. I searched for something else to say, hoping to stumble across something that would help push her out of the moment she was trapped in, but I knew it was pointless. I slipped my other arm, awkward in its cast, underneath her. My fingers pressed into her shoulder and drew her close until her back touched my bare chest. I closed my eyes and we lay there until our breath fell into sync and my heart pulsed against hers.

"Hey."

I turned to find Kate standing in the doorway.

"Can I come in?"

Nat had been sleeping for about an hour. Her breathing, ragged and shaking at first, had calmed. I nodded and Kate came in with a pile of folded laundry in her hands.

"I washed your clothes," she said, setting them down on the bed. "I also brought her some of mine, if she wants to change. They should fit, I think."

Bear's collar sat on top of the pile. I set it aside, then reached for my shirt, pausing at a flowery scent coming off of it.

Kate laughed. "It's lavender. Sorry, we only have girly detergent. Drives the guys crazy walking around smelling like flowers all the time."

"It's okay," I said. "Thanks." I slipped it on and finished dressing. When I was done, I stuffed Bear's collar back in my pocket.

"Oh, look who's here!" Kate exclaimed.

Nails clacked against the floor in the hall and then Bear leapt onto the bed and piled into me. He sniffed at every inch of me, burying his head underneath my arm, his butt wiggling. I rubbed his ears, then wrapped my arms around him and dropped my face into his neck. He smelled soapy and warm. A lump formed in my throat and I had to swallow hard to get rid of it.

"Jumped in the lake with us like he was a puppy," she said. "He even liked it when we threw him in the tub for a bath. We didn't have any dog food, so we fed him some hamburger we had sitting around. He pretty much ate a whole cow."

Bear settled down into my lap, licking contentedly at the palm of my hand.

"Where are we?" I asked.

"South Dakota," Kate said. "This is our friend Alec's house — well, one of his parents' houses. You'll meet him later."

"So you're all Fed?"

"I guess so. We're not very political."

I looked up at her. "But you have soldiers here. You said Sergeant Mitchell."

"He's the head of our security. Alec's parents hired him and his guys to look after us when they decided we'd be safer here than in California."

"Have you heard what's going on in Wyoming? Did it fall?"

"I haven't heard anything about it," she said. "But I was just coming to tell you we're getting supper together out on the back deck. Nothing big, just burgers and stuff, but it's a nice night. You should come and join us. Both of you."

I turned back and saw that Nat was awake. She lay in the dark watching Kate silently.

"Sure," I said. "Yeah. That'd be good."

"Okay," Kate said. "Cool. I'm just going to hit the shower and then we'll get started."

Kate gave my leg a pat and padded barefoot out of the room. Bear glanced up as she went, then resettled. Above us the air conditioner cycled on, breathing cool air out into the room.

"I'm fine," Nat said. "You go ahead."

"You should eat."

"I'm not hungry. I just want to rest. Okay?"

Music started up out in the house, filtering down through the hallways. A thump of bass pulsing beneath an electric fuzz. Silverware clinked together brightly.

I stared down at her lying motionless in the dark. "I'll bring you something back."

Bear jumped up to follow when I moved off the bed, but I nodded over toward Nat and he returned to her, crawling his way to the crook of her arm. Nat tried to shove him away, but he was persistent, wriggling closer until he had his nose buried in her neck. Finally she lifted one hand and began to stroke his side. I closed the door behind me and went out into the house.

Everyone fell silent when I slid open the screen door that led to the porch.

Kate was sitting on the opposite side of a large wrought-iron table with a magazine in her lap. Beside her, an Asian girl with a tattoo peeking out of her collar was drawing in a black leather-bound sketch pad. Reese sat across from them, slumped in his chair. The sun was just starting to fall, spreading golden light over all of them.

"Well, hello there!"

A stocky guy with exuberantly mussed blond hair stood at the head of the table, a bottle dangling from his fingers.

"Before you come any closer," he said, moving behind Reese and planting his hands on his shoulders, "I have to ask: Do you intend to follow through on stabbing this young man in the face?"

"Alec!" Kate said.

"Keep in mind that none of us are against this," he said. "I myself have always despised him because he's so much better looking than me. A good facial scar might take him down a peg."

The girl next to Kate spoke up, surprising me with a British accent. "Sorry, Alec, a good facial scar would just make Reese look tough as well as handsome."

"Thank you, Diane," Reese said.

Alec balled up his napkin and threw it at Diane's head. "We have to stick together, D!" Alec mock whispered. "He's prettier than you too!"

Diane laughed, then went back to drawing in her sketch pad.

"Over here, Cal," Kate said, patting the chair beside her. "Me and D will be like insulation between you and our obnoxious host."

"Obnoxious! Did you hear that, Reese? She called me obnoxious!"

"It's almost hard to believe."

I moved self-consciously around the porch as Reese and Alec argued playfully. The table was littered with food wrappers and green glass bottles covered in French writing.

"How's Nat?" Kate asked as I took a seat beside her.

"She's okay, I think. Tired."

"Right," Diane said with a gentle laugh. "If I'd been in a helicopter crash, I think I'd be pretty tired too."

"Yes!" Alec said, dropping back into his seat. "The helicopter crash. They tell me you were fleeing the Path!"

"Alec," Kate said. "Seriously?"

"What? Expressing curiosity about your guests is a virtue, Kate." Alec turned to me. "Now, what was it like? They were shooting at you and stuff?"

Alec was leaning across the table, his green eyes wide, almost hungry. I looked down at the silverware by my plate. "Yeah. I guess so."

"That is. So. Awesome."

"Uh, I don't think it was for their pilot, Alec." Diane said.

"Yes!" Alec said. "Sorry. Thoughtless."

"Obnoxious," Reese chimed in.

"Ha! Yes, that's true too. Sorry, Cal. Humble apologies. But that happens in war, right? Noble sacrifices? *Dulce et decorum est* and all that? The valiant private throws himself in front of a bullet to save the life of the general who will go forth and turn the tide of battle."

"He wasn't Army," I said quietly, pushing at the heavy silver knife. "He was just a pilot."

"Dinner has arrived!"

Christos came out from the house, bearing a massive plate that was overflowing with slabs of meat. Everyone pushed the debris on the table away so he could set it down. The array of food was mesmerizing — hamburgers and sausages and two-inch-thick steaks that were charred and dripping blood. Reese dashed inside and brought out bowls filled with potato chips, cut fruit, and a green salad studded with garnet-colored berries. A silver tray held a teetering pile of butter-slick corn.

"Gruyère?"

Christos had materialized beside me with a wooden board in his hands. It was covered with six overlapping piles of cheese.

Dumbfounded, I sat there with my mouth hanging open.

"On your burger?" He counted down the piles on the plate. "We have Gruyère, white cheddar, Brie, Havarti, a Danish blue, and . . . Diane, what is this one?"

Diane looked up from her sketch pad. "Gouda."

"Gouda! Any preference?"

"Go with the Gruyère!" Alec said. "When in doubt always go with Gruyère!"

"Gruyère it is!" Christos loaded a thick slice onto a bun, along with lettuce and tomato and a half-inch burger. He paused, thought again, and added another slab of meat and three mahogany-colored strips of bacon. "You look like you could stand to put on a little weight."

Everyone fell to their food. My body, used to canned tuna and desert reeds, was desperate to take in as much as it could. My stomach seemed to be bottomless.

"So are you from Wyoming too?" Diane asked, once most everyone had cleared their plates.

"New York," I said. "I'm on my way back."

"Alec!" Diane called. "Did you hear? Cal's from New York."

"That's great!" he said. "I love the Plaza. Do you go to the Plaza?"

"God, you are such a ridiculous snob," Kate said. "You're like a *New Yorker* cartoon."

"What? It's a nice place."

"Yes, it is, but I think what Diane was saying is that Cal here is from —"

Alec slapped the table, rattling the plates. "Hey! I just had an idea. It's going to be a beautiful night and I think it's time we got this party moving! Who's up for a swim?"

"Yes!" Reese agreed, leaping up from the table.

"Aren't we supposed to wait a half hour or something?" Diane asked.

Alec lifted a scholarly finger into the air. "Society," he declared, "has convinced us that the universe is a place of rules and regulations when, in fact, it is a . . . what?"

Alec leaned over Diane, palms planted on the tabletop, a ravenous look in his eye.

"Don't leave me hanging here, D."

Diane sighed. "Life is a cabaret."

"Yes!" Alec shot a fist into the air and led Reese and Christos from the table and down a hill leading away from the house. His voice rose up into the night, loud and off-key.

"Willkommen! Bienvenue! Welcome!"

Kate and Diane rolled their eyes as one and pushed back from the table.

"Come on, Cal," Kate said. "It's time to join the cabaret, ol' chum. You want to get your guitar, Diane? You might be able to drown out Alec's singing."

"Maybe we should just drown Alec."

Diane went back into the house as Kate gathered up some of the trays from the table. She stacked a loaf of bread and the board of cheese awkwardly in my arms and we left the porch, moving across a patch of lush grass that surrounded the house.

"Sorry about Alec," she said. "I mean, he's always been a handful, but he's been unusually intense ever since we got here. I think he flipped out when Daddy Dearest sent him away. Probably thought he was indispensible to the empire or something."

"What empire?"

"La-La Land? Hollyweird?" Kate laughed when she saw my confusion. "Don't worry about it. We'll take this one step at a time."

As Kate led me down the hill, I felt like I was moving through a dream. Below the house, there was a shallow valley with a small lake fixed in its center like a jewel. The sun was slipping below the treetops, spreading a rich orange light across the grass and the peaks of ripples out on the water.

Kate led me down to a wood-plank dock that reached out halfway across the water. We set our things down and took a spot at the edge. Kate slipped her sandals off and dangled her feet in the water. At the end of the dock, Alec and Reese were stripping their shirts off and getting ready to dive. Christos was lying stretched out on the deck, his skin almost bronze in the twilight sun.

"One! Two! Three! CANNONBALL!"

Alec and Reese leapt up into the air, tucking their legs in and slamming into the lake. A fountain of water exploded over the dock, soaking us all in icy water.

"Hey!" Kate yelled, laughing. I found myself laughing too, shocked by the water's chill. Christos didn't even move; he just closed his eyes and smiled up into the sky. Alec and Reese raced across the lake, their arms slicing into the steely water.

I looked back over my shoulder at the house. From the dock I could see how sprawling it really was. It stretched from one end of the hilltop to the other, a rustic brown expanse, more like a resort or a hotel than a house. The entire property was surrounded by towering pines that blocked out any trace of the world outside. I searched for bomb craters or scorch marks, anything that might suggest that this place existed in the same world I came from, but found nothing. A dreamy vertigo washed over me. For a second it was easy to believe there was nothing in the world but this.

"Camembert?"

"What?"

Kate was holding out a crust of bread with a slice of cheese on it.

"Oh. Thanks. Sure." I took the bread and sat with it in my hand, too thrown to even eat. "How long have you all been here?"

"Uh . . . about six weeks now, I think. I don't know. The days are kinda running together."

"You haven't had any problems with the Path?"

Kate bumped her shoulder into mine. "Forget about the Path. Life's a cabaret, remember?"

"Right. Sorry."

Kate smiled. "I was just kidding. We haven't had any problems.

We're pretty well hidden, and besides, Alec's dad was nice enough to hire a small army to look after us."

Kate tossed a bit of potato chip into the water, and a duck paddled over to nibble at it. The pier wobbled as Diane returned from the house, her guitar in hand. She sat cross-legged between us and began to tune it. When she was done, she played a song I didn't recognize. Her British accent disappeared within a lilting melody.

We listened as Diane moved from song to song and the sun fell. Once it was low enough, strings of white lights that lined the dock winked on automatically, surrounding us in a crystalline glow. *Fairy lights.* I remembered how Mom would hang them all through our back garden. Suspended within the flower patches and the vines, they filled the nighttime yard with a ghostly twinkle.

Kate gathered the remains of dinner into neat piles at the end of the pier. When she returned, she sat down beside me, the tip of her knee touching my arm. They looked strange so close, her leg smooth and white, my arm covered in old bruises and partially healed cuts just like the rest of me was. Kate lightly traced the boundaries of one of the bruises with her fingertip.

"Some of these are old," she said quietly, her voice slipping in beneath Diane's strumming. "You didn't get all of them in the crash."

I shook my head.

"You were taken," Kate said. "Weren't you? By the Path."

I turned to her, her violet-colored eyes shyly searching.

"How did you know?"

"A guess," she said with a shrug. "You said you were from New York but you were running from the West, which is mostly Path. How long were you with them?"

"Six years."

"Six years," she breathed, looking out at the water. "Since I was in . . . fifth grade."

"Does everyone know?"

"No," she said. "Not that they'd care, really." She thought for a moment, tossed another chip into the water. "After a while, everything outside of here starts to seem sort of . . . unreal. You know?" She looked back at me with a smile. "I think you're the most real thing that's come along in weeks."

Applause erupted as Diane finished one song and then launched into another, this one faster, punctuated by Christos stomping in time against the deck. Kate clapped along, moving closer to me as she did it, her shoulder warm against mine. The notes suddenly felt strident and jangling. Overloud. I thought of Nat and Bear lying alone in the dark.

"I should go," I said. "Check on Nat and Bear. Bring them something to eat."

"I'm sure they're fine."

"But —"

"It won't kill you to rest for a second," Kate said, a surprising command coming into her voice. "I promise."

"I . . ."

Kate took my hand as the song played on. Across the lake I saw Alec and Reese pulling back toward us. They planted their palms on the pier and slid out of the water, slick as seals. Alec stood at the edge of the pier, his pale belly hanging out, and began a lurching dance in time to Diane's playing. Reese and Kate cried with laughter and clapped along. Soon everyone was laughing, making a sound as crisp and bright as the fairy lights around us.

I felt Kate's hand take my shoulders and turn me around. I flinched away but she was firm, lowering my head down into her lap. Diane stopped singing and her guitar rang out alone. The sound of it was so familiar and so sweet.

I breathed easy for the first time in what felt like weeks. I closed my eyes, feeling like we were locked away in a bubble lit by fairy lights and so still. And even as the world revolved, we remained.

I glided up to the house with the moon's broad face above me. Diane and Kate were just behind me, talking quietly. The rest were strung along behind them down the hill, singing as they walked.

The glass door slid open and I stepped into the den. A second later, Reese and Alec came around behind me, heading into a hall at the dark end of the house. Alec brushed my shoulder as he passed.

"Night, buddy."

He drifted away, humming quietly to himself. Diane and Christos followed them off.

"Night, Cal."

"Sleep good, Cal."

Kate led me back to my room, where the light from my open door made her pale skin and her violet eyes glow. An anxious buzz started in my head and moved through my body.

"I'm the third door down," she said. "On the other side of the house. If you need anything."

"Thanks," I said, surprised to find my voice hoarse.

I expected Kate to go, but she looked at me intently for a moment and then down at the floor, her eyebrows drawn tight together. "I shouldn't . . ."

"What?"

"It's not my place," she said, seemingly to herself. "But . . . you noticed that Alec changed the subject when I brought up New York earlier?"

"Did something happen? Is New York —"

Kate placed her hand on my chest. "No, it's fine. It's just . . . a few days ago Alec and Christos decided they were getting bored, so they talked their parents into sending a plane to pick us all up. It'll be at a small airport not far from here in a couple days."

There was a wooden creak as someone moved through the house. A door opened and closed.

"I don't under—"

"Cal, we're going to take the plane and go to New York."

My heart pounded once, sending a tremor through my chest, and then everything seemed to go perfectly still, like the world was balanced on the edge of a cliff.

"I can't promise that Alec will agree, but Diane and I talked about it. We're going to tell him that if he doesn't take the three of you with us, then we're not going to go either."

"I don't know what to —"

"It's okay," she said. "You don't have to say anything. And we should probably be prepared for the possibility that Alec prizes Diane's guitar playing and my sparkling wit a little less than we'd hope. In which case the five of us might be stuck here for a while. Anyway . . ."

Kate dipped in and kissed my cheek. Her face lingered alongside mine afterward. The scent of lavender clung to her as it did to me. I closed my eyes, breathing in the flowery scent. When I opened them she was gone. The house was shadowy and still, quiet except for the phantom strains of Diane's guitar that replayed in my mind.

Something brushed against my calf and then Bear jumped up and planted his paws on my knee. He looked at me, his stump of a tail twitching frantically.

"You need to go out?"

Bear exploded out the porch door as soon as I opened it, disappearing into the trees. Even he seemed to be feeling better, his limping run a thing of the past. I went to the kitchen and filled one bowl with water and another with crumbled hamburger and leftover chunks of steak I found in the fridge. I carried the bowls outside and sat down at the end of the table. The sky was clear, so I found the North Star and used it to turn my chair due east.

I could feel Ithaca, sitting out there like a fire in the dark, tendrils of its warmth brushing my skin. I saw myself climbing onto a plane and rocketing toward it, a thrill in my chest so great it was almost an ache. I imagined finding Mom and Dad and even Grandma Betty out in the garden. Mom would have a glass of wine in her hand, listening as Dad played. Once dawn cracked the sky, we'd all drift toward the house and settle down to sleep. No one would ask about the last six years, no one would ask about James; we'd all slip into the future without a word.

Bear trotted out of the woods and threw himself into his food, snuffling and slurping as he ate. I looked across the table and saw that Diane had left her guitar behind. I popped the clasps of the case and pulled the guitar out and into my lap, leaning over its body.

"Want some dinner music?"

The Path didn't allow music outside of Lighthouse, so it had been a long time since I had played. My fingers moved across the steel strings, stretching against the restraint of my cast to press into the frets. I played slow and mechanically at first, chord to chord, but then it started to come back to me. I meandered for a while until a song settled in.

> *Moonlight road,*
> *Why don't you light my way home?*

My fingers tripped, sending the tune flat. I backed up and started again.

> *Moonlight road,*
> *Why don't you turn me on around?*
> *Moonlight road . . .*

"Hey."

Nat was standing in the open doorway behind me, barefoot in her filthy clothes. Bear left his empty bowl and ran to her, butting her shins with his forehead.

"She doesn't have any hamburger, buddy."

Nat lifted him up, setting his forepaws over her shoulder and cradling his bottom with one hand. Bear nuzzled into her neck as she dropped into the chair beside me. Bear adjusted, dropping off her shoulder and curling into her lap. He rooted around in her hand, opening it up and then licking it thoroughly.

Nat stared out at the shifting trees. She looked exhausted. Her face was drained of color and her eyes were deep and shadowed.

"Who are these people?" she asked.

"They're from California, I think. Their parents sent them here when the war was heating up. Sounds like they even sent a squad of Feds to look after them."

"Seriously? Fed soldiers?"

"That's who found us on the mountain. I guess they've got their own barracks out there somewhere."

Nat's brow furrowed as she turned to look deep into the trees around us.

"You okay? Sorry, that's a stupid thing to —"

"No," she said. "It's all right." A tired smile rose on her lips. "When they brought us here, that Reese guy patted my back and said, 'Just remember — everything happens for a reason.'"

"He's lucky you weren't armed."

A puff of a laugh escaped Nat's lips. It was welcome, but fleeting. She picked up a plastic lighter from the table and turned it in her fingers.

"I keep thinking about that parade," she said. "You know? The one they used to have at Thanksgiving?"

"Macy's," I said. "My parents took us down to see it one year when we were little."

"You remember how they had those helium-filled balloons? The big ones?" I nodded. "I feel like one of them. Big and empty and just . . . floating."

Nat sparked the lighter once, illuminating her face in flames, then tossed it onto the table.

"Me and James had never been away from our parents before," I said. "So those first few weeks after we were taken, it didn't even feel real. We kept thinking we'd just wake up one day and everything would be back to normal. Someone would come for us or . . ." I looked over at her, ashamed. I was saying everything wrong. "I know it's not the same —"

"No," she said. "I know what you mean. Does it get better?"

I wanted so badly to tell her that it did, that all it took was time and patience and then everything was okay again, but I couldn't lie to her.

"You think about it a little less," I said. "But it's always there. Eventually you go a day or two without thinking about it, but then you walk by a particular street or hear something familiar . . ."

"Yeah."

"And you're back where you started. And you hate yourself for ever feeling good, because it's like you're the one abandoning them."

"So what do you do? How do you . . ."

"I wish I knew."

Nat's gaze drifted to the table. Bear thrust his nose into the palm of her hand and Nat leaned down until their foreheads touched. She breathed in deep, shaking. I reached out and gently touched her arm.

"I should go in," she said. "Get something to eat, then go back to sleep."

Nat lowered Bear to the ground and rose from her chair. She was halfway to the door when I stopped her.

"They have a plane," I said. "In a couple days they're taking it and they're going to New York."

Nat stood with her back to me, staring at our reflections in the glass door. Bear went to stand beside her.

"Nat?"

"I'm tired," she said. "I should . . ."

"The Army won't take us. You know that."

Nat started to go, but I slid out of my chair and took her wrist. Her pulse beat a dull rhythm against my palm.

"Cal."

"There's nothing we can do here," I said. "All we can do is get as far away as possible. Ithaca isn't — maybe it's not perfect, but it's better than being here. I know that."

I slid my hand down her wrist and opened her hand so her fingers were draped across my palm.

"Just come. Okay?"

We were suspended there for a breathless moment and then Nat leaned in toward me. First there was the warmth of her breath on my cheek and then her lips touched mine, once, gently. Then she pulled back again.

I waited for something more but she turned away, striding across the porch and to the door. Bear and I both watched as she slipped into the dark house and vanished.

20

Diane scooted her chair next to mine when I sat down to breakfast the next morning.

"So Kate told me all about you being taken by the Path," she said in a conspiratorial whisper. "I hope you don't mind."

"No, it's okay."

"I just think it's soooo interesting," she said. "My father says the way Hill co-opted progressive ideas about economic justice and then mixed them with this kind of pastoral religious fundamentalism was an absolute masterstroke. And you know I don't believe any of that propaganda about the Choice and killing all those people. I mean, I don't want them to win or anything, but all that talk is just total religious bigotry. I mean, agree with them or don't, but they're people, not monsters. Right?"

Diane waited for a response, but I pretended to be absorbed in digging my fingernail into the rough grain of the tabletop. I was relieved when the rest of the group filed out of their bedrooms and collapsed into chairs around the table.

Everyone's eyes were half closed, their hair twisted into sleepy tangles. Christos brought coffee in thick earthenware mugs. Kate was at the end of the table. Her dark hair was bound with a paisley bandanna, her cheeks picking up a reddish glow from her rose pajamas. She glanced up at me over the edge of her mug and then quickly looked away. Diane shook her head and laughed softly. When Kate got up to get more coffee, Diane leaned over to whisper in my ear.

"Our Kate gets a little squirrelly when she decides she likes someone. Prepare for rough seas, sailor."

"What are you talking about?"

Diane patted my arm gently and went back to her drawing. "Don't worry, love, you'll figure it out."

Alec sauntered in, stretching his arms over his head. A slip of belly hung out under a Superman T-shirt. "Well well well," he said, clapping me on the shoulder. "Sleep okay?"

"I did. Thanks."

Alec dropped into his place at the head of the table, and Christos pushed a cup of coffee over to him.

"I had a dream that I stepped out onto the stage at Lincoln Center for my very first performance of *Hamlet* to find that I was not wearing any pants. It was disturbing for all involved."

Alec took a deep drink of the coffee and then looked over my shoulder. His eyes brightened.

"Well, this must be the reclusive Natalie! Come, join us. Christos, our lady needs coffee! Oh, and Bear's here too! Bear!"

Bear dashed across the floor and jumped up onto Alec's leg. Nat hovered awkwardly in the doorway to the dining room. She had transformed since I saw her the night before. The traces of dirt and blood had been scrubbed clean and her hair was washed. She was dressed in a clean pair of corduroy pants and a black T-shirt. Seeing her filled me with a strange sense of weightlessness. I caught her eye and nodded to an empty seat next to me. Nat quietly folded herself into it.

"Hey," I said.

"Hey."

"Morning," Kate said, with an odd edge to her voice, looking from Nat to me. Nat gave her an awkward smile and nod. "You look pretty this morning. You get enough rest?"

"Yes," Nat said, barely a whisper. "Thanks."

"Chris, we got a girl here who needs coffee and food, stat!" Alec shouted.

"I'm on it!"

Nat's hand moved beneath the table to take mine. It sent a tiny electric pulse through me. Our eyes met and she smiled.

"Breakfast is served!"

"Huzzah!"

As before, the food came out on platters, one after the other, an impossible abundance. It was an assault on the senses — vibrant yellow eggs shot through with gooey cheese and ham. I nearly laughed, seeing the stunned blank of Nat's face as she watched it all paraded before us. Bear had his paws up on the table, bopping from one person to the next, gracefully accepting offerings of egg and bacon and toast. I dug in, devouring what was before me, and then the plate was refilled.

I turned to Nat, eager to see how much she was enjoying her first real meal in days, but her plate was still full. The eggs gleamed and the bacon lay in piles. She had gone pale, staring down at it all, fork in hand.

"Hey," I said under my breath. "Are you —"

"So!" Alec announced to the table. "Who's up for some post-breakfast rock climbing and then maybe a little high-noon fiesta?"

"Let's do it," Christos said, followed by Reese and Diane.

"Sounds great!"

"Perfect."

"Awesome," Alec said. "Cal, your gimpy arm means you're useless to us, but I'm guessing Nat will be more than happy to show us all how it's really done. Right, Nat?"

Nat didn't look up. Didn't move. Everyone at the table went silent, watching her. I nudged her under the table and she looked up with a start.

"Ah, there you are!" Alec said, grinning. "I was just asking if —"

"Where does all of this come from?"

Nat's voice was flat and hard.

"Where does what come from?" Alec chuckled, his easy smile still gleaming.

"The house. The food. All of this."

Alec laughed, wiggling his fingers in front of him like falling rain. "It cascades from the heavens," he said. "Like manna. We go outside in the morning and there it is."

"Don't listen to him, Nat," Diane said. "Christos's and Alec's daddies are beyond super rich. Christos's dad is the last big Greek shipping magnate left, and Alec's dad is an überproducer in Hollywood. You guys know *Downtown Cop*, right?"

"You will not take this monkey alive!" Reese called out in a guttural, German-sounding accent.

"I will now dance the dance of my people!" Christos echoed.

"*Anyway*," Diane continued once the laughter died down, "it's about the biggest movie series ever, and Alec's dad produced them."

"Along with many other notable —"

"— independent and Oscar-winning films," Kate said. "We know, Alec."

"You see," Alec continued, "one of the benefits of being obscenely wealthy is that when you get tired of putting up with your children — who, let's be honest, are pretty big disappointments — you send them off into the wilderness with an army of Secret Service types."

"But if you're all so safe here," Nat said, "then why are you going to New York?"

"Because we're sick of each other!" Christos hollered from the kitchen.

"And we're bored!" Reese said.

"*And*," Kate added brightly, "we've been talking about starting a theater company since school. We're going to specialize in classic Roman comedy and the work that grew out of it. Commedia dell'arte. Molière. Maybe a little Shakespeare in the summer."

"But there's still a draft," Nat said. "Last I heard, the age was eighteen, so I'm guessing most of you should be eligible."

Alec glanced at Christos. "I suppose it was decided that our talents would be better used elsewhere."

"By whom?"

"Nat." I put my hand on her shoulder, but she batted it away.

"No, I want to know who decided!"

"Who decided what?" Alec snapped.

"That you deserve all of this."

"It doesn't have anything to do with deserving things," Christos said.

"Our parents made choices, hard choices, years ago," Alec said in the patient lilt of a grade school teacher. "And because of their sacrifices —"

"Their sacrifices!"

"Nat," I said. "Come on, let's just —"

"My mother was an Army ranger," Natalie said, a red fury burning her cheeks. "My dad just —" Nat dug her balled-up fist into the table. "My friends are all dead and you people sit here —"

"I'm sorry, Nat —"

"Oh, you're sorry."

"— but that doesn't have anything to do with us," Alec said.

"Your security guards should be in the Army," Nat said, standing up now. "They should be fighting the Path!"

"Yes," Alec said. "Absolutely. Because I'm sure this whole war would be over tomorrow if they were."

"Alec," Kate said.

"No, Kate." Alec shot up from the table. "I'm sorry you got dealt a bad card, Nat, but I'm not going to be blamed for it. It's the way things are and it's not my fault."

"Wait," Diane said. "It doesn't have to be like —"

"No, we gave them a place to stay and food to eat and now she wants to — Look, if you and Kate feel so strongly about this, then you two can stay and join up with the Feds too. I'm not making anyone do anything."

Alec turned back to Nat.

"And I am sorry if my dad's hard work allowed me to live like you wish you could. Honestly, I weep with guilt. But if you're telling me that you'd throw it all away if you were me, then you're either crazy or a liar."

Alec and Nat glared at each other across the table. Nat didn't say another word. She shot her chair away from the table and fled the room. Bear barked and ran after her. I looked back at the others, all of whom were glowering at Nat's back, except for Kate, who was staring at me.

"Guys, listen, I'm sorry, she's just . . . let me talk to her."

I left the table and caught up to Nat at the far edge of the living room. She spun around when I took her shoulder. Her face was seething red and there were tears in her eyes.

"Nat —"

"How can you want to go anywhere with these people?"

I turned to see the group was breaking up and moving toward the living room. I took Nat's hand and led her down the hall, away from the others.

"We're using them for a ride," I said in a hush. "That's all."

"We don't need them," she said. "We can't be that far from Rapid City. We'll get ourselves there and find a recruiting station."

"I told you. They won't —"

"We can talk our way in," she said. "I know it. And even if we can't, we can go back to Waylon and hook back up with Carlos and the others and enlist there."

I flinched at the sound of a TV snapping on in the living room behind us. Kate and Reese had moved into the room and were being joined by the others. There was a rush of static followed by loud, hurried voices.

"Cal?"

Nat's shoulders were squared, that aura of command pulsating off of her. I felt myself wilt beneath it.

"Listen, Nat, I . . ."

"Hey! Turn this up!"

I looked up at the edge of panic in Kate's voice. Christos grabbed the TV remote and keyed the volume higher. A harried-looking man was on the screen. He had his finger to a monitor in his ear and was writing notes furiously.

"Reports are coming in now," he said. "Some confirmed, some awaiting confirmation, but we'll tell you what we know for sure right now. After months of stalemate, major elements of the Army of the Glorious Path are pouring over the border into California."

"Oh God," Nat said. Her hand moved to take mine.

A map of the country popped up onto the screen with Path states in gold and Fed in blue. The map quickly zeroed in on California, a mass of blue with four sets of golden arrows pointing into it, two coming in from the east and two from the sea.

"Four A.M. Pacific time saw an end to a brutal series of aerial bombardments that began in major strategic areas in the north and south. Following these assaults, mechanized elements pushed into Southern California from Path-controlled Arizona, while in the north an amphibious assault began on Northern California of a magnitude not seen since D-day in World War Two.

"U.S. forces were quickly overwhelmed and we understand that by eleven A.M., regional military commanders and the California governor met with Path general Jonathan Moreland, where they officially surrendered their state."

On the map behind him, the blue of California switched to Path gold, linking up with other states to completely surround Nevada and Oregon.

"For more on what this means, we go to our senior military analyst, retired general Stanley —"

"Come on," Nat said. "No way the Army says no to us now."

She grabbed my hand but I pulled it back. "Nat, wait."

"What?"

I opened my mouth to speak, but it was like there was a hand around my throat.

"Cal, what's . . ."

I met her eyes and saw the realization hit her.

"You were never going to enlist with us," she said. "Were you?"

I swallowed back a cold lump in my throat. "The MPs were coming for me. You said you wouldn't help me unless I went with you."

"I never said that!"

"Nat, two people signing up right now isn't going to make any difference. You know that!"

"And what will make a difference? Running away to New York and joining their little *troupe*?"

"Please," I said, trying to keep my voice calm. "I know what happens to people who try to fight them."

Nat's glare hardened. "So do I."

"Wait." I reached out for Nat as she turned to go, but she jerked away from me.

"No," she said, glancing into the living room where Alec and the rest of them milled about the blank TV screen. "Maybe you do belong with them."

Nat turned her back on me and strode toward the door. Bear heard her footsteps and scurried out of the living room to follow her. Nat threw open the back door, and a blast of sunlight filled the hall. Bear barked out after her but Nat stalked into the light, a black silhouette and then gone. The door slammed shut behind her.

After Nat left, Mitchell, the Fed sergeant who oversaw the house's security, came in to brief us on the plan.

Their plane would be escorted into a landing at a nearby airport that evening. As soon as he had word that it was on its final approach, he would load all of us into a van and escort us to the airfield. Once we were safely away, he and his men would continue on to Philadelphia to join the forces getting ready to protect the capital.

Alec and the others took their last day in the house as an excuse to empty the place of food. Their party raged throughout the day, sending me down into the dark of a basement room to watch the news on a small TV with Bear in my lap.

What I heard changed from moment to moment as news teams struggled to keep up with a war that was moving almost too fast to be described. Reports of Nevada and Oregon falling were confirmed one moment, only to be retracted the next. There was talk of Path terrorists and hijacked planes and nuclear weapons, of pleas to Europe for assistance that were made and ignored. Late in the afternoon, there was breaking news that President Burke had been assassinated, but that too was disavowed within the hour.

All that was clear was that California was now in Path control and fighting was intense as they tried to push their advantage as far as they could.

The news cycle fell into a loop with ever more scant updates and one talking head after another. They were discussing a massive Midwestern blackout when I finally snapped the TV off for good.

A tense silence sat above me. No music. No movement. The glowing numbers on a digital clock across the room read 8:45. Where was Mitchell?

"Come on, Bear."

Bear jumped down, staying right by my feet as we climbed up into the house. It was practically trashed. There were holes in the walls and burn marks on the furniture. Bottles and cans stood in piles among thickets of trash. The few scattered lights that were on filled the house with an eerie gloom.

Christos and Diane were passed out under a heavy blanket on the couch, their arms wrapped around each other. I tried to shake them awake, but they groaned and turned away.

I opened the porch door and stepped out into the night. Bear was tentative, sniffing at the empty porch before pressing his body into my calf and following me down to the lake. The fairy lights glistened over the dock and the water, filling the little valley with a white glow.

There was what sounded like a distant roll of thunder somewhere to our south and the ground shook. Bear whimpered, his head down and tail tucked between his legs as we continued on.

Alec was lying on his back at the end of the pier, arms spread wide and his feet in the water. Out on the lake, Reese was drifting on a large inflatable armchair.

"Cal?"

I turned. Kate was sitting cross-legged on the grassy shore, half in and half out of the light. She reached out to Bear, but he eyed her warily and moved behind the cover of my legs.

"Where have you been?" she asked in a sleepy drawl. "We were having fun."

Even in the low light, I could see that her pupils had gone wide and were fringed in a maze of red.

"Inside," I said. "Watching the news."

"Any of it good?" she asked through a strange chuckle.

"The Path is on its way east," I said. "We need to go. Has Sergeant Mitchell come back to —"

"What do you think it'll be like if they win?"

"Kate."

"Christos says it'll be weird for a while, but sooner or later everything will go back to the way it was before because of, like, market forces, which are an inherently moderating force. Do you think it'll be like that? Like a wheel? Or do you think it will be like something else?"

I felt a twinge of disgust and said nothing. A hard glimmer came into Kate's eyes.

"Where's your friend?"

"She left."

Kate nodded, then went back to staring at the water. "It wasn't nice, you know. What she said to us."

"You should get ready to leave."

Bear and I left her there, crossing the dock to where Alec lay sleeping. Out on the water Reese's chair spun in lazy circles. When he saw me, he raised one hand in greeting, then paddled away into the dark.

"Alec," I said, nudging him in the shoulder. "Alec, it's Cal. Wake up."

His eyes opened slowly. In the fairy lights they were shockingly blue with wide black pupils.

"Cal!" he said, then reached out to ruffle Bear's fur. "Little dog!"

"Alec, you have to talk to Mitchell. We need to get —"

"Relax," he said, moaning as he forced himself to sit up. "All is as it should be. Have a seat."

"We don't have time," I said. "We have to get —"

Alec slapped the side of my leg. "Mitchell is getting ready as we speak, Cal. Now come on. Sit."

Alec reached into the water and fished out a six-pack of cans. He tore two off and held one up to me. I looked back at the house, then took it and sat next to him. Alec cracked the can, and Bear settled down between us. There was another faraway rumble and the sky lit up in the distance.

Reese's voice drifted to us from across the water. *"And the rocket's red glare, the bombs bursting in air . . ."*

Alec peered into the sky and began to recite — " 'If destruction be our lot,' he said. 'We must ourselves be its author and finisher. As a nation of freemen we must live through all time, or die by suicide.' Honest Abe himself said that back before his Civil War started."

"I don't . . ."

"Everybody thinks this is just like Lincoln's Civil War," Alec said. "But this isn't two sides fighting it out for the soul of a country. This is a suicide."

Alec drained his can and threw it out into the water, where it spun among small eddies. He leaned forward, staring gloomily into the dark water, one hand on Bear's side.

"We should start getting everyone together," I said. "Get ready to —"

"We're not going to New York, Cal."

Everything around us seemed to cease all at once. The water went still and so did the sway of the trees and the air in my lungs.

"My dad got us clearance into Canada," he said. "We fly west to meet him in Vancouver, then after that . . . I don't know. We were thinking São Paulo, maybe. Or Shanghai."

"Alec, if this is because of what Nat said —"

"I don't blame you for that," he said. "I asked my dad if we could fly to Toronto so you could get to New York from there, but the word is, it has to be Vancouver." Alec turned to face me. "Look, you can still come."

"Alec —"

"New York is *done*, Cal. This whole country is. There's no point pretending that it's not."

He waited for me to respond, and when I didn't, Alec rolled up onto his feet and threw his arms over his head. He stood poised for a moment and then dove into the lake, barely making a splash. He sprang up to the surface again and pulled away from me on his back with easy strokes.

"Think about it, Cal. The future is coming whether you like it or not. I promise you, in a few years, we'll all wonder what it is we got so worked up about. No one will even remember this dump!"

Alec began to sing as he pulled away, aiming at Reese in his revolving chair. Soon his voice and the splash of his strokes dissipated and the water re-formed its glassy surface behind him.

I sat at the end of the pier feeling everything inside of me grow more dense by the second, like I was collapsing in on myself. Was Alec right? Would it really be so bad to leave with them? To leave all of this? I thought of Ithaca, trying to re-ignite the flame that drove me this far, but home felt so far away and so cold. This place was dying. I looked over at Bear, leaning eagerly over the side of the pier. Why should we die along with it?

I recoiled from the thought; even the barest edge of it felt like a betrayal. I set my knuckles against the wood of the pier and pushed until the grain bit into my skin. The pain snapped me into focus. Mom and Dad were waiting. Home was waiting. I wouldn't let the Path turn me away now.

I scrambled for a plan. Walking out would be crazy. It was too far, and with the fighting heating up, I couldn't imagine that we'd make it long before being picked up by one side or the other. We needed another way. Something fell into place. Philadelphia. I counted the miles between there and New York in my head and then jumped up and ran back to the house with Bear beside me.

I guessed that Mitchell and his men were quartered somewhere to the west of the house, so I passed it by and moved into the forest. When we came out the other side, we found a black passenger van at the end of an asphalt driveway, flanked by two Humvees.

Four soldiers were hurrying between one of the Humvees and a dock, loading it up with ammo and provisions. When I looked closer, I saw that Nat was one of them. She was dressed in scuffed combat boots and a set of fatigues that were too big. She set a wooden crate in the back of the Humvee and went for another. Bear ran to her, and I jogged over to keep up.

"What are you doing?" I asked.

"Go away, Cal." Nat pushed Bear aside and bent over to pick up a crate of ammo.

"Where are you going?"

She hefted the box and brushed me aside. "Virginia."

"Virginia?" I said, trailing her. "I thought after they dropped off Alec and his friends, Mitchell was heading to Philadelphia."

"He is," she said, slinging the crate into the back of the Humvee. "But the rest of us figured that instead of protecting a bunch of rich politicians who are in no actual danger at the moment, we'd go to Virginia, and help the people who actually are."

"Think we're set," one of the other soldiers said.

She shut the hatch while the others took their places inside the Humvee.

"Nat, don't do this."

"California is *gone*," she said, turning to confront me. "Pretty soon they'll have the entire West Coast, and the odds are that Philadelphia won't be far behind. So how long do you think you and your family can hide out in New York and pretend that none of this is happening?"

The Humvee's engine rumbled to a start.

"Yo, Natalie, let's go!"

Nat moved closer and I was surprisd to feel her hand taking mine, drawing me to her.

"You could help us," she said. "You could help me."

The anger in her had drained away, replaced by something raw and trembling that reminded me of sitting on that classroom floor with her and Bear, her armor of command wiped away. I started to speak but strangled the words off at the last second. Alec hadn't turned me aside and neither would she.

Nat stood before me a moment more and then her boot heels turned and thudded across the asphalt. Bear went after her, barking as he ran around to the side of the vehicle. The door slammed shut and the engine revved.

"Rup! Rup rup rup!"

The Humvee pulled away down the dark drive. I stood there for a long time without moving. Eventually, Bear gave up the chase and returned to my feet, a small whimper in his throat.

"They about ready down there?"

Sergeant Mitchell had come out of the barracks and was standing by the loading dock. I nodded.

"Well, let's get a move on, then. Don't worry, kid, you and your friends will be singing 'O Canada' before you know it."

"I'm not going with them," I said, pushing my voice out harsh and quick. "I want to go to Philadelphia with you."

"Looking to join up, huh?" he asked with a pleased grin. "Fight the big bad Path?"

Sergeant Mitchell waited for an answer, but the lie stuck in my throat. All I could do was nod.

Once the rest of Mitchell's men got Alec and his friends in the van, we spent the next few hours creeping along back roads behind the remaining Humvee.

I was in the middle row of seats, with Bear in my lap. Kate was to one side of me, Diane to the other. Alec and Reese were in front of us, bouncing their heads in time to whatever was coming through their oversize headphones. Christos stared out the window at the dark.

Everyone was lit in the ugly green glow of the radio that sat between Mitchell and the private riding shotgun. Transmissions came through it in staticky bursts of code, panicked voices calling for assistance while gunfire snarled in the background. Eventually, Mitchell flipped the radio off and we were left with the rush of tires against the road.

An hour later we merged onto a highway that was clogged with refugees heading east. Mitchell forced his way through the jammed traffic and pulled up to an exit blocked by two Fed Humvees. We came to a halt and Sergeant Mitchell and his private got out to talk to the sentries.

Alec pulled one of the headphones off his ear and cupped his hand over the side window to look out.

"I would *not* want to be one of them," he said. Reese turned to see what he was looking at and laughed darkly.

A rusty pickup truck had pulled off to the side of the road, just beyond the roadblock. One of its back tires was lying on the ground in shreds. A skinny man in a tattered blazer sat beside it, his head in his hands; a jack and a deflated spare lay in front of him. Standing behind him was a young woman staring at his back and clutching the hand of a small boy.

"What'll happen to them if they're here when the Path comes?"

Kate had turned away from the window and was staring back at me.

"They'll be given the Choice," I said.

"Is that really what people say it is?"

I nodded and Kate turned back to the family at the side of the road. The man was standing now and waving his arms for help, but everyone passed by, studiously ignoring him.

"We should help them," she said.

"Sure," Alec said over his shoulder. "Maybe we can cram all of South Dakota in our plane and fly them to Canada."

"Alec —"

Before Kate could finish, Mitchell was climbing back into the van. Up ahead, the sentries drew aside and our Humvee pulled through the roadblock. Mitchell put the van in gear to follow. Kate pitched forward, about to say something, but as the Humvee started to move, she swallowed it and collapsed into her seat.

Behind us, the man by the pickup had given up trying to flag anyone down. He sat in a heap, the useless tools in front of him, watching us as we slowly rolled away. I pulled Bear closer to me and looked away too.

We went through the checkpoint, and the two Humvees re-formed the roadblock, like a gate slamming shut behind us. Mitchell switched the radio back on, filling the van with static and disjointed communications. Up ahead, the Humvee bristled with rifle barrels poking out of every window, scanning the trees. The turret gunner stayed low but kept his weapon moving, sweeping back and forth. The private in our van leaned out his window, his face lit by the glow of his rifle's night-vision scope.

The war sounds were nearly constant, distant still, but seeming to come from everywhere at once, like hearts beating out in the darkness. The air felt warmer too and dense, weighing down on us. Even Alec and Reese noticed. They pulled the headphones off their ears and sat up straighter, watching out the side windows as bursts of yellow and orange lit the sky above the tree line.

I wondered where Nat was right then. Had she and her friends gotten stuck in this fight? Or had they managed to push through, eager to throw themselves into an even fiercer one ahead? I could still feel the heat of her hand on mine and hear her voice, hushed, asking me to come with her. Why did that sound make me feel so small?

I shut my eyes and counted out the miles from Philadelphia to New York. Once we reached the capital, all I had to do was slip away from Mitchell and all of this would be over before I knew it. I tried to fill my head with green forests and the crash of waterfalls, but the memories were slippery, gone as soon as they came.

Diane said something and as I opened my eyes and turned to her, a blast of yellow light erupted on the road ahead. The sound of the explosion followed a half second later, tearing through the inside of the van like a tidal wave. I bent over my lap, clapping my hands onto my ears. The world outside spun wildly and then there was the squeal of brakes, and the next thing I knew, the side doors were flying open. The world outside the van was lit in flickering yellow and orange.

"Everybody out," the private ordered. "Move move move!"

He pulled Diane out first, followed by me and Kate. I reached for Bear but the private shoved me away and went back for Reese and Alec. Mitchell was at the rear of the van, his rifle locked into his shoulder, firing into the tree line. Christos crashed into me and I stumbled farther into the road, where I saw the Humvee lying on its side, consumed within a wall of flames.

"Across the road!" Mitchell yelled over the gunfire. "Run!"

Diane and Christos blew past me, but I turned back for Bear. I made it to the corner of the van just as Alec and Reese were jumping out the door. Reese hit the asphalt and dodged away, but as the private reached up for Alec, a volley of gunfire exploded from the tree line. The private crumpled to the ground and when Alec tried to jump past him, there was another roar. He took the full force of a blast in his chest and was pitched back into the van.

Someone screamed behind me but I couldn't move. Alec was half in and half out of the van, his legs hanging out of the door, still. The private was on the ground in front of him, his chest torn, surrounded in blood.

"Run! Get across the street!"

Mitchell pushed Kate into my arms. We tangled together as she tried to get past me and reach Alec. It was like time started up again. I shoved her away and kept her in front of me as we ran. We made it halfway across the road when I saw Bear. He was between the van and the Humvee, claws dug into the asphalt, barking at the gunfire that was pinging off the roadway. I handed Kate off to Reese and sprinted across the street. Terrified, Bear sank his teeth into my arm when I grabbed him but I held him tight and raced into the trees.

I found the others at the bottom of a hill. Reese was holding himself up with one hand braced against a nearby tree while with the other he mopped at blood pouring from a gash on the side of his face. Christos was on the ground, his face ghost white, his body limp. Kate was deeper in the woods, wailing, her fingers sunk into the flesh of Diane's arms.

"We have to go back!" she screamed. "We have to get Alec!"

There was a crash behind us and I turned, expecting a squad of Path soldiers. It was Mitchell. He raced down the hill and dropped to his knees in front of me.

"Took us too long to get here," he said, panting as he freed a spent magazine from his rifle and tossed it aside. "Drone took Rashad's Humvee and now there's movement everywhere. Path. Fed. I don't know. You have to get them moving. Head west."

He seized, digging one hand into his side. It came back shiny with blood.

"Sergeant —"

He knocked my hand away. "The plane is on an airstrip two klicks west," he said. "Last we heard, no one controls it yet. You have to get there before they do. Get to it and get on it, all of you."

"But you're —"

"Go!"

Mitchell slammed a fresh magazine into his rifle and ran back toward the hill. Bear was barking again, wild and high-pitched, mixing in with the chatter of weapons fire and crackling flames coming from the road. Reese was the only one still on his feet, so I grabbed him first, turning him to face me.

"We have to go. Get Christos. Do you hear me?"

Reese nodded and lurched away. Kate was on her knees, slumped over with Diane at her shoulder. I took her arm but she thrashed away from me.

"We can't just leave. We have to get Alec!"

"He's dead, Kate."

She looked up at me, eyes wild, uncomprehending. There was no time for this. I glanced at Diane, and she jerked Kate up without a word and got her moving.

Bear and I led the way, running until we were nearly out of sight of the road. I took one last look behind us and saw Mitchell on his back, arms thrown up over his head, his weapon on the ground next to him. Dark figures, silhouetted in the Humvee fire, were crossing the highway toward us.

Gunshots zipped through the air, slicing into branches and rocks all around us. There was a clear trail dead ahead, but I led the others off of it and into heavier woods. We ran over dark and uneven ground, crashing to the earth and pulling each other up again and again until the firing behind us finally died down.

We came out of the woods and entered a shallow valley that was filled with a pall of gray smoke heavy as fog. Explosions made deep bruises of red and yellow within it, and the rattle of gunfire came from every direction. Seeing no other alternative, Bear and I led the others into the smoke, trudging across ground that was a mix of torn grass and ankle-deep mud. It was like walking underwater.

I kept us as close together as I could, but there were moments when I'd look back and someone would have evaporated into the gray, only to reappear seconds later. Only Bear stayed by my side, but he was limping again and cringing at the rattle of fire. Every time we paused I dropped my hand to his side, petting him to try to still his shaking.

We'll get them in sight of the airfield, I thought, willing it to somehow bridge the gap between us. *And then they're on their own. We'll find the highway east and mix in with the evacuees.*

We moved on, catching bits and flashes of the fighting through the haze. Men and women grappling hand to hand. Scattered, torn bodies facedown in the muck. Ranks of artillery like smokestacks vomiting fire and smoke into the sky. Once, we all dropped into the mud and watched as a company of tanks passed within feet of us. Close up, they were massive, their flat gray hides making them seem like something mythological — eyeless creatures clanking and grinding and spewing fire.

More than anything else we saw our own mirror images — ghostly scores of refugees shambling half blind in every direction. I shuddered to see them, feeling a sudden bone-deep terror that said there was no airfield at all, only this smoke and this battlefield, and we would all be out here wandering in the gray forever.

The base of a hill emerged from the smoke and I waved everyone to it. We all dropped to the ground, exhausted. Bear cringed against my leg, trembling at the blasts that shook the ground without a pause.

Kate and Reese looked to be the worst off, pale and blank eyed, their clothes torn and weighed down with muck. Reese's wound had stopped bleeding but his face and neck were covered in blood. Christos looked unhurt but he was strangely listless, sitting draped over his knees and breathing shallow. Diane was as dirty and worn as the rest, but she seemed sharper than she had been before, more focused. She was crouched beside me, searching the hillside methodically.

There were pockets of other refugees all around us — men, women, families — all of them clinging to the hillside like it was a life raft.

"Look."

Diane pointed about a half mile above us just as the wind shifted, revealing a thin road that rose up the hill and, at the end of it, a small island of light. Within it I could make out the rotating lights of a control tower and a tall steel fence.

Diane moved forward, but I held her back. We weren't the only ones interested. Muzzle flashes bloomed along the length of the hill, like strings of firecrackers.

"What do we do?"

I looked to our right where the ground ran straight and clear along the base of the hill and into the woods. The highway east was only a few miles on the other side of those trees. This was my chance.

I heard my instructions to them in my head — *Keep your eyes on the lights of the airport. Keep running. Don't stop no matter what.* But when I turned back, Reese and Christos and Kate and Diane were all watching me. Behind them some of the other refugees had drifted down around our circle, all of them waiting.

"Cal," Diane said. "What do we do?"

Bear was on the ground in the center of our group, turned in a ball, his head tucked into his belly. I placed my palm on his back and felt his warmth move through me.

"You follow me."

Bear and I sprinted up the hill toward the road. Kate and Reese were behind me, followed by Diane and Christos. The other refugees were spread out below us, like links in a chain. Two or three at a time, spaced thirty seconds apart.

The hillside was a slurry of mud and debris that sent all of us down into the muck every few feet. Each time, though, we dug in and got back up and kept running, focusing on the lights of the airport and trying to ignore the sounds of the valley being ripped apart behind us.

I hit the road and made it halfway up before I was stopped by a roadblock of Humvees. They raised their weapons and shouted, but we darted off the track and back into the trees. An instant later I heard the swoop of a helicopter, and the roadblock was obliterated. The shock wave sent me into the mud. Bear dug his snout into my side, urging me up. I pushed him aside and started to move.

"Cal!"

Behind me, Diane and Christos were running up the hill to Reese and Kate. Kate was standing but Reese wasn't. He was on his back, conscious but moaning and clawing at the mud. When I reached him I saw that his leg was shattered midway down his shin.

"What do we do?" Kate asked, her eyes electric with fear.

"Keep going," I said and pushed her up the hill. "Christos!"

Christos left Diane and dropped by his friend's side. Reese was sweating and pale, covered in mud. He gritted his teeth to try to keep from screaming.

"I'll get his arms," I said to Christos. "You take his knees."

"But his leg —"

"Do it!"

Christos hooked his arms under Reese's knees, and I slipped my elbows beneath his armpits. Reese shrieked as we lifted him, the veins in his neck bulging, his skin going scarlet. It got even worse

218

when we began moving up the uneven ground and I was climbing backward, slipping and stumbling. He screamed until his throat was shredded and then he passed out.

We hobbled up the hill that way until the sky went bright around us. At first I thought it was another explosion, but then I saw my feet move from mud to asphalt. Floodlights were beating down on us. I looked over my shoulder and saw the open gate of the airfield. Kate and Diane had run ahead out onto the tarmac, where a single plane waited. Christos and I made it through the gate and then hit the ground when we couldn't take another step. Bear rushed to my side, digging his nose into my arm.

He flattened to the ground when a drone shot over the airfield with a scream. It loosed its munitions on the valley. Where they fell, it was like a seam had been ripped into the earth and you could see all the way down to its molten core.

Two of the other refugees came over the lip of the hill at a run and moved Christos and me out of the way as soon as they saw us. They took Reese in their arms and brought him the rest of the way toward the plane. Its engines were spinning now, filling the air with their urgent whine.

Diane returned for Christos and then someone tugged at my arm. "We have to go!"

Kate's violet eyes were electric in the floodlights. She knelt down beside me and covered my hand with hers.

I looked over her shoulder at the gleaming white of the jet as the refugees filed inside. I saw myself in one of its seats, strapped in and climbing into the night sky, leaving behind the Path and the Feds forever. It should have made me feel like I was being sprung from a prison, but it didn't. It was like there was a stake running through my body and deep into the earth and if I tried to leave, I'd be torn apart.

"Come on," Kate said. "It's over."

Her hand slipped from mine as I backed away. Kate called out to me but I had already turned and started running. Bear's claws scrabbled against the tarmac behind me, racing to keep up. I heard Kate's voice one last time as we ran through the gate and turned east toward a patch of trees where the land dipped down into the valley. We hit the edge of it just as another bombing run completed out in the valley. The ground shook and my foot hit thin air, sending me tumbling down the embankment.

Rocks and twigs raked my arms and back as Bear and I went spinning down the face of the hill. We hit the bottom with a jolt and rolled into a thin stream of icy water. I lay there buzzing and numb, holding my breath against the rush of pain I knew was coming.

Far above me, there was a swell of engines, loud even over the sounds of the battle, and then the jet's running lights appeared as it strained against gravity and rose into the sky. Trails of tracer fire chased it but they fell short. In seconds the jet was swallowed up by the dark.

I imagined all of them looking down at fires in the valley and then the snaking lights of the evacuees on the highway, relieved to see them grow smaller and fade away. I wondered how cold that relief would feel when they looked back and saw the place where Alec was meant to sit.

There was a whimper behind me and I turned to find Bear lying in the water, dazed and still.

"Bear?"

I crawled across the ground, grimacing from the pain, and reached out for him. Bear's teeth flashed as he snapped at my finger.

"Hey. It's me."

Bear kicked himself back into the muck near the stream, coiling up and eyeing me warily. He growled when I went for him again, so I held up my hands and eased back onto my knees to examine him from a distance.

"Shhh. Shhhhh."

There was a shallow gash on his belly and another on his side, but it was one of his front legs that was the real problem. It was bloody from a deep cut that ran nearly its length and the paw was badly swollen. It was the paw he had been avoiding on and off for days. It looked like one of the thin bones just back from his claw had snapped. I looked down the length of the ditch. It had to be a mile or more to the highway.

The fighting was still raging in the valley behind us. We had no choice. I plunged my hands in the scummy water of the ditch and scrubbed the soot and sweat from my face before drinking deep to purge the acid from my throat.

Bear growled steadily as I reached for him. Moving as slow as I could, I got one of my hands on his side and held it there. His fur was hot and his heart was racing. His growl rose in pitch as I moved closer. He snapped again, drawing blood, but I managed to get my hands hooked under his front legs and lift. My wrist throbbed and he yelped in pain but I got him up onto my shoulder, holding him steady and letting him settle as the icy water of the stream coursed around my feet.

When I felt his head fall to my shoulder I held him tight and started moving. I stayed as low as I could, stroking Bear's back and whispering in his ear as I crept the length of the ditch. We finally came to a place where the water ran into another concrete pipe. I could hear honking horns and idling engines just above us.

I climbed the embankment around the pipe, awkwardly leaning forward so Bear's weight wouldn't throw me off balance and send us tumbling backward. He began a steady whine in my ear. The sound of it gutted me. I wanted nothing more than to stop and hold him until it passed, but I kept pushing us on, focused on the highway sounds ahead. A couple feet from the top, I set Bear down and belly-crawled the rest of the way until I could peek between two thin trees.

The highway was choked with a river of cars and trucks stopped dead. Horns and voices blared and miles of brake lights glowed bloodred, from where I stood out to the horizon. Bear stood watching it all, his injured paw held tight to his chest.

"Hey! Over here!"

A rusty Chevy sat a few cars down from us. The passenger-side window was open and a gray-haired woman was leaning out of it and waving us down. Bear lifted his head and then hobbled over to her. When he reached the car, he jumped up on his hind legs and hooked his one good paw over the window. The woman produced a bag of crackers and fed them to him one by one.

"This your puppy?" the old woman asked.

I nodded and dropped down beside Bear. "You know there's Path just on the other side of those trees."

"Yep," she said. "Saw 'em a ways back and they waved us right by. Word is they decided that it was better to hand the Feds a refugee crisis than deal with it themselves. Say one thing about those Pathers — they ain't dumb!"

She cackled, then turned to the man driving the car and exchanged a few words. Bear moved down the length of the car, sniffing around the backseat where an old mutt was curled up among their things. He lifted his head when he heard Bear and pressed his nose against the glass.

The woman leaned back out the window and waved me over. "Listen," she said, her voice low. "The rest of these jerks are more than happy to leave people like you behind but we got room and, sorry to say, but you two don't look so hot. Why don't you jump in? We're heading to my sister's lake house out in Bull Lake, Montana. You guys can snuggle up with Roscoe back there. Rest a few days with us before moving on."

I shook my head. "We're heading to New York."

Bear hopped back to us, and the woman continued to feed him, watching me over his shoulder.

"Not my business," she said. "But I can't say I like your chances, son."

I looked down the miles of road that lay ahead. How many of them could I walk with Bear on my shoulder before we fell over? The woman's offer made sense — go to Montana, rest, then continue on — but thoughts of Grey Solomon loomed. Surely these people would hit a Path checkpoint eventually. What if they were still looking for an escaped novice traveling with a dog? Did I want to see this woman lying by the side of a road too?

I watched as Bear devoured the food from the woman's hand. Despite our time at Alec's house, his ribs still stood out under his coat. He was filthy too, caked with mud and the blood from his injuries. I could only imagine what kind of infection was working itself into him from the filth of that sewer ditch.

Brake lights blinked off and the cars far down the line started to move. I looked back again and Bear was panting happily as the woman rubbed his ears. I felt a suffocating weight pressing down on my chest and imagined that my voice was something separate from me.

"Can you take him?"

The woman stilled Bear with one hand on his shoulder and looked over him at me. "You sure?"

As if he sensed something in the air, Bear came down off the car and limped over to me, pushing his nose into my leg. It took everything in me not to look down at him.

"Got a long way to go yet," I said, fighting the hitch in my voice, trying to get it out before I stopped to think. "And he's hurt."

People behind us started to honk as the cars just ahead of the woman's began to pull away. She said something to the man at the wheel and then reached behind her to pop the back door.

I threw my arms around Bear's neck and pulled him close to me. I closed my eyes, burying my face in his side. He yipped and wiggled, his whimper growing sharper and more distressed. The cars ahead moved down the road. The honking grew louder.

"A cabin sounds pretty great," I whispered into his ear as he squirmed and whined. "It'll be better. Okay? There's a long way to go still, and I don't know if I can take care of you."

"Rup!"

His anguished bark hit me like a punch to the chest. As much as I wanted to keep my arms around him, the honking horns were growing more insistent. People had begun to shout for the couple to move their car. I swept Bear up in my arms as an awful pressure built in my chest.

"Rup! Rup rup rup rup!"

The woman's dog cleared out to the far side of the car as I laid Bear onto the backseat. Bear jumped up, barking, but I slammed the door before he could get out.

"We'll take good care of him. I promise. Son?"

I couldn't look at her. Couldn't look at Bear. I ran toward the tree line to escape the sound of his claws scrabbling madly against the raised window.

"Rup! Rup rup rup! Rup! Rup! Rup!"

His barking grew louder and more broken-sounding, mixing with the angry horns of the piled-up cars. All I could do was keep moving, stabbing my boots into the unsteady gravel as fast as I could to get away, into the safety of the trees.

"RUP! Rup! Rup rup rup rup rup rup!"

The woman's car drew alongside of me and then the engine thrummed as they pulled down the highway. Bear's barking peaked into an anguished wail as they passed and then it faded and I was alone.

I reeled through the woods, reaching from one tree to the next to hold myself up. Without Bear, the night seemed like a hand pushing me into the ground.

I walked until I couldn't anymore and then fell onto a mossy bank in the midst of towering oaks. Skeletal branches and black sky hung over me. I rolled onto my side, curling around a keen emptiness, a void where the heat of Bear's body should have been. I could still feel his chest rise and fall beneath my hand and hear the little yips and barks that escaped his lips as he slept. I tried to imagine him safe and warm in the back of that car, but it was no use. How could I have let him go? How was I going to make it home without him?

Exhausted, I felt myself dragged down and I passed in and out of fitful sleep throughout the night. When I woke for the last time, I was covered in sweat. I struggled to sit up, my body feeling like it was made out of lead. My head was pounding and my stomach churned. I planted one hand in the dirt and rolled myself up, legs shaking, half bent over. I made it twenty or thirty feet from my camp, then fell to my knees just off the highway's shoulder.

There was a pause like being held over the edge of a cliff and then my gut clenched and I vomited up the foul ditch water until I was breathless. The sickness came in waves, one after the other. When there was nothing left in me, I collapsed onto my side, spent and trembling.

The wind moved through the trees all around me, but I couldn't feel it. A fever was smoldering in my skin and I was slick with sweat. Cramps moved up and down my body, subsiding and then flaring up without warning.

There was a grinding metallic sound and then a bright light rose up all around me. I looked down the length of the road, squinting at the intensity of the sunrise coming up between the trees. No, not the sun. Headlights. Floodlights. I scanned the roadway through bleary eyes and saw that I wasn't alone. Bodies emerged from camps on the highway's shoulder and from their places at the backs of pickup trucks. They all turned to stare into the ball of light down the road. I stumbled forward, drawing closer to it, shading my eyes with a quivering hand.

One of the cars started up and began to pull away from the others, but there was a sound like a string of firecrackers going off and the car exploded into an orange ball of fire. I fell onto the roadway, watching the flames and some dark writhing thing deep inside the burning.

I wanted to run, but I couldn't move. I watched as Path soldiers stepped from vehicles and into the headlight glare, fanning out, rifles in hand. One refugee charged forward and was shot. The others drifted together into a small grouping, trapped. I saw it then. The main body of the evacuees had passed; now it was time to deal with the stragglers. A figure stepped from a Path vehicle and positioned himself directly in front of the group.

"My name is Beacon Radcliffe," the man said. "And I am here to offer you all a choice."

Somehow I found the strength to run. The trees and the roadway blurred, shifting into patterns of black and gray with flecks of yellow from the fire behind me. But then I felt a crash and I was on my back, staring at the stars. *How did I get here?* I wondered, delirious, as two sets of hands reached down and grabbed me. I thrashed senselessly, trying to pull myself out of the grasp of the dark bodies that had gathered around me, but I was too weak.

"He's burning up," someone said. "He's sick."

My back hit the road again, this time surrounded by the glare of a truck's headlights. There were voices all around, murmuring shadows.

"What do we do with him?"

"Son? Son? Can you hear me? My name is Beacon Radcliffe."

"Where's James?" I moaned, barely aware of the words leaving my mouth. "Where's Bear?"

"Give him the Choice and move on," said a voice far above me.

"He's delirious," the beacon said. "He isn't able to make a choice. Get a stretcher."

"Sir, we don't have room for any more. We can't —"

"I answer to God and Nathan Hill, Sergeant, not you. Now, have one of your men get a stretcher. Once he's better, we can give him the Choice."

There was a thump of boots, and the beacon was beside me again, his hand heavy on my arm. I screamed as they lifted me to get the stretcher underneath my back. Every muscle in my body was filled with gravel and glass. Somehow I bit back my screams, but tears coursed down my cheeks. They got me into a troop carrier, dropping me roughly onto the deck, and then the engines started and we pulled away.

What I remembered after that came in a series of bursts as I crashed in and out of consciousness — the weary faces of the other captives in the back of the truck, their hands tied, bodies bent and exhausted; the nauseating lurch of the truck as it went from crawling to racing over uneven roads beneath the pounding of rocket fire; the way the green canvas cover above me lit up, almost beautifully, as bombs burst around and above us. When I closed my eyes to block it all out, there was still the constant shriek of machine-gun fire mixing with screams of pain and fright and the smell of smoke and sweat and fear-soaked urine.

All of this was entwined with the fierce heat of the fever that had moved into every inch of my body. It seemed to grind muscles and bones as if they were in a mortar. I turned my head to vomit onto the floor. My body wasn't my own.

Time slipped and lurched. Along with the present, the past was there too. I could feel a lake and trees and the winds moving through the flowers of home, like a hand brushing through someone's hair and then letting it fall. I was lying in the hammock late at night, happily sleepless, with James below me.

Then I was nine and in school, tiny behind my big plastic desk, so much smaller than all the other kids in my class. I felt the weight of the textbooks in my hand, their glossy pages and the rough grocery store paper-bag covers. School let out and I ran out the doors and met James. We found our way down to the creek, where we would leap from boulder to boulder, the slate-gray water coursing just beneath us.

But now it wasn't only me and James; Bear was there too, barking happily, his tail up and wagging, hesitating at a boulder's edge until we coaxed him to leap toward us. He would land, his sides shaking with fright at what he had done. James or I would scoop him up and tell him he was a good boy and brave, and we would carry him down the trail until he wriggled out of our arms and took off, leading us on.

> *Moonlight road,*
> *Why don't you light my way home . . .*

The future was there too, but it was so hard to tell from the past, like a circle turning back to itself. I was older, tall for the first time, and living in the same blue house at the end of the street, only now it was my house and it was me who sat in the garden and played guitar late into the night. James was somewhere close, but I wasn't sure where. Living down the street maybe or in a nearby town. Bear was at my feet, ageless, sleeping, his stub of a tail pounding the grass in time to the guitar. As the night fell deeper and cooler, the back door opened and two women stepped out. It was my mother, beautiful with her gray hair, and Nat walking side by side. They came to join me, but when they did, my fingers fumbled on the guitar strings.

"Where's Dad?" I asked. "Why isn't he here?"

Nat looked to Mom, and Mom reached down and scratched Bear's sides until the dog wiggled over onto his back, his legs kicking contentedly.

"Where is he?" I asked.

Nat took my hand.

"Mom?"

But she just went on stroking Bear's sides while Nat held my hand. I asked again, standing up at the edge of the garden, but no one answered me, no one even looked at me. It was like they were caught in some loop, immobile, out of time, and I was barely even there.

"Mom?"

"She's not here, son."

My eyes ached as I opened them. Someone was dabbing my forehead with a cool cloth. I was in the present again. We had stopped and the truck was empty except for me and Beacon Radcliffe, who was sitting on one of the wooden benches that lined either side. He was leaning over me, the cloth in his hand, his beacon vestments stained with dirt and bulky from the body armor he wore underneath them.

"You have to pray," he said. "Do you know how to pray?"

I closed my eyes again and my knees were aching from kneeling for hours with the other novices in Lighthouse with Beacon Quan. He had us repeat our prayers over and over again until we could say them without thinking. Until the words weren't words anymore, but ritual movements of air and lips and tongue held in muscle memory.

"If you pray hard enough," Beacon Radcliffe said, "then God may allow you off this Path and onto another. Just pray. God makes the world. He can make yours."

What would I have to do? I wondered. How hard would I have to pray for God to put me on the path home, along with James and Bear and Mom and Dad? Because if he won't do that, then I had nothing to pray for.

I turned my head from the beacon and he finally relented and disappeared. There was a great stretch of blackness and then I was rising up into the air, free of the close stink of the truck. There were hundreds of voices all around me as well as the sounds of engines and boots and the rotors of helicopters flying low.

Had I slipped back in time again? Was I back at Cormorant, about to start my time as a novice all over again? My heart seized. How much longer then until I sat by that lake and listened to the Choice being given to all of those people who had trusted me? How much longer until I watched Grey Solomon die? Or Alec? How much longer until I abandoned Bear?

The sound dropped out again and I was somewhere cool and filled with only the softest rustling of feet. My clothes were torn away and what felt like steel wool dipped in freezing water was worked up and down my body. I was left alone, shivering and sweating at the same time, my skin livid. I tried to open my eyes, but they were so thick with tears and grime that all I saw was a fiery light filled with a black blur of distorted bodies.

What did I do to deserve this? asked part of me, but another part of me knew.

PART THREE

21

"Where am I?"

A white-robed companion was sitting at the edge of my cot. There was a bowl of water and a cloth in her lap.

"They're calling it Kestrel." Her voice was tentative with a light Southern accent. Her eyes were soft shadows beneath her mesh veil.

"How long have I been here?"

"About a week," she said. "Your fever broke a few nights ago."

"What was it?"

"Something waterborne, they think. We've been seeing a lot of it."

The companion filled a cup from a water pitcher near the bed, then slipped her hand beneath my neck to lift me up so I could drink. I was lying in a large canvas tent that was packed with cots just like mine. Companions and medics glided through the room, ministering to the sick. Outside were the familiar sounds of a Path base, helicopters, Humvee engines far off near the command center, voices giving crisp orders.

I ran through the flashes of my memory — the truck, voices, sounds of engines and helicopters.

"We're at the front," I said.

"A few miles south of it," she said. "Near Richmond. Everyone they take is being brought here now. Getting ready for the big fight, I guess."

"Have they taken Philadelphia?"

"Not yet," she said. "But Oregon and Nevada fell. Everyone says Philadelphia is next."

The companion dipped a cloth into her bowl and mopped the sweat from my forehead. Cool water ran down the side of my face, loosening knots that seemed to run through my entire body.

"So it's almost over," I said, dreamy, my eyelids drooping. The companion moved on to wash my neck and my chest.

"Mara!" the shepherd called from across the room.

"Rest," the companion said, laying a reassuring hand on my shoulder.

When she was gone, a lonely stillness fell over me. Somehow the bustle of bodies moving around me only made it worse. I reached under the sheets to my pockets but my clothes had been traded for Path-issued pajamas. The jeans I had been wearing were in a neat stack by the bed. I leaned over and rifled through them, digging one hand into my pants pocket until I felt a bit of metal. I drew out Bear's collar and held it under the sheets, both hands pressing into the tough fabric. I felt an empty place inside me, but I imagined him in that cabin sitting by a fire, safe, and the gnaw of it eased a bit. I closed my fist around the collar and held it tight, wishing he were here, thankful that he wasn't.

There was a gap in the tent flap across from my cot. Through it I could see a thin trail leading away from the tent and out into the camp. Bodies dressed in forest camo passed and a black helicopter streaked across the sky and disappeared. Despite the ache and the exhaustion, I could already feel a drumbeat starting up inside of me. Get up. Get dressed. Keep moving. I drew the blanket off my legs but stopped when I saw another companion standing across the aisle.

She was watching me, ignoring the rush of medics and orderlies around her. Blurred beneath the veil, her face was visible only as shadows and worried lines. I could tell she was new just by the way she stood, her body drawn in tight like she was trying to collapse in on herself and disappear.

The other companions were being led in prayer by their shepherd at the far end of the tent.

"You just got here," I said.

The companion nodded. I waved her over and she drifted across the aisle, stopping at the foot of my cot.

"Don't be afraid," I said. "Just do what they tell you and you'll be fine."

"Is that what you did?"

I sat up slightly. There was something familiar in her rasp of a voice. "What do you mean?"

The companion checked the far end of the infirmary and then drew closer, coming up along the side of the cot.

"Don't," I whispered urgently. "If they see you they'll —"

Her hand grasped the side of the cot and she leaned down by my ear.

"Looks like I was wrong, Cal," she said. "I guess *this* is where you really belong."

I peered through her veil until the lines of her face resolved into a sharp jaw and amber-colored eyes.

"Nat?"

I reached for her arm but she jerked it away from me. The shepherd called out to her across the infirmary.

"I guess we both do now," Nat said. Then she backed into the aisle, sweeping across the infirmary and melting into the white sea of her sisters.

I sank into the cot, any scrap of energy I had gone, my head buzzing with a flat hiss of static. If they got Nat, then what chance did I have? What chance did any of us have? Beyond the tent flap, soldiers marched back and forth and engines revved. I held on to Bear's collar and searched for the drumbeat that would urge me on, but there was nothing there. We were all lost.

Two days later I was put on my first work detail.

A young corporal showed up with a pair of standard-issue novice fatigues and led me out of the infirmary to where I would be helping to dig latrines.

I covered my eyes from the blast of sunlight that came when we stepped out of the gloom of the infirmary tent. My body was still weak, loose limbed, from days on my back. I kept my eyes on the corporal's back and tried to keep up as he led me through the base.

Kestrel sat in what had once been a grassy clearing before it was trampled into muddy ruts by thousands of Path boots and Humvees. It seemed to be laid out in a mirror image of Cormorant, only bigger and more hastily put together. One quick walk through it and I had picked out the novices' and citizens' barracks and the sequestered ops center. A canvas-walled Lighthouse towered over everything in the center of camp.

The base was surrounded by a high fence topped with rolls of razor-sharp concertina wire. Plywood guardhouses, stacked with sandbags and bristling with heavy weapons, sat at every turn. The camp had clearly been constructed with a typical Path focus on security, but it was new and partially unfinished. I told myself there had to be a hole somewhere, that all I had to do was find it, but then I remembered all the years that James and I spent in Cormorant thinking the exact same thing.

I scanned passing groups of companions, looking for Nat, but I didn't see any trace of her. She hadn't come back to the infirmary since the day we spoke and part of me wanted to believe I had imagined the whole thing, that she had been some kind of fever dream. The idea that Nat could have been taken, and that she would have submitted to the Choice if she had been, seemed too impossible to be real. Of course, I knew it was. The Path had swept across the whole of the country, and now controlled nearly two-thirds of it. Anyone could be taken, and once they were, no one was immune to wanting to live.

The corporal led me up a hill at the southern edge of the camp and gave instructions to me and a group of ten or fifteen other novices. Since I still had my cast, I was on gofer duty, ferrying supplies and water, while the rest of them dug in the noonday sun. It took us till nearly sundown to finish the pit and construct the latrine housing. The group was almost ready to drop when the corporal led us to the novices' barracks, where we were allowed a tepid shower before being shuffled off to dinner and prayers.

The Kestrel Lighthouse was nowhere near as impressive as Cormorant's had been — it was simply a large tent full of chairs facing a makeshift altar. Drained from the sun and the day's work, it was actually a relief to find my place among the others and rest on the flat pew. I helped a bewildered young novice find the right page in the book of prayers and then Beacon Radcliffe emerged and began the service.

"I am the Way and the Path . . ."

The voices around me fell into a tentative unison. The beacons stalked the aisles, their eyes hardest on the newest of us. Luckily, the service was still deep in my bones and I followed along easily, making myself nearly invisible in the cadence of the prayers and the flow of kneeling and standing. The rhythm of it was so familiar that I felt myself dissolving into it.

After prayers I followed the men to the novices' barracks and found an open bunk, falling into it without even bothering to turn back the thin blanket. The men talked for a while and then one by one the lanterns were blown out and the tent fell quiet.

I was tired, but sleep seemed impossible. One look at the bunk above me and for a second I felt sure that all I had to do was stand up and James would be there, reading *The Glorious Path* by candlelight. When I turned onto my side and set my hand on the rough wool blanket, all I could feel was the warmth of Bear's fur.

I slipped out of my bunk and stepped into my boots. A private was supposed to be keeping an eye on us but he had stepped away. I ducked through the flap in the barracks tent and into moonlight. Kestrel was restful in the dark, quiet except for the rhythm of helicopter landings and the distant artillery booms out at the front.

The ops center glowed with its electric lights. A few soldiers moved importantly from building to building within it. I could predict their every twist and turn: from the command center to the drone operators' room or, if it was the end of their shift, to the cleansing tent to pray for forgiveness amid the scent of sandalwood. I hated the part of me that grew calm watching them. I kicked at a tent pole as I passed it, welcoming the jolt.

I found myself at the northern edge of Kestrel. Directly in front of me was the perimeter fence and a guard tower. I could see the soldiers inside, one leaning against a wall while the other stood over a machine gun, barrel pointed north. There was a blind spot along the side of a plywood hut. I stepped into it, pressing myself against the boards to watch.

Over the course of an hour a guard with a dog moved along the base of the fence and then vanished around a bend in the line. Later, two new guards emerged from their barracks and crossed toward the tower. The replacements climbed the ladder, and once inside, the four of them gathered in the center of the platform. I could hear a whisper of talk and even laughter. Lighters flared as illicit cigarettes were lit. The place may have looked like Cormorant but these were not her soldiers. I felt a twinge of disgust at their lack of discipline.

Gravel shifted out in the dark. I turned as a figure stepped out of a doorway and down the far side of the street. The last thing I saw before it disappeared into a dark patch was a flutter of white robes. There was no reason a companion should have been out at this hour.

The guards in the tower were still talking among themselves, so I slid along the length of a deep shadow, then across the road. I spotted the companion again, moving through a tight alley behind a line of tents. She stayed low, moving quick and decisively, not like a scared capture, like a soldier. I knew at once that it was Nat. But what was she doing?

Keeping my distance, I followed until she came to the end of the alley and crouched down with her back to me. She pulled her robes off and hid them just behind a tin garbage pail. Underneath them she was wearing nondescript gray coveralls.

The eastern fence was directly ahead of her, a hundred feet down a shallow slope. When she moved, she didn't look left or right, she just ran straight toward it. Once there, she knelt near the struts of an unfinished guard tower, disappearing into the darkness.

Of course, I thought. Nat would have been looking for an escape route from the second she was taken. I couldn't say I was surprised that she had already found one. I was just happy she saved me the trouble. A rattle of steel came from the fence line, followed by footsteps dashing away across the grass on the other side. I hesitated, certain I should go back and gather supplies, food and water at least, but then I heard the guard dog bark across the camp. His master was bringing him back this way. I left the cover of darkness and raced across the yard, running for the fence.

I was just barely able to keep up as Nat moved from empty streets and crumbling homes into an industrial area of boarded-up shops and abandoned warehouses.

There was a lull in the fighting at the front but there were signs of old battles all around me. Fast-food restaurants bombed into barely recognizable ruins, pitted streets, and the charred husks of destroyed vehicles. We weren't alone now, either. Here and there other refugees — whoever hadn't been swept up in the Path's net as they ground forward — skulked about in the thin moonlight, scavenging for whatever they could find. They were all horrifyingly thin, with sunken eyes and wasted limbs, little different than the packs of stray dogs that emerged from every alley and shop I passed, their old tags chiming. I tried not to linger over the dogs' matted fur and too-prominent ribs.

Their mournful whimpers as I passed were like fingers probing a raw wound.

Nat stopped at a street corner by a string of warehouses. I thought she was taking her bearings in preparation for moving on again, but she backed into a dark doorway and didn't emerge for some time. What was she doing? Was this as far as her escape plan had taken her? If so, I was safely away from the base. I could press on alone from here — keep moving north and hope to find a weak point in the Fed line.

I was about to start down the street again when the faint rumble of an engine rose behind me. I pressed myself into a doorway as a civilian pickup truck appeared on the street. Its lights were off and it moved slow, navigating around the craters and piles of debris in the roadway. When it came up alongside me, I saw there were two men inside.

Nat didn't wait for the truck to stop; she emerged from the shadows and climbed into the bed as it rolled past her. Once she was in, the truck turned a corner and was gone.

Even better, I thought. If Nat had hooked up with Feds who were helping to move refugees across the border, then all I had to do was follow along. I shadowed the truck as it weaved through the streets, ducking into an alleyway when it came to a stop in the parking lot of a warehouse. Two men stepped out and, after scanning the buildings and street around them, knocked on the side of the truck's bed. Nat emerged and the three of them crossed the parking lot and went inside. I stood in the quiet dark, watching the building. The front was a few miles to the north. What were they doing here?

A rusty-looking set of stairs was bolted to the side of the building, leading up to a second-floor entrance. I made it across the street and started up it, freezing at every creak and rattle of the old metal. At the top was a landing and a door with a narrow window set above the handle. I peered through it and saw a faint glimmer of light coming from the first floor, but there was no trace of Nat or the men.

I eased my shoulder into the door and stepped inside, finding myself on a narrow catwalk high over the warehouse floor. Below were empty boxes and wooden pallets lit by the beams of flashlights. I stole along the length of the catwalk until I came to another staircase, then flattened myself against the deck.

Nat was standing below with her back to me, facing the two men from the truck and another two who held the flashlights. The men were all in civilian clothes, old jeans and flannel shirts, but each of them moved with what I recognized as military precision.

One of the men took a hammer from a bag on the floor and carefully pulled the nails from the top of a wooden crate that sat in front of Nat. He lifted off the lid and reached inside. It was hard to tell what it was he pulled out at first. All I saw were canvas straps and lengths of white material. Nat held her arms up over her head, and the man lowered it over her body.

It looked like a bulletproof vest except it was larger and the fabric was far too thin. The man circled Nat, tightening straps until the vest fit snug against her body. When he was satisfied, he reached into the crate and set another box at Nat's feet.

When he pulled out what was inside, a sick chill ran through me. I understood what it was that Nat was wearing.

The gray bricks he took out of the box looked like blocks of modeling clay, but the explosive power in each one of those slabs of C-4 was enough to demolish a small car.

He fit the bricks of explosive into slots that had been sewn into the canvas vest Nat was wearing. Two in front, two in back, and one on each side under her arms. Then he took a small battery out of the crate and ran wires from it to each of the bricks. The wires were gathered into one cable and concealed in a channel built into the vest. At the end of the cable he attached a trigger that was about the size of a small lighter.

Once Nat was wired up, the rest of the men moved around her, critiquing the bomb maker's work and making adjustments. When they were done, the vest hugged her body so tightly that her companion's robe was sure to conceal it. No one would notice what she was wearing until she pressed the trigger.

The men gathered into a circle while Nat stood before them. They murmured among themselves, then returned to Nat, slowly removing the vest and packing it into an ordinary-looking backpack. Nat slung the pack over her shoulder and was led out of the warehouse by the two men who had brought her.

The men with the flashlights spoke for a moment more, then went their separate ways. A door below opened and then whispered shut. The warehouse was perfectly dark and silent.

I lay on the edge of the catwalk, a dull buzz in my head, too stunned to move. It wasn't possible. Surely I hadn't seen what I thought I just did. Nat would never —

An engine cranked outside, shocking me out of my daze. I scrambled up the catwalk and to the door, stepping onto the landing just as the truck pulled away, retracing its steps back to Kestrel.

The ground trembled as the nightly barrage of artillery fire began. I turned toward the front, imagining soldiers on both sides of the border running in a hundred different directions with a hundred differ-ent concerns — certainly the least of them would be one raggedy-looking kid slipping across the border. Every muscle in my body was taut with anticipation, ready to run, but the image of Nat standing in that ware-house — motionless as those men dressed her — wouldn't fade.

Far up the road the pickup truck accelerated, turning deeper into the warren of crumbling buildings. In seconds it would be gone. I took a last look at the front and then followed.

Nat slid out of the pickup's bed at the same corner as before and set off through the streets, the backpack around her shoulders.

She took a different route back, veering from the warehouses into a winding suburb of abandoned houses. She dipped in and out of patches of moonlight through overgrown yards and cracked drive-ways. I trailed her around the fenced-off edge of a drained swimming pool, but when I came around to the other side, she had vanished.

I stood panting amid a wall of hedges and scanned a trio of houses across the street, trying to see into the woods behind them. Nothing. Everything was gray and still. My heart was pumping hard, on high alert. *Where did you go, Nat? Where* — A branch cracked near the middle house. I took off after it but the second I passed the row of hedges, I knew I had made a mistake.

Something slammed into my back, knocking the wind out of me and sending me sprawling to the ground. My cast hit an exposed root and I nearly screamed from the pain. Nat emerged from the bushes, a thick branch cocked over her shoulder like a bat.

"Nat, wait — it's me!"

She paused, her face lost in the darkness. The branch didn't move.

"Who else is with you?"

"No one," I said. "It's just me."

Nat checked down the street and in the dark between the houses. "You followed me?"

I nodded.

"Plan on running to your friends in the Path and telling?"

"I told you. They're not my friends."

"You didn't look too upset digging latrines for them."

"I was captured. What did you expect me to do?"

Nat threw the branch into the bushes. "Nothing."

I pushed myself off the ground and followed as Nat crossed the street, heading for the dark woods behind a track of houses.

"This is insane. You can't do this." Nat ignored me, head down, striding away. "Do you think your dad would want you to do this? Or your mom?"

Nat whipped around to face me. "I don't think it matters what they want anymore."

Her glare was cold and blank. The breath froze in my lungs and I couldn't meet her eyes. "I'm sorry. That was a stupid thing to — But killing a couple Path officers . . ."

"It won't *be* a couple."

"A hundred, then. A thousand. It doesn't matter. They have the West Coast. At this point —"

"He's coming here, Cal."

"Who?"

Nat stared back at me.

"No. There's no way he'd —"

"We hooked up with a Marine unit not long after we left you," she said. "They were doing border raids into Arkansas and we decided to help them out. One day we came across a courier. Just one guy traveling alone. No phone. No radio. All he had was a satchel filled with encrypted messages. Once we broke the encryption, we were able to read them."

"What did they say?"

"Hill knows this is the last battle," she said. "He says God wants him to give a speech to the troops before it starts."

"So tell the Feds," I said. "If they know Hill is there —"

"We took it to them," she said. "But they think as soon as the Path realizes the courier is dead, they'll decide he was compromised and cancel Hill's plans."

"They're probably right."

"You know they aren't," Nat said. "If Hill believes that God is telling him he has to come here, do you think a lost message is going to keep him away?"

I searched for an argument, but she was right. If Hill thought coming here was his path, nothing would stop him.

"When?"

"We think tomorrow night," she said. "In the Lighthouse. They're already getting set. Flying in supplies. More security."

"No," I said, shaking the idea out of my head. "The Feds can't make you do this."

"No one is making me do anything," Nat said. "I volunteered."

Half in the moonlight, Nat's skin was smooth and gray. She was thinner than I had last seen her, making her cheekbones stand out in thin ridges. Her eyes were sunk deep in their sockets. I reached out to her but she pulled away from me.

"There's a soft point in the Fed line three and a half miles to the west," she said. "That's how my people got through. The password of the day is *streetcar*. Say that to a sentry and you're on your way home."

"Nat, wait."

"Go on," she said. "Mommy and Daddy are waiting."

Nat turned her back on me and there was a whisper of grass beneath her feet as she slipped into the dark. A flash of sickly light came from the front, throwing Nat's shadow across the trees and the abandoned houses. There was a deep rumble beneath us and when it passed she was gone.

The house in front of me was two stories with a soaring front porch and large picture windows, all of which were shattered. Its door hung limp on its hinges. I climbed the stairs and pushed it open. The floorboards creaked as I moved from the hall to the dining room and into a kitchen.

A winding set of stairs led up to the second floor. There were four bedrooms there, each one larger than the last. I visited each of them in turn, walking around fallen curtains and the strewn clothes that people had left behind as they fled. Inside the last one, there was a small bed stripped down to a dirty mattress. Next to it was a nearly empty bookshelf and a single window with torn Spider-Man curtains.

I drew the curtains out of the way. The neighborhood spread out below, black and pale gray where the moonlight struck. I tried to picture the place before the war, the drab houses painted in bright shades of yellow and blue, surrounded by yards so lush they seemed to smolder beneath the summer sun.

Now the empty houses made me think of seashells washed up on the beach. I imagined you could put your ear to them and hear the echoey sounds of the people who had lived there — bodies moving from room to room, distant voices.

I ran my hand down the dusty spines of the books that had been left behind on the shelf. An odd warmth came over me as I recalled a time when James was four and I was six. We had both fallen to the flu and collapsed into our beds for three full days, sweating with fever and groaning from aches that made it seem like our muscles had been tied into thousands of tiny knots.

Those three days had been torture — I knew that — but when I recalled them now, the pain and fear seemed distant, like things I had heard about but never actually felt. The only times that seemed to have any weight at all were when Mom and Dad crowded into our room to feed us ginger ale and read to us in low soothing tones. I could still feel my mother's palm resting on my forehead, and my father's voice, and the feeling of the four of us in that room, bound together in a way that seemed unbreakable.

It was strange that memory could do this, reach into our history and twist it into simpler, happy shapes. But didn't I already feel the agony of our trek across Utah's desert less keenly than the warmth of Bear in my lap as we watched the stars turn? Wasn't the horror of our first days with the Path less present in my mind than the nights James and I laid up in the barracks whispering back and forth in our bunks? I wondered if this was a gift our memory gave us, or a curse.

There was a flash and the walls of the house shook from another bombardment out at the front. I looked down at the bed, which seemed as small as a dollhouse toy now, and then left the house to stand on the overgrown lawn.

The fighting had kindled a fire out on the northern horizon, a red streak singeing the black. Beyond it Ithaca sat like a bend in the earth, the gravity of it pulling at me. One word and I was through the lines and on my way. And if Nat succeeded, the war might be as good as over. Ithaca would remain untouched.

I pictured myself there and wondered how long it would take before the sting of the price Nat paid for my freedom faded in my memory too. A year? More? When would her death seem like just another detail, known but not felt?

Would the memory of Grey fade then too, along with James and Bear and Alec and all the rest? And if they did, if I looked back into my past and nothing was there, who would I be then?

A helicopter came in over the treetops, heading for the front. I stepped back and then made my way quickly through the streets, past the houses and the woods and the ragged little town. The next thing I knew, I was crouching in the brush outside the perimeter of Kestrel. I found the break in the fence and slipped through and across the silent camp.

I fell into a bunk and lay there sleepless, hoping I had the strength to carry out the plan that was clicking together in my head.

22

When Beacon Radcliffe arrived at the Lighthouse the next morning, he found me feigning sleep at the tent's entrance.

"Son?"

His hand touched my arm. I leapt away in terror. "I'm sorry, sir," I said, cowering away from him. "I didn't mean to —"

"It's all right," he said, backing off with his hands up to reassure me. "Don't be afraid."

He took a step closer and held out his hand. I regarded it warily for a moment and then reached out to take it.

"Rough place to sleep," he said as he pulled me up. I shrugged and kept my eyes on the ground. "There's a little time before services still. Why don't you come in?"

Radcliffe threw aside the tent flap and I peered inside.

"Come on," he said. "It's all right."

I stepped through the tent flap, moving hesitantly like I expected someone to come along and strike me at any moment. Radcliffe followed and let the opening fall back into place. There were already a few lanterns burning, filling the Lighthouse with an amber glow. He set his copy of *The Glorious Path* on the altar and said a prayer.

The place had changed since I'd been there just the night before. A stage had been built beneath the altar, raising it high above several added rows of pews. Racks of folding chairs sat in one corner, ready to be placed behind them. When they were, I guessed the Lighthouse would hold a hundred more people than usual.

"Is there something going on tonight?"

Radcliffe looked over his shoulder. "Oh. Yes. There's a . . . special service. I'm sorry to say that very few novices will be invited."

"Oh. Okay. Well, I can go if you need to —"

"No. Please. How can I help you, ah . . ."

"James," I said.

"There's no need to be afraid, James. Sit down. Please."

I took a seat in the second row of pews, and Radcliffe sat in front of me. He was a kindly enough looking man, plump, and bald on top with a weathered face. I looked up at a brand-new Glorious Path symbol hanging over the altar. The old one had been brass and aluminum. This one's gold and silver curves gleamed in the lantern light.

"Couldn't you sleep in the barracks?"

I kept my eyes on the altar and made my voice far away and dreamy. "It was fine, I just — I guess I felt . . . drawn here."

The beacon smiled. "Yes. I feel like that too," he said. "I used to be an accountant. Can you believe that? I sat at a desk all day long, looking at pages of numbers and fiddling with a computer. Now I never want to be more than ten feet from this place." Radcliffe looked down at my cast and my old bruises. "You were badly hurt when we found you. Sick too."

I nodded, cradling my broken wrist and wincing as I did it.

"What happened?"

"There was a battle," I said. "Not far from where I lived. After it was over, there were so many injured people but there was only one doctor. He used to work for my dad, so I got this cast, but everyone else . . . they waited for more doctors to come, from the Army or the government, I guess, but no one did."

Radcliffe shook his head. "It doesn't seem fair, does it?"

I stared at the floor and answered him with silence.

"Why did you come here, James?"

My head throbbed at the sound of the name. Why had I chosen it? "Some of the other men said they had to make a . . . a . . ."

"A choice."

"Yes. They said when it came time for me to do it, I should just tell you whatever you wanted to hear because you'd hurt me if I didn't."

"And do you think that's true? Do you think that's how it works?"

I raised my shoulders weakly. "The doctors told me I might have died if you hadn't been there to save me."

"Well, I'm glad we could be, then," he said. "There are a lot of rumors about the Choice. But do you know what it really is?"

I shook my head, and Beacon Radcliffe turned toward me on his pew.

"We believe there is a light inside all of us that comes from God. The Choice is simply you committing yourself to following the path that it illuminates."

"How do I . . . ?"

Beacon Radcliffe returned to the altar for his copy of *The Glorious Path*. He kissed its cover and whispered a prayer before opening it in his lap.

"All you have to do is repeat after me."

Radcliffe read from the book, and I repeated all he said back to him, making sure to fill the words with all of the cautious reverence I could muster. As I spoke, I felt a strange doubling inside me, like past and present were synching together.

When I was done, Beacon Radcliffe smiled warmly and I returned his smile in kind. He said I should go get something to eat before duty but that I'd be welcome in his Lighthouse anytime. He left me then, returning to his book and his altar.

I stayed in my pew, staring up at the Path symbol. "I am the Way and the Path," I said, full of devotion, and just loud enough for Radcliffe to hear. When he turned back to me I left my pew and headed up the aisle.

"Wait!"

I froze in place, making sure to erase my smile before I turned back.

"The service tonight," he said. "I think perhaps we can make an exception. Be here at seven."

After morning mess and prayers, Corporal Connors led us up the hill to the site of our newly dug pit and set us to building the latrine structure around it. On one trip across the hill to fetch a bucket of nails, I found myself looking down at the Lighthouse.

Thirty or forty soldiers had surrounded it, followed close behind by several horse-drawn wagons. As soon as the wagons were parked, the soldiers threw themselves into the task of unloading them. More canvas. More folding chairs. The walls of the Lighthouse were taken down and half the soldiers set about expanding it to nearly twice its size.

Even though no announcement had been made, everyone knew something big was happening. An electric tension jumped from person to person in the camp.

Was Nat watching the preparations too? Or was she serving meals and tending to the sick with the vest strapped under her robe, sweating beneath the weight of the explosives? Was there any part of her that wished she'd be caught and stopped before she could step into the Lighthouse and press that trigger?

I worked the rest of the day in a dream, floating from one assignment to the next. It felt like barely any time had passed before the sun began to sink into the trees and Corporal Connors led us off the hill and down to the barracks.

The Lighthouse towered in front of me. The flaps were drawn back, and inside I could see the ranks of chairs, split by a razor-sharp aisle that led to the raised altar. The Path insignia glowed in the candlelight. I shuddered and imagined Nat standing before it in her white robes, her finger falling on the trigger, felt the breathless moment before the detonation.

"Okay, everybody. Showers. Let's go."

The men around me moved with a weary groan, but I was distracted by a flash of white as a group of companions moved across the camp. They were heading toward the soldiers' barracks, and as they passed a wooded rise near the outer fence, one companion drifted away from the group unnoticed. As the rest continued on, she climbed the hill and disappeared among the trees.

"Hey. Kid. Let's move."

"I . . . I'm having a hard time, sir," I said, looking up at Corporal Connors, with one hand clutching my middle. "I'm wondering if I might run to the med tent."

"We got a schedule kicking into high gear here."

"I know, sir. I won't miss anything. I'm on Path, I promise."

Connors considered a moment, then waved me away. I moved slowly until he got the men into the barracks and then I skated around behind the med tent and climbed the hill.

The trees at the top were few but thick and gave a small umbrella of shade. I crossed into the shadowed ground, and Nat turned at my footsteps. She was still in her companion's whites. The backpack lay at her feet.

"My mother trained me to fight since I was six, Cal. If you think you can take it from me —"

"I don't."

"You can't talk me out of it, either."

"I know."

"So why are you here?"

I took a step back and then found a place near the edge of the hill among the roots of a nearby oak. Below, soldiers poured from their duty stations to the barracks and the mess. Lit from within by scores of flickering candles, the Lighthouse glowed. There was a pause and then a rustle of fabric as Nat crossed the hilltop.

"Where's Bear?"

Nat was standing alongside a nearby tree with the backpack at her feet.

"Had to give him up."

"Oh," she said. "I'm sorry."

She sat down and pulled the backpack close to her. It was gray with black piping and a small logo, no different from one a thousand kids threw on their backs before jumping onto a school bus.

"Did they make it out?" she asked. "Alec and the others?"

I shook my head. "Alec is dead. Two of the soldiers too. I think the others made it."

There was a sharp draw to her breath but Nat said nothing. Her fingers went white on the straps of the pack as she pulled at them and looked down at the camp.

"How did you get into the service?" I asked.

"They always want a few companions around to do their bidding. I played the pious game until I got an invite."

Bells within the Lighthouse began to chime and the first wave of soldiers responded, flowing from the mess toward the open tent. Soon the novices would follow and then the companions.

"Do you know when you'll do it?" I asked.

"As soon as he gets on the stage."

"Too many people will be watching then," I said. "After he speaks he'll probably do the Receiving. Security will be expecting people to come up, and by the time the companions get there, they won't be paying as much attention. That's the best time."

Nat stared at me a moment and then she nodded and hooked her fingers beneath the backpack's straps. When she stood, she pressed one shoulder into the oak beside her to steady herself. I followed her into the copse of trees, where it was nearly dark and smelled richly of grass and honeysuckle. Nat set the pack at her feet. Her hands trembled as she unzipped it and lifted out the vest.

"Let me help you," I said.

Nat hesitated a moment and then handed me the vest. She lifted her arms up over her head and I stepped forward, lowering it onto her shoulders. I tightened each strap until it fit her like a second skin. Next came the explosives. I lifted each brick and slipped it into its slot in the vest's pockets. I did the sides and the front and then the back.

"The detonator," Nat said. "It's in the front pocket."

I pulled out the battery pack and a tangle of wires that ended in the trigger. Nat turned around and I paused, staring at the connections. Maybe if I could find a way to disable it now, then I wouldn't have to —

"Is everything okay?"

"It's fine," I said. "I'm just adjusting the —"

"Let me."

Nat turned around and took the battery and trigger from me. She stepped away and finished up herself, tucking the battery into a pocket at the small of her back and running the wires into their channels. When she was done, she pointed to her robe and I helped her with it. Once it was back on, the bomb was invisible beneath its snowy folds.

Nat looked up at me. She was shaking now, her veil in one hand, and the bomb's trigger in the other. Down below us the Lighthouse bells chimed. There was no breath in my lungs. My blood had gone still.

"Do you believe in God, Cal?"

My throat tightened. I didn't know the answer. Didn't know what to say.

"I thought after Mom and Dad and Steve, I would stop," Nat said. "But I didn't."

Nat's tears came silently, sliding down her face and darkening the collar of her robe. I put my arms around her and pulled her toward me. She dropped her forehead onto my shoulder. Her breath was hot on my neck and ragged. I could feel her heart pounding through the plates in the vest.

"Maybe we can still go," I said. "We know the way out. Maybe there's still time to —"

"No," she said. "There's no more time."

Nat raised her head and kissed me, her fingers curled into my back as she pulled me tight against her and I pressed her closer to me. When the bells rang again, Nat broke away. Her eyes closed tight as if she was making one last desperate wish. When she opened them again, they were dry and clear. Her hands no longer shook.

Nat lifted her veil and set it down to cover her face. Her robes fluttered behind her as she descended the hill and walked out into the camp.

23

I fell in behind a few citizens crossing from their barracks toward the Lighthouse. They were all talking excitedly, but I was thousands of miles away in my head.

"Have you heard, brother? They say he's come to see us. They say it's Nathan Hill."

"Glory to the Path."

"Glory."

And then I was inside and the flaps were closing, trapping us in air that ran thick and hot. The first rows of pews were already full with soldiers, all of them with board-straight backs and heads held high. Only three other novices were considered devout enough to attend and I was moved with them into a precise row behind the citizens.

The temperature inside seemed to mount every second along with the waves of voices rising and falling. You could hear the intensity packed behind every word. The soldiers and most of the novices were practically vibrating, threatening to shake the very walls down to the dirt. It became harder and harder to breathe.

A blast of cool air washed through the space. Everyone turned as the tent flap lifted and a band of veiled white moved into the theater and took their places behind the men. Nat was standing on the aisle. There was no bend to her; her shoulders were thrown back, her head was up, staring resolutely at the stage. Her right hand, the one that held the trigger, was down by her side, closed in a fist.

Behind the companions, two armed guards stood on either side of the tent flap, their hands on the sleek black of their weapons. Weapons outside of the ops center, much less in the Lighthouse, were forbidden. They clearly weren't taking any chances. I turned, sure to keep a look of religious awe on my face as I searched out the rest of the guards.

There were three along each wall and one at either side of the stage. I recognized some from Kestrel, but others were strangers to me. Hill's private security forces, I guessed. I scanned their faces, all of them filled with the same unyielding focus, until one stopped me cold.

He was standing at the edge of the stage. Average height, sunburned skin, dark hair. Unremarkable. That was, until he turned and I saw the scar along his cheek. Then, I saw him not as he was but as he had been, standing in the midst of a desert, a mad gleam in his eyes as he raised a baseball bat to his ear and let it fall.

Rhames.

My skin went cold. Of course. Cormorant housed the top special forces the Path had, most of whom were focused singularly on the overthrow of California. Now that it had fallen, where else would they be but by the leader's side?

Cormorant is here, I thought, and then, with a jolt, *Is James?*

I had no time to wonder. There was a rustle of uniforms as the soldiers snapped to attention. The theater fell silent. Every eye was on the stage.

There was no fanfare. No warning. He simply emerged from the darkness at the back of the stage and walked toward us, the glowing Path insignia over his head. No one clapped. No one breathed.

I had seen Nathan Hill in pictures and had heard him described in awed detail by the people who had been in his presence, but still I wasn't prepared for the experience of being less than fifty feet from him. I don't think anyone was. I heard a sharp intake of breath beside me, and when I turned, a bald man I had entered the theater with was weeping.

Hill had the kind of face that seemed ageless. It was unlined, almost boyish, but wise and deeply troubled at the same time. His eyes were dark blue beneath gently curving brows and waves of red-brown hair. Peaking out from the collar of his uniform I could see the topmost edge of the burn scars he received in Saudi Arabia. Everyone said they covered the whole of his back and arms and chest.

But none of those details really meant anything. He could have been tall or he could have been blond. It would have made no difference. Something radiated off of him — a force, gentle as the wind, but overwhelming. Even I felt calm descend upon me as he looked out over us. It was a feeling of rightness, of certainty, of being one of the few people who had the honor to be standing at the axis of the world.

I held my breath as he began to speak.

"With these words, I consecrate my life to the Glorious Path."

The congregation repeated his words back with one voice.

"God, lead me to my Path. Let me be a light in the darkness and the rod that falls upon the backs of the defiant. The lives of my brothers and the lives of the Pathless are in my hands. If I allow them to fall into the darkness, then so must I. Their loss is my loss. Their death is my death."

Hill opened his eyes and looked up at us again, his full lips turned up in a smile.

"A lot of very smart people told me not to come here tonight," he said. "And since I know they're smart, I guess it follows that I must be monumentally stupid."

He smiled again, giving permission for the laugh that rippled through the audience.

"We have been told that this great thing could not be done and now here we are, standing on the edge of it. There was once a great light that shone from this country and illuminated the whole of the world. Every one of us lived through that light's dimming. We were there as brother reached out to brother, not to help him up but to tear him down. We were there when a million backs turned from God to venerate worldly things. When I think of that time, I think of a pit of dogs driven mad by a hunger that can't be quenched."

He stepped back and the silence hung, crystalline.

"But then I stood in the desert of Saudi Arabia with my brothers, Riyadh burning behind us, and I was struck dumb by the beauty of the world. There was sand and there was sky and at night there were stars. Finally, I thought, I can find my way."

He paused again and the silence was crushing. I wanted to turn, to look for Nat, but I couldn't move.

"We decided then that we would not make a new world. We would find our way back to the one we were never meant to leave."

The crowd rose as one, applauding wildly. My paralysis broke and I moved low and fast toward the aisle. The Receiving would come soon, and I had to be ready. Just as I expected, the beacons moved toward the altar to assist Hill. But Hill bypassed it and came to the edge of the stage. He stepped off into the crowd and my stomach sank. What was he doing?

The Path discipline vanished and the crowds rushed toward him. Hard-faced soldiers and novices alike knocked aside their chairs until there was a wall of bodies pressing their hands through a circular perimeter that security quickly came in to establish. I looked to where I had last seen Nat, but she was gone.

Hill moved through the space, and the crowd accommodated him, splitting ahead to re-form behind. They all reached out to touch him, and Hill struggled to meet every hand, beaming as he did so. People's cheeks shone from tears. Their faces glowed.

Bodies pressed in all around me, pinning my arms to my side and dragging me along. I managed to look behind me and saw a band of gray uniforms, unbroken except for a single dot of white making her way through them toward Hill.

Nat was twenty feet out and closing quickly. I tried to push through the crowd, but there were so many people. Hill appeared and disappeared in the confusion, reaching out to grasp people's hands, to embrace them, to kiss them, tears in his eyes. But then there was a gasp and the movement of the crowd ceased moving and a hush fell.

I pushed through the final layer of bodies until I saw Hill, barely five feet away from me. A young novice, overcome with emotion, had thrown himself past Hill's security to fall at the man's feet. Hill touched the novice's arm and drew him up. Once he was standing,

Hill embraced him and then turned the young man around for all of us to see.

The novice beamed up at Hill, his face rosy, joyous. Hill smiled, lost in the moment, but then his eyes fixed at a point across the circle. Everyone turned to follow his gaze and came to a lone companion who had just stepped out of the crowd.

Nat's face was bare of her veil, but no one was looking at her face. Every eye in the room was locked on her right hand and the silver cylinder that rested in her palm.

There were screams and then the rush of security as they swarmed through the crowd and raised their weapons. I recoiled, anticipating a roar of fire, but then Nathan's voice rose over the crowd.

"Stop!"

The soldiers hesitated. Hill lifted his hand, then slowly lowered it until it rested once again on the boy's shoulder. As one, the guards returned their weapons to their sides. The crowd pulled back, but I stayed where I was, ending up alongside the first line of soldiers, Nat to my left and Hill to my right.

Nat's eyes were red and swollen, moving from Hill to the novice boy in front of him.

"You've been crying."

As soft as Hill's voice was, it filled the Lighthouse. Nat didn't move, didn't take her eyes off him. Her hand was out before her like a lance. The room felt very small as everyone in it except Nat and Hill and the boy seemed to fall away.

"People you love have been killed in all of this," Hill said. "Haven't they?"

I moved behind the front line of the crowd, drifting closer to Nat.

"Let him go," she said.

"Was it your parents?"

"I said let him go!"

"Were they soldiers?"

The muscles in Nat's jaw stood out like bands of iron. "My mother was a soldier."

"And your father?" Hill asked. "A firefighter? No. A police officer."

Nat said nothing and Hill nodded, sadly.

"My dad was a cop too," he said. "He was killed in the line of duty after patrolling a neighborhood in Dallas for twenty-five years. I didn't really know my mom. Your parents were killed trying to protect you. Weren't they?"

Nat nodded, uncertain. A line of sweat was breaking out on her brow.

"They gave you an amazing gift," he said. "Why would you reject it now?"

Her hand began to tremble and tears had started to form at the corners of her eyes. Nat gritted her teeth to hold them back, but they came anyway. Hill eased the boy into the crowd and then waved them all back to a safe distance. He took a step closer to Nat.

"Kill me if you want to kill me," he said. "The Path will go on."

As if on cue, the canvas walls shook like they were caught in a sudden gust. A jet flew overhead and then another. I slipped closer to Nat, my eyes on her thumb as it hovered over the trigger.

"Would your family want you to die defending a world that was already gone?"

Nat's fingers went pale around the metal cylinder. Her thumb rose over the trigger.

"I don't give a damn about the world."

I leapt out of the crowd and hit Nat hard, throwing my arms around her waist and knocking us into a pile on the floor. There were screams above us and a rush of bodies. Nat struggled to get out of my grip, finally managing to lift her hand free and bring it up between us. The trigger flashed. Her thumb fell toward it, but I wrenched it out of her hand before she could press it.

Hands fell on my arms and back and I went flying away from her. A black mass of security grabbed Nat and pulled her away while she thrashed, eyes wild, screaming.

"What did you do?! What did you do?!"

The soldiers tossed me aside and I crashed into the floor on the other side of the Lighthouse. I felt a hand on my shoulder, pulling me up, and I suddenly found myself staring into the wryly smiling face of Nathan Hill.

"My hero," he said.

A soldier appeared at Hill's side. "Sir, the Feds are heating up at the front. If they know you're here —"

"Take the girl to Shrike with us," he said. "We'll talk to her there. Our hero is coming with us too, so make room."

"Yes, sir!"

Hill clapped me on the back. "Can't let anything happen to my rescuer, can I?"

Another soldier appeared to hustle us off toward the exit. The battle sounds outside were louder now and closer. I looked over my shoulder as we ran. Rhames and the other security guards had Nat on her knees, her robe and bomb vest stripped off, her hands cuffed behind her back. Her eyes burned through the air at me. I turned and followed Hill.

A line of vehicles was idling behind the Lighthouse — two Humvees with .50 cals on top and a Stryker armored personnel carrier. A soldier patted me down thoroughly, then pushed me into the back of the Stryker. I settled onto a bench and watched out the open hatch as the horizon north of Kestrel lit up with tracer fire and the glare from artillery strikes. A flight of Apaches and Kiowas spun up and lifted off their pads, angling out toward the front.

Hill conferred with a group of soldiers just out of earshot. He talked to them quietly and slowly, turning his attention to each in turn. Behind them, Rhames and a scrum of soldiers dragged a bound Nat into an armored Humvee. I imagined her sitting in the back of it, a would-be assassin surrounded by soldiers who looked at her target as only one step removed from God. Hill told them he wanted to talk to her, but that would only keep her alive a little while longer. My plan had bought us some time but if we were going to get out of this, I had to stay focused.

Once Nat was locked away, Rhames broke off from the group and came toward Hill. I pushed myself into a dark corner, out of sight.

Had Rhames recognized me? And if he had, would saving Hill's life be enough to keep me and Nat alive until I could get to the next part of my plan?

The back hatch of the Stryker slammed shut. I looked up to find Nathan Hill was sitting on a bench directly across from me. He leaned forward, elbows on his knees. His hands, surprisingly thin and small, were clasped in front of him. Scars stretched from his knuckles up into his sleeve.

"So," Hill said with his ever-present, gentle smile. "Why don't you tell me about Benjamin Quarles."

24

I stared at him, openmouthed, without words.

"Sergeant Rhames told me his version. I'd like to hear yours."

Anything I said could cause those hands clasped in front of him to reach out and take me by the throat. I grasped for a lie but nothing came.

"Callum?"

"I . . . found a dog," I said. "Quarles was going to kill him. Me too."

"And so you killed Quarles first."

I swallowed back a dry spot in my throat and nodded.

"How did you feel?" he asked. "After you killed him?"

I saw Quarles lying there on his belly and smelled the sunbaked dust of the market mixing with the metallic stink of his blood.

"Sick," I said.

"But later? After that had passed."

Hill waited, but no words came.

"You knew you had done the right thing," Hill said. "Didn't you? Rhames told me a little about the man. The things they found out about him once he was gone. He was so far off Path he never should have been in that place. People like that" — Hill looked toward the back of the Stryker, his eyes far away — "my father was a shoe salesman, and to relax after a long day at the shop, he liked to garden."

Hill saw my look and chuckled, caught.

"Yes. It's true. I lied to the girl with the explosives who was trying to kill me. There was a vacant lot near the house where I grew up. It had been an old basketball court, I think, only then it was just cracked concrete and trash, and Dad decided that the neighborhood would be better if it was a garden. He was a good gardener, but his biggest problem was weeds. He'd poison them, but they'd always come back, choking off everything he had planted. Eventually he had to get down on his knees and tear every one of them out by the roots with his bare hands."

The blue of Hill's eyes seemed to pulse in the dim light, binding us together.

"Is that true, sir?"

Hill smiled. "Does it matter?"

The Stryker shook as it took another hill.

"Good men try to do good things," he said. "Great nations try to make the lives of their people better, but there are weeds that hold them back. Weeds like Mr. Quarles. Are we supposed to value the weeds above the garden?"

I kept my eyes steady on Hill's and slowly shook my head.

"But it wasn't just that," Hill said. "Was it? Why you left, I mean."

"No."

"Mr. Rhames said Captain Monroe was about to make you take part in the Choice."

The Stryker shook from an explosion nearby and then accelerated. Hill didn't even flinch. I dug my hand into the bench beneath me to steady myself.

"Stupid," Hill said. "The Choice is necessary, but it's not a place for children. I don't blame you for protecting yourself against a monster, Callum. I don't blame you for running, either. Sometimes I think you have to stray far from your Path in order to find your way back again. It's a truth not many people understand, but you do. Don't you?"

There were helicopters above us now, at least three, flying low. The Stryker strained up a hill, then fell onto a roadway, and the ride went smooth and fast. Hill was waiting. I said that I did.

Hill reached across and took my hand in his. His grip was strong and firm. My fingertips lay along the waxy plain of his scars.

"You were sent to me in a time of need, Cal. I can't repay you for my life, but if there's anything I can offer you, tell me what it is and it's yours."

This was it. I knew I should play the selfless novice and deny him at first, but there was no time for that.

"The girl's name is Natalie," I said. "We came to Kestrel at the same time. You were right. Her parents had just been killed. She was in pain, confused. The Feds took advantage of her. They made her do this. She can find the Path. I know it. Please spare her life."

"She's been in contact with the Feds, Callum. She has to talk. Tell us whatever she knows about their plans."

"I can talk to her," I said. "She'll tell us everything she knows."

"And she has to choose," he said. "She may have done it before coming to Kestrel, but she needs to make a real choice for the Path. An honest one."

Somehow I managed to not let my eyes slip from Hill's.

"She will," I said. "I promise."

•   •   •

The Stryker came to rest and the hatch fell. The war was far enough away that I could only hear an occasional thump, like a book falling from a shelf. I searched for the Humvee carrying Nat, but it wasn't anywhere to be found.

We were parked outside a low concrete building, one of many that were huddled within a tall perimeter fence. Streetlights glowed around us. I could see signs of an old battle. Charred walls and broken windows. I guessed that Shrike must have been an old Fed base the Path took over as it advanced.

The soldiers swarmed Hill as he moved from one to the next, taking in information and issuing orders. Rhames stood on the outer ring of the group, glaring at me, but once Hill spoke with him, he turned away and didn't look back.

"Callum," Hill said, returning to me with a heavily freckled soldier. "Sergeant Parker here will get you something to eat and then take you to have your talk with the girl. You'll report to me when you're done."

"Yes, sir," I said, falling easily into the crisp obedience of my days at Cormorant.

Hill flew up a set of concrete stairs and was gone, leaving me with Parker.

"This way, Private."

"I'm just a novice," I said as I followed him up the stairs and inside.

"Well, looks like when you save the president's life, you jump to the head of the line. Congratulations. Come on, I'll grab you a uniform and show you to the mess. You missed dinner, but I'm sure they can find a hero of the Path something to eat."

I had to hustle to keep up with him. Hero of the Path. All I could do was ignore it and stay focused. Parker and I weaved through a stream of soldiers, most of whom were wearing more stripes and stars than anyone I had ever seen. You could feel purpose sparking off the place like a live wire. They all knew they were about to win.

"Here you go."

Parker held out a stack of camouflage and a pair of boots. A private's stripes hovered over the Path insignia on the arm of the shirt. I hesitated, knowing I should reach out and take them but unable to do it.

"Let's move, Private. Latrine is that way. I'll give you five."

I took the clothes out of Parker's hands and pushed through the latrine door. The bathroom was empty and stark, smelling of bleach and soap. I dressed as fast as I could, struggling with the awkwardness of my cast. I moved my good hand through my unkempt hair, trying to smooth it back and match the men I had seen in the hallways outside.

When I was done, I stared at the strange figure in the mirror. A flash of gold winked and I reached up to touch the pin on my collar, a sun bisected by a single line. There it was again, that feeling of the present rushing into the past like two rivers into one.

Parker banged on the door. I knelt by my old clothes and dug through them until I found Bear's collar. I stuffed it in my pocket and then stepped out of the latrine.

As Parker and I made our way down the hall through the masses, I walked faster, my shoulders squaring to match the others. The mess was empty except for a few novices moving from table to table, cleaning up plates and glasses from dinner. Silverware clattered as it dropped into their trays. Parker sat me down at the end of a table and returned a moment later with a tray full of meat, corn bread, and green beans.

"Real Texas barbecue," Parker said. "President Hill insists on it everywhere we go. Some of us think that's what the whole war is really about: bringing proper beef barbecue to the heathen masses. You have fifteen minutes for chow. I'll be waiting down that hall in the third office when you're done."

"Yes, sir," I said, and then Parker was gone.

I drained the glass of milk next to my plate in one gulp, then lifted my fork and poked at the glistening pile of meat. Real Texas barbecue. Just looking at it made me ill, but I forced it down, watching as the novices scrubbed and polished the mess. It was hard to believe that an hour north, an entire world was slipping away.

"Are you done with that, sir?"

"Yeah. Thanks."

I pushed the tray toward the novice's hand, but the tray and everything on it crashed onto the linoleum floor. Shards of glass glittered amid the charred pile of beef. I looked to see if the novice was okay and was met with a rush of vertigo. The room spun around the young novice's face and I sat there, mouth open, fingers splayed weakly on the plastic tabletop.

"James?"

25

I knelt by the table and helped James gather the shattered dishes into a bin he carried. He reached for a piece of glass and it pricked the tip of his finger.

"Careful," I warned.

"I got it."

James glanced out the open door into the hall.

"What are you doing here?" he asked as he picked up the remaining shards. "If you're a spy, President Hill will find out."

"So it's President Hill now?" James glared at me, then went back to his work. "Someone had a bomb at his speech and I saved his life."

"Why?"

It was a knife-edge of a question and I didn't know how to answer it. A speck of barbecue sauce flew off his rag as he scrubbed, striking his uniform. James hissed and rubbed at it with his thumbnail. I took the rag and found its single clean corner.

"Here."

I held the cloth of his uniform between my fingers and worked at the stain until it began to fade. If I closed my eyes, I could have sworn we were back at Cormorant.

When I was done, I stepped away and caught James staring hungrily at the private's stripe on my shoulder. He had been dragged across the country to scrub floors and clean plates and he still lusted after a stupid stripe. I remembered dogs in Quarles's kennel that were the same way. The harder you kicked them, the more they tried to please.

"Private Roe!"

James jumped to attention as soon as he saw Parker standing by the door.

"Everything okay here? This novice bothering you?"

"No, sir. Everything is fine."

"Good. Then let's move out."

I nodded and Parker strode away down the hall. James started toward a door to the kitchen.

"Wait." I took his arm but he snatched it away from me. "James —"

"I didn't tell Monroe anything when I got back. Nothing. But if you're planning to do something here —"

"I'm just trying to get home."

"Fine," he said. "Do it and leave us alone."

James shoved the door open and disappeared into the kitchen. I wanted to tell him what I thought of a kitchen boy's smug superiority, but then a single thought came from nowhere and stopped me dead.

It's because of me.

There was no one in Cormorant more on Path than James, and yet he had been stripped of his place as a valet and hauled across the country to scrape food off trays. How better to humiliate the brother of a traitor? It wasn't Monroe who had done this to him, it wasn't the Path, it was me.

I backed away from the door. I had done enough to James. It was time to leave him alone.

A cheer broke out down the hallway. I left the mess as the hall filled with soldiers. I joined the stream, bouncing from officer to officer.

"Sir!" I said. "Sir, what's going on?"

A major grinned mid-stride. His hand found my shoulder. "It's about over, son," he said. "We just punched a hole in the Fed's lines north of Richmond. We're taking territory faster than we can secure it!"

"Philadelphia?"

"We're on our way!"

I eased out of the flood of bodies and into a nearby doorway. The major ran a key card through a reader next to a set of double doors down the hall. He stepped through and before the doors could close, I saw banks of computer screens and the dark silhouettes of soldiers. In the middle of it was Nathan Hill.

"Roe!"

Parker was standing beside an open door. Inside was a small room with a table and two chairs. On the far side of the table was Nat, her wrists cuffed and secured to the table.

He pushed a notepad and a pen into my hands. "We'll be recording everything you two say, but we also want a signed confession and details on Fed forces."

"Yes, sir."

Nat didn't look up when I entered the room. She was wearing a gray pair of Path work pants and a gray T-shirt. Her feet were bare. Her skin was waxy-looking, but I couldn't see bruises on any of the skin that was showing. So far Hill had kept his word. She hadn't been hurt.

The door shut behind me, and a lock was thrown.

"You're a private now," she said, her brown eyes sunken and dark. "Not bad pay for a job well done."

I sat down across from her. There was a large black microphone in the center of the table. I pulled the notebook toward me and began to write.

"Do you need water?" I asked, pausing for an answer I knew wasn't coming. "Something to eat? Are you injured at all?"

I held up the notebook so she had to see it.

I won't apologize for wanting you to live.

Nat looked at the paper without reaction.

"I was able to make a deal with President Hill —"

"President Hill," she said.

"I explained to him why you did what you did and he's prepared to forgive you and let you go."

"You explained why I did it?"

"Yes."

"And why did I do it, Cal?"

I took the notebook back and started to write. "You were distraught over the deaths of your parents. Like I said, the president decided to be merciful and is willing to let you go. You just have to tell him everything you know about the Federal forces."

"I don't know anything about the Federal forces."

I held up the notebook again.

The Path broke the Fed line a few hours ago. They'll be in Philadelphia by the morning. Say something about forces at the front. True or false, it won't make any difference now.

When I put the paper down, Nat had a thin smile on her face.

"I'm not afraid to die, Cal."

I scribbled another note.

Do you think all they'll do is kill you?

Nat's smile vanished. Her chains rattled as she put her hands flat on the table, like she was bracing herself.

"We're going to win," I said. "We were always going to win. Keeping things to yourself won't do you or anyone else any good."

Nat said nothing.

Please, I wrote.

Nat flexed her hands into fists and then let them go. Her hair hung down in greasy locks along her cheeks. She looked so tired. I wanted more than anything to touch her.

"Their numbers aren't what you think they are," Nat said, her voice steady but lifeless. "They have maybe ten or fifteen thousand good fighters left. They moved them all to the front so the Path would assume they must have more in reserve. They're going to rely heavily on armor and artillery, which they have a lot of. More than the Path."

Nat took the pen and a sheet of paper from the notebook. Moments later she pushed it back at me.

"Show them that."

Scrawled on the paper was a rough map of the front, indicating where their artillery was, along with the location of a small airfield and a brigade of armor. The plastic pen clattered to the desktop. We sat there beneath the buzz of the fluorescent lights.

"What else, Cal?"

The microphone was crouched between us like a rat. I wanted so badly for this to be over, to take Nat's drawing and walk out of the room, but I forced myself to meet her eyes.

"You have to make the Choice, Nat. You have to say the words."

She stared back at me, motionless.

"Once you do, this is all over. You're free."

"Free to be what?" she asked. "A companion? Ministering to men of the Glorious Path in my robe and veil?"

"You'll be alive."

"No," she said. "I don't think so."

Sick of the paper, I covered the microphone with my hand and whispered.

"They're just words."

Nat pushed my hand away and spoke directly into the microphone.

"My name is Natalie Marie Whitacker. My mother was Staff Sergeant Eliza Whitacker of the U.S. Army rangers. My father was Deputy John Whitacker. Both were murdered by Path forces. In retaliation, and to defend the republic, I attempted to assassinate the traitor Nathan Hill. I am proud of my actions."

Nat dropped into her chair.

"Those are just words too," she said.

There was a metallic click behind me as the door opened. I crumpled the notes I had written Nat in my hand and stuffed them in a pocket. Parker's presence was heavy in the doorway.

"Nat, please."

She said nothing as Parker stepped inside and unlocked the chain that bound her to the desk. He took her arm and led her out into the hall and away.

"Private Roe?"

A young novice stood in the doorway behind me. "President Hill has asked that you meet him in his ready room in one hour. He thought you might want to go to your quarters until then. They're this way."

I followed him out of the building and through the streets of the base, mixing with the soldiers and the novices. The sounds of the war filtered in from far away. I stopped across the street from a long building with a peaked roof.

"That's our Lighthouse."

I looked over the novice's shoulder at another building. "My quarters are that way?"

"Yes."

I thanked him and crossed the road. Flickering amber light warmed the windows of the Lighthouse and spread onto the concrete below. I remembered years ago when Beacon Quan explained that anyone looking for light should always be able to find it in God's house.

The Lighthouse was large and empty, carpeted in burgundy with black walls and a thin stage that held the altar. It looked like it had been a movie theater before the Path came. The air was warm from the lanterns hung all around and the thick candles that lined the stage.

The Path insignia hung over the altar, radiant in gold and marble. It was more than simply quiet within the Lighthouse. It was as if time stopped within its walls.

I dropped into one of the seats and thought of Nat, wishing that time could stand still for her too. In less than an hour I would meet with Hill and he would know that I failed to bring her to the Path. After that it wouldn't be long until someone like Rhames showed up in Nat's cell. I wondered if she would welcome him when he came.

"Cal?"

Startled, I turned and found James standing behind me in the aisle. He had changed out of his dirty kitchen things and into rumpled novice fatigues.

"Mind if I . . ."

I moved over and James sat next to me. He closed his eyes and mouthed a prayer. His copy of *The Glorious Path* was on his knee.

"Not where I expected to find you," he said.

"Just looking for someplace quiet, I guess."

James sunk down into his seat, gazing up at the altar, its varnished lines gleaming in the candlelight.

"You remember the first time we came to Lighthouse?" he asked.

I nodded, remembering the two of us as we were then, fresh from the Choice and trembling in our pews as we sat through services for the first time.

"I was so scared."

"I know," James said. "You were holding my hand. I remember thinking — why is my brother holding my hand? And when will he stop?"

James laughed and I glanced over at him. "All of this always just felt right to you. Didn't it?"

"No. I fought it at first too."

"I wasn't fighting it, James. I was —" I cut myself off, hating the angry snap of my voice. I looked over my shoulder at the Lighthouse door. Time was still turning on the other side. Why had I come in here? What had I hoped to accomplish?

"You remember those nights we would sleep in the backyard?"

James was looking up at the altar, a half smile on his face.

"Our bunk beds," I said.

"I remember how Mom and Dad would go to bed and we would stay up talking, you know, just about —"

"Your crush on Mrs. Hurley."

"I didn't have a crush on Mrs. —"

"You told Mom and Dad that if they didn't get you into her class, you were going to run away."

"Well, what about you and — what's her name?" James asked. "That girl down the steet. The redhead. Cassie!"

"No no no," I said, waving him off. "I *definitely* didn't have a —"

"I saw the poetry. I *saw* it. Would you like a quote? 'Oh, Cassie! With hair of fire —'"

"Enough!"

James laughed and so did I, the sound echoing off the walls and brightening the inside of the Lighthouse. Once it faded, James and I sat side by side, a little breathless.

"The best thing about home was me and you," James said.

"Yeah," I said. "It was."

"I can't believe this is a coincidence. God wanted you here."

"Why?"

"You have to ask Him."

"God doesn't talk to me, James."

"You don't listen."

An old anger began to smolder and I tried to hold it down. "How can you — I mean, the things Hill does. The Choice —"

"We're trying to fix something that's badly broken," James said, repeating the line we had heard from a dozen beacons. "The Choice is a tool. Once we get where we're going, it won't be necessary anymore. Until then —"

"How can you say that?" I asked, my voice rising. "How can you *believe* that?"

"Because it's —"

"How did they get to you?"

"No one got to me! I just —" James stopped. He closed his eyes for a moment and then continued. "I was just as scared as you after they took us. Just as angry too. Without Mom and Dad, everything just seemed . . . It's like we were in the middle of this hurricane all the time. You know? But then I went to Lighthouse one night and Beacon Thomas explained that there was a path that ran through the center of the world. He said that no matter how chaotic things seemed, there was a plan and everything and everyone had their place in it. He said that once I pushed the fear and anger and doubt out of my head, I would know mine."

A glow washed over James as he remembered.

"And he was right," he said. "Once I saw it, once I *let* myself see it, I couldn't see anything else. I didn't want to. And it can be the same for you, Cal."

"James."

"I know you don't believe it, but you have a path too. There's a reason that you —"

"Maybe there are some things we just shouldn't talk about."

James fell silent. He turned away from me, staring down at the concrete floor, his hands on *The Glorious Path*.

"Yeah. Maybe."

Neither of us said anything more for some time. The quiet in the Lighthouse made it feel like we were trapped in amber.

"Guess they'll want everyone at their duty stations soon."

I nodded weakly, and James left his seat and started toward the aisle. The feel of him drawing away stopped my breath. If he left, if he opened that door, time would start up again and everything would be lost.

"I don't know what to do," I said.

James stopped. "I thought you were going home."

"I think there's something I have to do first," I said. "A friend I have to help. But I don't know how."

James's footsteps whispered down the carpet until I could feel him standing just at my shoulder.

"I don't know if I even can."

"God's not cruel," he said. "He wouldn't put you on a path you couldn't reach the end of. You have to trust that."

I turned around. James stood like a pillar in the middle of the aisle. The way the candlelight struck his face, deepening the hollows of his eyes and cheeks, made him seem so much older. It was like we had switched places and he was the older brother now and I was the younger. Or maybe it had been that way for a long while and I had never noticed.

"Good luck, Cal."

The noise of the war broke the spell of the Lighthouse as he opened the door. When it closed again, that same timelessness gathered around me — only now, I could feel the lie of it. Seconds ticked away inside of me like the fall of an axe.

I leaned forward over the seat in front of me. The altar and the glimmering sign of the Path seemed huge, overwhelming. Without thinking, I laced my fingers together and closed my eyes. Terror of the beacons had led me to spend months hiding in our barracks, rehearsing all the gestures and expressions of faith until I had them down perfectly. But sitting there in that Lighthouse, peering into the darkness of my closed eyes, a prayer unspooled deep inside me and for the first time it felt like something reaching out from the very center of me.

"God," I prayed. "Lead me to my path. . . ."

． ． ．

I stepped out of the Lighthouse and into the chaos of the battle. A siren was screeching and scores of soldiers ran by in a blur of camouflage, sprinting for their duty stations. There was a flash as a missile battery on the outskirts of the base fired. Veins of smoke shot into the sky, and seconds later, there were three explosions high overhead.

With all the confusion, it was hard to be sure, but I thought I heard small-arms fire just beyond the perimeter of the base. I joined the rush of traffic headed into the command building.

"Cal!"

James was running from the kitchens and I shoved my way through the mob to meet him.

"What's going on?"

"I don't know," James said. "Something's gone wrong but no one will say what."

Down the hallway, officers were streaming in and out of the ops center. "I'll be right back," I said. "Stay here."

A soldier swiped his key card by the doors and I timed my stride to slip in right behind him. The room was packed with generals and their men, all of them huddling over communications gear and glowing computers. I eased back into the shadows and looked for Hill.

He was standing with a group of officers before a large screen that showed a map of the United States. Path forces were displayed as gold circles and Fed forces were blue triangles. One look and it was easy to see what fueled the chaos in the room. There was a lot more blue on the board than gold and much of it was south of the

Path's frontlines. It looked like Federal forces were streaming in from the east and west simultaneously and quickly overwhelming Path forces.

"I want to know what the hell is going on," Hill said. "The Feds were not supposed to be able to do this."

A general in a disheveled uniform stepped forward. "Mr. President," he said, struggling to keep his voice calm. "There was a wave of drone and cruise missile attacks followed by large-scale beach landings and paratroop drops from stealth aircraft in Virginia, North Carolina, and Maryland."

"Which we weren't prepared for," Hill said.

"Sir, I —"

"Your assessment said that the Feds weren't supposed to have *half* this many troops left."

"We're working on it now, sir," the general said. "If we have more time, I'm sure we can come up with an —"

A junior officer spoke up from a bank of communications gear. "Sir, it's confirmed."

There was a pause as the general turned to the young man. "We're sure?"

"Yes, sir. We have multiple visual confirmations."

The general seemed to deflate. He glanced to a tech seated by the side of the main computer screen. "Go ahead. Change them."

With the press of a button, a large concentration of the Federal blue triangles to our south and east turned into the Union Jack of British forces. Throughout Maryland and Pennsylvania, what had been marked as Fed forces changed into the blue, white, and red of France. Other flags appeared in smaller numbers across the map. Israel. Spain. Brazil. Germany.

"Sir, we're ready to confirm that a coalition of at least six different countries is currently operating within our eastern theater," the general reported. "There are also indications of Russian forces attempting landings in California, and the Canadians breached the lines at Washington State."

Another communications officer spoke up. "Sir, the Two-Three reports sightings of small team forces within our own fence line."

The general pulled a red folder from a nearby case and held it out to Hill. "Are we ready, Mr. President?"

The room went silent. Hill stared at the red folder in the general's hand but made no move to take it.

"Sir? They knew the consequences when they did this."

"Have the men from Cormorant repel the coalition forces within Shrike's perimeter," Hill said quietly. "Commit everything else to Philadelphia."

"But, sir —"

"Do it!" Hill snapped as he took the red folder out of the man's hand. "I need to pray on this."

Before anyone could say another word, Hill left the group and strode past me and through a door to an adjoining room. The officers looked from one to another while the blinking armies advanced and retreated behind them.

The door Hill went through opened with a soft click when I turned the knob. I stepped inside and closed the door. The small room was almost suffocatingly hot due to the dozens of candles that lined the desk and shelves, filling the place with a flickering glow.

Just inside the door, there was a desk made of darkly polished wood. A belt was draped across it, holding Hill's holstered sidearm and his combat knife. His uniform was on a hook near the door.

Hill was across the room, kneeling with his back to me, in a nook where an altar had been set up. He was shirtless and barefoot. Waxy burn scars covered the whole of his back. The way the light hit them made them look like flames.

"Have a seat," he said without turning. "I'll be done soon."

I crossed the room to a small couch. The red folder sat on a table in front of me. When Hill had finished his prayers, he stretched into a khaki T-shirt and sat across the table. He said nothing for a time, eyes locked on the folder.

"Sir, I wanted to talk to you about the girl who —"

"You're from New York."

"I . . . yes, sir."

"But not the city."

"Ithaca."

"There's a lake there," he said. "Did you sail?"

I sat forward on the couch. "Sir, I'd like to —" Hill fixed me with his icy-blue eyes. "No, sir. I didn't."

"I sailed with my father," he said. "He took me out on the water the day his store finally went under. Everyone told him he should just torch the place and collect the insurance money, but Dad said that when he started out in business, he promised himself he'd be honest. A man of his word. He wasn't going back on that just because it made his life a little easier."

"Sir, Nat —"

"Sergeant Parker made a report, Cal. The girl will be dealt with in the morning."

"But if I could have a little more time with her, I could —"

"Your friend admitted to treason and refused to join the Path."

"But the intelligence —"

"Was worthless," he snapped. "Anything that girl knows is out of date. It's over."

I started to speak again but Hill was done. He reached for the red folder, drawing out the papers inside and regarding each carefully. A cord of tension inside of me evaporated and I fell back against the couch, feeling foolish for my whispered prayers. I imagined Nat in a cell somewhere within the base. Did she already know this was her last night?

"It's terrifying, isn't it? The things God requires of us."

Hill had dealt the papers out across the table so they sat in a snowy line between us. He was regarding them carefully, his chin in his hand. I looked closer and saw the name of a city printed at the top of each paper — Moscow. Berlin. London. Paris. Ottawa. Madrid. Below each name was a map and a list of numbers. A chill went through me as I remembered something Grey had said about a promise Hill made to any country caught interfering.

This was a list of targets.

The cities were the capitals of each country joining the coalition against him. The numbers detailed the quantity of warheads, their yields, and the estimated casualties. The numbers in the last column ran into the hundreds of thousands for each city. There was one more piece of paper sitting in the folder. I reached across the table and drew it out.

At the top of the paper was one word: *Philadelphia*. I looked over the page to find Hill's otherworldly blue eyes locked on me.

"God can't want this," I said.

"Why?"

James's voice fell into my head. "Because he's not cruel."

A peaceful smile settled across Hill's face, but his gaze didn't falter. "When God does it, it isn't cruel. It's what's meant to be."

Hill leaned across the table.

"God brought you across the country and set you down in that room, at that time, and gave you the courage to save my life. Why? To ensure that his will was done."

"Sir, you can't —"

Hill swept the papers into the folder and crossed the room to his desk. He reached for the uniform hanging by the door.

"Don't worry," he said as he pulled on a shirt and laid a tie around his neck. "There'll be a place for you after this. And for your brother too! Sergeant Rhames mentioned he was here. Kitchen help, I think." Hill chuckled. "I'm guessing we can find something a little bit better for him than that."

I watched Hill as he knotted his tie in crisp strokes. I thought of Alec pulling away from me out into the moonlit lake. Maybe he was right. Maybe the future was coming and there was nothing I could do about it. All I had to do was be still and let it come. James and I would be together and safe.

Hill slipped on his jacket and buttoned it. I saw Grey Solomon standing on the side of the road, and Nat, defiant, in the interrogation room, and a prayer started to unspool in my mind. It was a whispered voice growing stronger by the word.

I am on a glorious path. I will not turn from it even if it means my death.

Hill turned as I threw myself across the room, reaching for the sidearm that lay on his desk. My fingers grazed the belt, but Hill came at me in a blur. One fist slammed into my ribs and then his knee found my stomach. The air shot out of me and I hurtled into a shelf, shattering it. I rolled over, groaning, and saw Hill's belt on the ground. The gun was gone but the combat knife was within reach. I snatched it out of its sheath and slashed at Hill as he reached for me again. The blade bit into his flesh, buying me the second I needed to get up and stumble out to the center of the room.

I staggered backward, swinging the knife in front of me to keep him away, but Hill was too fast. He glided in between swipes of the blade, taking my cast in both hands and slamming it onto a corner of the table. I screamed and then a backhand to my temple sent whatever energy I had pouring out of me. The knife fell out of my hand and I tumbled backward, crashing into his altar.

I tried to get up, tried to keep fighting, but I had nothing left. I lay there, my arm throbbing, one eye swelling shut while the other filled with blood. My consciousness slipped in and out. I thought I heard gunfire and sirens coming from somewhere nearby. Hill stepped through the blur of my vision and fell on top of me, his legs pinning my arms to my sides. He found the knife by my side and held it over me.

"No one can stop what God has put in motion," he said, barely out of breath.

I closed my eyes as Hill lifted the blade, but there was a crash by the door. Hill turned toward it, and three sharp reports rang out across the room. His body jerked and he collapsed over me. His chest struck mine. His face fell by my cheek. Streams of his blood poured down my sides.

I forced myself out from under him, scrambling until I struck the far wall. I coughed and wiped the blood from my eyes as someone staggered into the room from the open doorway. The knife was lying by Hill's body. I grabbed it and held it out toward whoever was coming. A gun clattered onto the floor and a body came into focus.

James fell to his knees beside Hill's feet. He stared at the body in front of him, his arms limp at his sides, his eyes wide. His chest began to heave.

"James?"

I dropped the knife and reached for him as several small explosions shook the walls of the office. There were shouting voices just outside, followed by the back-and-forth chatter of small-arms fire.

"We have to go," I said, reaching for Hill's gun, which lay beside James. "James?"

The door to the ops center flew open and three black figures appeared. I scooped up Hill's weapon and fired half blind. Three shots shredded the door frame and forced them back. I stuffed the gun into my waistband and took James by the shoulders.

"Come on," I said, but James didn't move. "Get up!"

I grabbed James's shirtfront with my one good hand and hauled his limp body up. My muscles screamed and the effort sent me crashing against the wall beside me. There were more gunshots out in the hall and fire alarms began to wail. I wiped the blood out of my eyes and dragged James toward the door.

There were bodies strewn across the ops center, generals and their servants torn apart and still. The computers and the communications gear had all been destroyed and were smoldering, filling the room with a haze of smoke. My eyes stung as we made it through and into the corridor outside. Weapons fire seemed to be coming from all directions. Somewhere there was the boom of a grenade.

I searched through the gloom and saw a door just past the mess. The glass was shattered and I could see streetlights shining on the other side. The way to it was clear, but we couldn't leave. Not yet.

"Where would they keep a prisoner?" I asked, trying to shake James out of his shock. "James?"

He nodded down a hall across from the mess and I moved toward it, pulling him along, trying to ignore the pain that came with every step. The battle sounds grew louder, the deeper we ran into the base. I followed James's direction, ducking into doorways at any sign of the soldiers who stalked the hallways, never knowing if they were Path or Fed. We passed bodies, fallen singly or in groups, torn, bloody, eyes open.

James pointed down a corridor where a young Path corporal was collapsed over a small desk, a pool of blood gathering around his temple. Behind him was a hallway lined with close-set rooms.

I set James down in the hallway, then searched the corporal for his keys. I found them and moved down the line of rooms, opening door after door, only to find the rooms empty or their occupants dead.

I stuck the key in the second door from the end and when I opened it, a body flew at me from a far corner. A fist connected with my jaw and I hit the floor in a heap, fireworks lighting up my vision.

"What are you doing here?"

Nat was leaning over me, one hand grasping my collar, the other ready to strike.

"We came to get you out," I said, and when her glare didn't soften, I shoved her away from me. "Trust me or don't. You're free. Do what you want. James, let's go!"

I pushed us both into the hallway just as another volley of fire erupted. James flew out of my hands with a grunt, slamming into the wall and hitting the floor.

"James!"

He was sprawled on his back. His right side was gushing blood and he was breathing in ugly gasps. His skin was the color of paste. I pressed my hands into the wound to stop the bleeding and James screamed. I was dimly aware of Nat pulling Hill's gun away from me. There was more gunfire and then silence. James's eyes had gone wide and dark and then began to close.

I draped James's arm over my shoulder. He cried out as I took a halting step forward. My knees went weak and I began to fall but then the weight suddenly lessened. Nat was beside us, James's other arm around her shoulder.

The building was a maze, corridors blocked by bodies and collapsed walls. There were fires everywhere and clouds of smoke that burned our eyes and tore at our throats. We blundered through, coming to dead end after dead end. James hung between us, barely conscious, his lips moving soundlessly as he prayed.

"This way!"

Nat turned us down a hallway and I saw it. The door by the mess. We were almost there. Nat threw her shoulder into the door and we collapsed on the other side, coughing the smoke out of our lungs.

"James?"

His head lolled back and forth on the pavement. His eyes were closed and he was mumbling silently, incoherently. Buildings and wrecked vehicles burned all around us. Bodies littered the ground, and soldiers ran in and out of the darkness, firing constantly.

"Get somebody," I said to Nat. "Get anybody. Please."

Nat ran out of our small circle of light and disappeared down the street. There was a dead soldier facedown on the ground nearby. I took his combat knife and canteen and returned to James. His torso was slick with blood. His pants were dark with it. I stripped off his shirt and washed away as much as I could, revealing the ugly tear of a wound on his side. When I pressed the wad of bandages into his side, blood flowed between my fingers, but James didn't make a sound. He pawed at my hands and I knocked them away.

"It's okay," he said weakly. "I'm okay."

His eyes opened, shockingly bright. The sky lit up nearby and the pavement shuddered.

"Where are we?" he asked, in almost a singsongy kid's voice. "It feels like we're on a train."

I smoothed the hair off his brow. His skin was hot and wet. "Yeah," I said. "We're on a train."

"Where are we going? We going home?"

"That's right," I said. "We're going home."

I lifted the canteen to his lips and poured a stream of water across them. He gasped and drank. When he was done, I set the canteen down and took his hand in mine and squeezed. A strange smile rose on his face.

"Why is my brother holding my hand?" he said dreamily. "And when will he stop?"

I searched the dark of the base for Nat and saw nothing. A scream was rising in my throat, but I swallowed it.

"My friend is looking for help. She'll be back any time now."

"I killed him, Cal. I was looking for you, and then I heard the fight. I just saw someone on top of you. I didn't know who it was. I didn't —"

"You saved my life."

James shook his head, and then his eyes narrowed like he was searching for something in the sky. Across the street three figures emerged from the dark and were coming our way fast. I gripped the combat knife and leaned over James, but when they moved into the light, I saw it was Nat followed by two soldiers. I waved them over frantically.

"James, we're going to get you out of here, okay?"

When I looked down, his eyes were wide with horror, staring up into the dark. Tears ran across his cheeks.

"James?"

". . . I didn't know it was him."

26

More than a month later, I stepped out into what used to be Camp Kestrel.

It was a bright day and hot, dusty from the dried mud kicked up by the Fed vehicles tearing through the streets. I gathered my things and left the barracks I had been staying in since Nat helped convince the Fed MPs that James and I weren't a threat to national security.

I walked through the camp toward the infirmary, watching the Fed soldiers. Some went about the work of packing for the push south diligently, but most lounged on hillsides and across the hoods of vehicles. They smoked cigarettes and laughed. Their uniforms were ragged. The officers tried to keep order but few listened.

Path tents lay in molding piles of canvas all around the camp, but the command buildings still stood, gutted of intelligence and repurposed. Fed drone crews now sat in the place of their Path counterparts.

I paused by a blighted rectangle of ash and trampled grass. The Lighthouse had been the first thing the Feds destroyed, torching it to the cheers of their men. The altar was now a pile of scorched wood. The Path insignia had fallen and was facedown in the dirt, black and twisted. Soldiers still gathered to have their pictures taken with it, thumbs up and grinning. I knew I shouldn't have cared, but for some reason, I was glad I hadn't been there to see its destruction.

When I arrived at the infirmary, an orderly was pushing James's wheelchair out into the sun. James looked as much like a ghost as Kestrel did. His skin was a waxy gray and all the weight he had lost gave him a skeletal look. His deep-set eyes seemed to stay permanently fixed to the ground. He'd barely spoken since we arrived.

"You ready?"

James said nothing. I passed the orderly a small wad of cash and he gave me a bag of medicine that I tucked into my backpack. After he left I reached for the back of the wheelchair, but James waved me away.

"James . . ."

"I can walk on my own."

He planted his hands on the wheelchair's armrests and pushed, his face white with strain. He wavered once but he closed his eyes for a moment and it passed. I led him around the infirmary and pulled open the door of a rust-and-blue hatchback. James dropped into the backseat and I shut the door.

"Nice of them to give you a new cast."

Nat was standing on the other side of the car in a swirl of dust. I had only seen her a few times since we'd arrived at Kestrel. Each time was from a distance, as she tried to talk her way into companies of Marines heading south to pursue the Path.

"Yeah," I said, holding up the clean white plaster. "The old one had seen better days, I guess. They say I still have a few weeks with this one, though."

I came around the front of the car and saw the backpack on the ground next to her. Behind her a group of soldiers were loading supplies into a trio of Humvees.

"They finally let you sign up?"

Nat shook her head. "They're dropping me off at home on their way to California. Figured I could help with the rebuilding for a couple years until I can enlist."

"President Burke says it'll all be over by then."

"Yeah," she said with a roll of her eyes. "I heard that too. If he thinks this guy who took Hill's place is going to fold, he's crazy or stupid."

"I'm betting on stupid."

I threw my pack into the front passenger seat and shut the door. Nat peered into the car where James sat staring out the back window at the base.

"How is he?"

"Fine," I said quickly. "It'll take some time, I guess."

"They should give him a medal."

"Captain Assad tried," I said, spreading my arms wide to present the rattletrap hatchback. "But I said we wanted this instead."

Nat's laugh was small and reluctant, but it was good to hear. "So you're headed home too."

I nodded. "Assad slipped us enough cash to get there and not eat MREs for a while too. We should be okay."

There was a clap behind her as the soldiers closed the Humvee's hatch.

"Nat."

She looked back at one of the men and nodded.

"Well, I guess I better . . ."

"Yeah."

Nat started to go but then she jumped forward and threw her arms around me. She pulled me close and her head fell to my shoulder. Everything seemed to go very still around us. I lifted my arms to her back and held her, breathing in the dusty heat that clung to us. I closed my eyes.

"Thank you," she breathed into my ear.

"Whitacker!" one of the soldiers called. "Let's move!"

Nat stepped back, her amber eyes shining, the sun lightening her brown hair. She slipped a piece of paper into my hand and then ran to catch her ride. I stood by the car, watching as she slung her pack over her shoulder and jumped into a Humvee. Her door slammed and they pulled out, joining the long line of vehicles waiting at the main gate.

The car door opened with a rusty squeak. I got in and unfolded the piece of paper. On it was a phone number and an address in Wyoming. I stared at it a moment before putting it into my pocket and checking the rearview.

James was watching the line of departing Fed transports as they pulled through the gate and then vanished in a cloud of dust. Sitting closed on his lap was a small green book, stained with faded blood. His hands lay on it as if he was warming them over a fire. The gold leaf of the title, torn and dull, said *The Glorious Path*.

Time, I thought, pushing past the sick feeling in my gut. *That's all he needs. All any of us need.*

I cranked the ignition and guided us away.

We spent the morning driving through a landscape struggling to return to normal. A steady stream of refugee traffic surrounded us, moving north past bombed-out restaurants that sat next to gas stations that were open and lit in neon.

A detour brought us directly through DC, where we saw the worst of it. Even though the government had moved out years before, the Path had hit it with a vengeance. The roads were rubble-strewn and pitted, and most of the gleaming white government buildings we could see were covered in black scorch marks. The White House and the Capitol were ruins of white marble.

Only the ivory needle of the Washington Monument stood nearly pristine. A tent city had sprung up on the mall around it and along the edge of the reflecting pool. Refugees milled about in tattered clothes beneath a ring of American flags.

The signs of war became less frequent as we moved up into Maryland. For miles at a time it was possible to forget the last six years except for the occasional checkpoints staffed by bored-looking privates in lightly armored Humvees.

Once we crossed the border into Pennsylvania, I sat up straighter and gripped the steering wheel. I counted the miles, sure I could feel the bright line of the next border in the distance. One hundred. Fifty. Twenty.

My pulse raced. Even James was sitting up now, peering out the windshield, *The Glorious Path* on the seat next to him.

"Look!"

A sign appeared at the side of the road, green and white, just beyond the line of trees. The car's engine gave a wheezy complaint when I stood on the gas, but I didn't care. The sign grew larger by the second and then we were on it.

WELCOME TO NEW YORK. THE EMPIRE STATE.

I held my breath as we blew past it, and New York surrounded us. And this wasn't the ugly glass and steel of New York City, this was trees and grass and the rolling hills. This was small towns and snaking rivers and crumbling barns. We passed Binghamton and then Whitney Point, turning west onto 79 for the final stretch that brought us through the dense green of state parks. The side of the road teemed with ferns and white oak and maple trees. I rolled the window down and let the wind blow around us. It smelled of damp leaves and grass warmed by the sun.

I could feel home sitting out beyond the trees, sending tremors through the air and the ground, until my heart pulsed along in time. I knew James felt it too when his hand, thin and weak, clasped my shoulder. I heard myself laugh as the little car struggled on.

We rode the last miles in a silence greater than the inside of any Lighthouse. Even the engine settled into a quiet thrum. James leaned forward between the seats and, as I urged the car faster, everything around us faded into a blur of motion. Only the road remained, a bright seam cutting through the forest. At first it was pockmarked and rough and then, as we grew closer, there was the slick whisper of fresh asphalt that made me feel like we were flying.

I could see Mom's face and Dad's and Grandma Betty's. It was like we had just left only days ago.

We came around a bend in the road, and the trees parted and shops appeared with hanging signs and shining windows. We went over a bridge above a seething falls and the Cornell campus rose and fell away. We were flying again, alone on the road beneath a bower of branches, winding through the bright day. We crested a hill and houses emerged from the woods, one or two at a time and then clusters of them, paneled in wood and brick and surrounded by runs of hedges and sun-dappled lawns. We came to a hill leading to a cul-de-sac and there it was, down at the end of the lane. Cobalt-blue walls surrounded in roses.

"James," I said, my voice thick with wonder. "James, look . . ."

27

I parked at the top of the hill and cut the engine.

Down the street, brightly colored mailboxes peeked out from ranks of lilac and honeysuckle. *Gutterman. Royce. Egan. Bell.* And then, at the edge of the cul-de-sac, surrounded by rosebushes — *Roe.* The simple black letters seemed to pulse against the white of the mailbox.

I felt rooted to my seat, unable to move. The back door creaked open and I watched James step onto the sidewalk, dazed. He took a few tentative steps before turning to me and waiting. I pushed my door open and tumbled out of the car and onto the sun-warmed road.

We descended the hill without a word, each of us holding our breath. Most of the houses we passed had signs of wartime neglect — curtainless windows, overgrown yards, peeling paint.

And then the hill flattened and we were there. I stared down at the base of our front gate, the white paint dry and chipped, exposing the graying wood beneath. Crabgrass and dandelions grew in untidy clumps. The gate squeaked as James opened it and stepped through to the other side.

"Look," James said.

The grass at his feet was brilliantly green and the rosebushes that ran the length of the fence were voluminous and dotted with red and pink and white flowers. He climbed the front steps and stood framed in the front door.

I tried to call out to James as he reached out for the doorknob, but my voice was strangled in my throat. The door was locked, so he reached down into the bushes by the porch and, after searching a few moments, retrieved a small stone. He slid open its compartment and exposed a single brass key. Laughing to himself, he fit the key into the lock.

I thought of an ancient ship locked inside a glass bottle. What would happen if you broke the seal? Would all those accumulated years rush in at once, turning it to dust?

I called out to James as he turned the doorknob, but it was too late. The door swung open. He looked back at me and then stepped inside. I closed my eyes as his footsteps clicked across the wood floor.

"Cal, come on!"

The stones of the front walk passed slowly beneath my feet, giving way to brick stairs and then slats of blond wood stretching out before me, gleaming in the sun. I ran into the house, following the sound of James's voice as he called for Mom and Dad. I moved from room to room, a giddy energy bubbling through me as I saw how little had changed.

The living room was a dim cave with thick brown-and-gold carpet. A TV sat at one end and at the other was the lumpy brown couch where Mom and Grandma Betty would drink wine while Dad played guitar. The kitchen glowed in shades of pink and yellow, with dishes sitting unwashed in the sink and stacks of mail teetering by the coffee machine.

"Mom! Dad!"

I threw myself at the door to our bedroom and there was our red shelf full of books and our stacks of games. Loose Legos were scattered across the floor between our beds in piles of red and yellow and green, like raw jewels. I bent over laughing, out of breath, wanting to throw them all into the air. I felt James in the doorway behind me.

"Can you believe it?" I said as I turned. "Mom and Dad are probably just out. They'll be here any —"

James was holding a yellowing piece of paper. On the front it said JAMES AND CALLUM.

"Go ahead," he said. "Read it."

I paused, thinking of that crumbling ship, but then James pressed it into my hands. I unfolded a single sheet of paper covered in our mother's neat hand.

> Boys,
>
> It's been five years now and we haven't heard a word about either of you. I can only pray that you found some way to stay safe until all of this is over.
>
> The war seems to be going badly now and the last few years have been very hard on your grandmother. The rationing has made getting her medicine increasingly difficult, so your father and I finally decided that we had no choice but to try to get into Canada before they close the border for good. We're leaving first thing tomorrow morning.
>
> We never thought we'd have to leave the house you both grew up in. It's sad how so many things that would have seemed unthinkable only a few years ago are now so

*commonplace. Maybe in times like these, all we can do
is survive and hope for the day when we'll be able to live.*

*We plan to head northeast toward Wellesley Island,
where they say there are still people who can get us
across. Where we'll go after, if we even succeed, we have
no way of knowing. The refugee camps near Ottawa are
full and we hear that they're pushing people farther and
farther west. We'll do all we can to leave word for you
wherever we go.*

*We love you both and pray for the day when we'll all
be together again.*

Mom and Dad

The letter slipped from my hands and fell to the floor.

"Cal . . ."

I found myself running back through the house and toward
the front door. This time I saw the layers of dust and the empty
shelves I had missed before and smelled the musty air of a place
abandoned.

"Cal! Wait!"

I collapsed onto the front porch, my head in my hands, breathing
in the cloying smell of the roses that had grown unchecked all around
the house. The floorboards creaked behind me.

"It's been six years," James said.

I nodded but couldn't speak. Couldn't think. James hovered a
while and then he drifted inside. I looked up at the empty houses
tucked in among the oaks and the grass-lined streets.

I remembered how the school bus would let James and me off at
the top of the hill and we would race each other down the sidewalk,

kicking at the russet piles of fallen leaves, before bursting inside and yelling for Mom. I remembered lying in the front yard in the summertime, the warm air around me full with the hum of Dad's lawn mower and the smell of cut grass. I remembered our neighbors and our friends and how I ran thoughtlessly through the streets to the shores of the lake.

I tried to remember the bad things too, the unhappy things, hoping they would drive away the ache of the loss, but it was no use. As hard as I tried, all I could remember were the times I had been so happy.

It was after nightfall when I made my way through the dark house and slid open the door to the back porch. James had built a small fire in the middle of the garden and he sat reading by its orange light.

The grass in the garden was overgrown and the flowers had gone wild and weed-strangled. Our hammocks still hung between the twin oaks though they were threadbare, the white ropes frayed and gray with mildew. James sat on the crumbling stone border that surrounded the small pond.

"Where've you been?" he asked, setting his book down beside him.

"Walking," I said. I drifted across the yard and sat down a few feet from James, staring into the flames at his feet. "Most of the houses in the neighborhood are abandoned. The Guttermans. The Bells."

James pushed a tin plate my way. "Warmed up some of the rations we brought with us."

It was spaghetti with red sauce and bits of sawdusty meat. I pushed at it with the plastic fork James gave me. "Guess we can go out tomorrow and spend some of Captain Assad's money on real food."

James said nothing. He cracked a branch in two and tossed half into the flames. It flared and crackled. Sitting on the cracked stone next to him was his copy of *The Glorious Path*. The cover was battered and stained. I took it and rifled through the dog-eared pages. Almost every one was worn glossy. The margins were filled with James's careful handwriting. I set the book back down and stared into the fire.

"You're going back, aren't you?"

James poked at the campfire with a stick, arranging the coals. The fire surged and brightened.

"I was studying to be a beacon," he said quietly. "I never said anything because I knew you wouldn't like it. Beacon Quan told me he knew a place in Oklahoma that he thought would be good for my apprenticeship. It's this town called Foley. It grows wheat and corn. Just a few hundred people living on farms with a small Lighthouse."

James sat forward and stared into the flames.

"The Choice is wrong," he said. "I know that, and I know other things are wrong too, but . . ." James stopped, struggling for the words. "Even now, I close my eyes and I pray and I can feel my path. It hasn't gone away. I wish it would, but it hasn't. And I know it doesn't end here. Maybe if I'm there . . . maybe I can try to help make things better."

"They'll kill you if they find out who you are."

"I know," he said.

I took another branch and fed it to the fire.

"I keep thinking about the day they took us," I said. "Maybe if I hadn't been so afraid, we could have escaped, or if I had stood up to the beacon —"

"They would have killed us," James said. "You were trying to keep your little brother safe, Cal. Just like you've been trying to do for the last six years."

James moved off the stone border and sat down next to me.

"You put us on a path," he said. "I know you don't believe it, but I do, and I think it's the one we were meant to be on. I don't regret it."

"Not even Hill?"

The wind blew through the trees, sending sparks across the yard like a swarm of bees. James turned to me, his eyes warm in the firelight.

"Not even Hill."

We sat there in silence until the fire died down to a few orange coals. We kicked dirt over them and then we made our way inside. I paused at the porch door, looking at the tattered remains of our hammocks swinging in the breeze. I closed the door, and James and I drifted toward our old bedroom without a word.

The wood floor between our now too-small beds was hard and cold, but it felt right to be there, him on one side and me on the other. We brought in a couple dusty blankets and pulled the shades back from the window. Outside, moonlit trees swayed against the black.

"James?"

"Yeah."

"I don't know what to do now."

James thought a moment. "Well, last time we were here, you said you wanted to be Batman. Maybe you could get started on that."

I found a loose Lego and tossed it at his head.

"Ow."

"Maybe it was stupid to come here."

"It wasn't stupid," he said. "It just isn't the end of the line."

James had propped himself up on one elbow and was looking across the room at me.

"It's been more than a year since they left," I said. "And even they didn't know where they were going."

"Where they are doesn't matter," he said. "Wanting to find them does."

I said nothing more and eventually James lay back down. I sat up and looked out at the stars hanging above the trees across the street, restlessness buzzing through me. I found my shoes and my jacket and headed for the door.

"Where you going?" James asked sleepily.

"Just for a walk."

"Want me to —"

"No," I said. "I'm okay."

Outside, the night was full of the rhythmic call of insects and the wind in the trees. The front gate opened with a squeak and I stepped through and out into the street. I didn't remember the names of roads, so I followed a kind of muscle memory. I'd reach the end of one road and wait to feel a tug one way or another, following what felt like a compass that had been buried inside of me years ago. Most of the houses I passed looked empty but a few were lit, spilling their yellow glow out into their yards. In a few the bluish lights of TVs shone and voices came out onto the street.

The roads wound through trees and hedges, like the turnings of a knot. More than once I felt sure that I had become hopelessly lost, but every time I was about to turn back and go home I'd feel that tug and I'd press on. I followed a meandering lane through the yellow pools of streetlights until it came to a chain-link fence. I could hear cars passing on the other side.

There was a strange scent on the wind, something clean and mineral. It was like two hands had grabbed me by the shoulders and were pulling me along. I hopped the fence and crossed a string of two-lane roads. On the other side, there was a curtain of trees with a sign among them that said no trespassing after dark. I passed it by with a laugh, remembering all the times James and I ignored it when we were kids.

I ran across a parking lot and then more grass and I was there. I stripped off my shoes and socks and my feet sunk into sand and wind-smoothed pebbles. The air was full of the salty smell of decay and the breeze blowing across the top of rippling water. I dropped onto the sand and looked out across the face of Cayuga Lake.

The shores on either side of me, rolling hills against the dark sky, stretched into the distance, embracing water that was like a black mirror reflecting the moon and the stars. The red and white running lights of a few distant boats bobbed on its surface. The only sounds were the small waves crashing at my feet and the night murmurings of insects and frogs. I picked up a handful of pebbles and threw some out into the water, where they landed with a gentle plunk.

How many times had James and I come here after school? How many times had I stood in this exact spot, looking at this exact view? I almost expected I could turn and see another me standing there. A little boy with his brother by his side, their parents laughing on a park bench just up the hill.

As familiar as it all was, though, the restlessness that had forced me out of the house hadn't faded. It was like a ragged edge running straight through me, keeping the contentment I had expected to feel to be back in this place, the *rightness* of it, at arm's length.

I wondered where Mom and Dad were right then. Were they lying awake and thinking of us? Did some part of them think we would appear at any moment as they turned a corner or walked down an unfamiliar street? Or had they moved on, forcing themselves to accept the fact that their only sons were never coming back?

A cold weight settled in my stomach. James and I had been gone for more than six years without a word. Was it possible that Mom and Dad thought we were dead?

And worse, did they blame themselves, sure that if only they hadn't sent us west, it never would have happened? I sat there on the shore, trying to imagine the torture of believing that day after day, but it was too big, too awful.

I let the rest of the stones in my hand spill out by my side. When I looked across the lake again, its waters seemed flat and gray. The distant shores nothing but black swells in the land. It was like a painting of another time, perfectly made and impossible to touch. I hadn't come all this way for these things. James was right; the path I was on stretched far beyond this place.

I stepped into my shoes and walked away from the shore, striding into the dark without another look back.

28

"Careful. You're going to cut my arm off."

"Not if you stop squirming."

My arm was laid out on the kitchen table. James jockeyed for position until he found the best angle and then slipped the teeth of the garden shears beneath the dirty plaster of the cast.

"You sure about this? Maybe the hacksaw would be better."

"Do it."

James put all his weight into it and the plaster cracked. He made it past my wrist and then across my palm, backtracking to cut through the thumbhole. When he was done he dug his fingers into the seam and pulled. The plaster crunched and then snapped in two.

I lifted my arm out of the debris. It was pale as milk, and the skin felt damp and puckered. I flexed my fingers and turned my wrist in a circle. There was a deep ache still, but the relief to have it free again was so great it was almost unbearable. James tossed the shears onto the table.

"There you go," he said. "Free at last."

James went out into the living room and pulled one of Dad's old flannels on over his T-shirt. I was amazed it fit as well as it did. A month's worth of rest and food had done him good. He had put on weight and when he walked, his hand no longer went instinctively to the scar at his side. He picked up his backpack and stuffed a pair of jeans inside.

"Sure you don't want to wait another day? They say the fighting is dying down a bit," I said. "Maybe —"

"Border's gonna get tighter," he said, filling a water bottle at the kitchen sink. "War's not even over and the Path is already building a wall. If I want to get across, I have to move now."

"Okay, but you should take the car."

"Nah, you keep it."

"What? You're going to walk the whole way? You're really pushing this whole biblical prophet thing."

James set the bottle by his pack. "I never learned how to drive, Cal."

"Oh. Right."

I pulled a small box from my pocket. It was wrapped in the comics section of an old newspaper with twine ribbon. "I got you this."

"What is it?"

"A going-away present." James hesitated. "It's not a bug, I promise."

James took the box and unwrapped it. When he saw what was inside, he sat back against the edge of the sink.

"Got it before we left the base," I said. "Good thing about those Feds is that they're pretty easy to bribe."

James reached into the box and pulled out a white asthma inhaler with a pale-blue stopper.

"Got a couple replacement cartridges too but they wouldn't fit in the box." I waited for him to say something but he was stuck, staring at the inhaler. "James?"

"I haven't had an attack since that night in the desert."

"And you won't," I said quickly. "Just think of it as a — Look, I don't know what you should think of it as; just put it in your pocket and forget it's there, okay? For me? Your big brother?"

James looked up and smiled. "Thanks, Cal."

He pocketed the inhaler, then went over everything he had in his pack and zipped it closed. I expected him to head for the door, but he stood looking out the window at the back garden. With little else to do over the last month, James and I had cleaned it up the best we could. The grass was cut and the weeds had been pushed back so the flowers had a little room to breathe. We even managed to get the hammocks repaired and rehung, which naturally led to a discussion about sleeping in them instead of our cramped bedroom. In the end, we decided that nostalgia was a thing you could take way too far.

"You don't have to do this," I said.

"I know." James settled the pack onto his shoulders. "When you find them . . ."

"I'll explain," I said. "It'll be all the ammo I need to finally be declared the good son."

I followed James through the house and out into the front yard. He stood at the gate, looking across the street at sidewalks and trees and empty houses before pushing it open and stepping through. He looked back at me, his brown hair light in the morning sun as it rose. He waved one last time, then he turned to go.

Even though I had been preparing myself for weeks, standing there in the moment of James's leaving was overwhelming. Every part of me wanted to follow him, but I held myself steady, eyes shut, and listened as he climbed the hill to the main road. His footsteps slowly faded away. After he was gone, there was a long silence. The emptiness around me seemed impossibly vast. I told myself that he'd always be out there, like a jewel in a box, or a heart beating in the darkness. No matter what happened I'd be able to turn south and for a moment feel like we were together again.

I drifted back through the empty house, my lone footsteps echoing off the bare walls. I moved from room to room, gathering up anything I thought I could use — matches, food, a half-dull kitchen knife — then pulled a crumpled road map out of my pocket.

Wellesley Island was circled in red ink, a speck of land on the Canadian border. I ran a finger along the route, feeling the lonely grind of the miles there and then all the ones that would come after. I had no way of knowing how long it would take me to find Mom and Dad, or even if I could. The only thing to do was start, but there was something that held me in place. It was this feeling like I was standing in a half-finished room, or the way a song, shut off before the end, stays inside of you, anxious until it can resolve.

I folded the map and stuffed it in my pocket. There was no sense dwelling on it. I reached for my pack, then remembered that I had traded the clothes the Feds had given me for some of Dad's shortly after we arrived. I figured I could use the old ones as spares.

I found them in a pile in our room. The shirt was sweated through and full of holes, but the rest was worth taking. I stuffed the jacket into the backpack and then reached across the floor for my old jeans. There was a soft jangle of metal as I pulled them to me.

My heart lost a beat when I heard it. I reached inside and pulled out a thick pink band with a black buckle and a silver tag. I didn't breathe as I drew the collar across my shaking hands. The collar felt impossibly heavy, as if all of those months and all the hundreds of miles had been compressed into its fibers. *Bear.* I traced the letters

319

of his name with my fingertip and then held the tag in my hand until the metal grew warm. I could feel the heat of his fur and remembered his summery smell.

I imagined him in a cabin, safe and well fed, and wondered if it was home to him now or if he still thought of me. Did he wonder why I left him even now? And did he lie among the woman and her family, awaiting the day I'd come back for him?

The map rustled as I flattened it out on the floor. I found what I was looking for in a corner of Montana way out on its own. *Bull Lake.* A dot of a town next to a blue patch of water. I pulled the pen out of my pack and circled it in red.

Looking at both of the marks on the map, Bull Lake and Wellesley Island, I felt something snap into place, like my path had emerged before me, clear and straight.

I left the house with an old song turning in my head, its melody bright but distant. I hummed it out loud as I got into the car and set my pack and Bear's collar on the seat next to me. I looked down the road and then I started the engine and drove away.

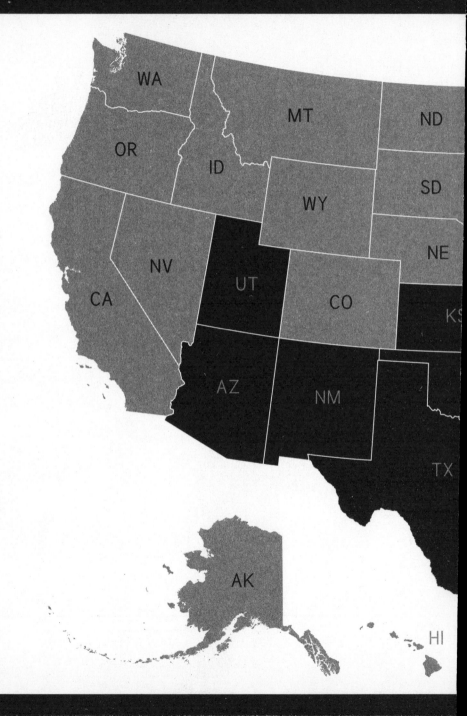

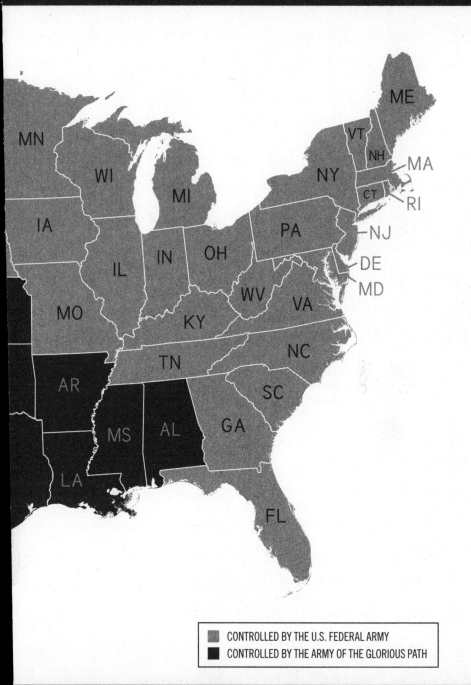

CONTROLLED BY THE U.S. FEDERAL ARMY
CONTROLLED BY THE ARMY OF THE GLORIOUS PATH

ACKNOWLEDGMENTS

Like with every book, I'd be absolutely nowhere without the peerless agenting of Sara Crowe, and without the fine, fine folks at Scholastic, especially Cassandra Pelham, David Levithan, and Lauren Felsenstein. For early and absolutely essential constructive criticism, thanks to Eliot Schrefer (if you haven't read *Endangered* yet, go get it!), Phoebe North (if you haven't read *Starglass* yet, go get it!), Ken Weitzman, and Ryan Palmer.

Thanks also to every teacher and librarian who invited me out to their school this past year. One of the best parts of this job is getting out there and meeting the next generation of readers!

Beyond these usual suspects, an awful lot of new folks helped me out on this one. Appropriately enough they largely fall into one of two categories — military folk and animal folk.

As for the military folk, who fielded questions big and small from this hapless civilian, I want to say thanks to Sergeant Major Kevin Spooner, U.S. Army; Specialist Heather Zenzen, U.S. Army Reserves/ Minnesota National Guard; and Chief Aviation Electronics Technician Daniel Bramos, U.S. Navy (retired).

On the animal side, thanks to Jeff Hiebert, President of Search and Rescue Dogs of the United States. Also, huge thanks to all the nice folks at Pets Alive in Middletown, NY, for rescuing a little mini pinscher with gigantic ears from the side of a highway in Puerto Rico. If they hadn't, my wife and I would have missed out on an awful lot of fun this past year and I never would have had the inspiration for Bear. It was pretty awesome to spend a year writing this book with my inspiration cuddled up to me every day.

Talking with these folks got me thinking about how much great work they do and how they can always use a bit of a hand. If you'd like to join me in lending one, I hope you'll consider making (or pestering your parents until *they* make) a donation to Pets Alive (www.petsalive.com) or Operation Homefront (www.operationhomefront.net).

ABOUT THE AUTHOR

Jeff Hirsch is the *USA Today* bestselling author of *The Eleventh Plague* and *Magisterium*. He graduated from the University of California, San Diego, with an MFA in Dramatic Writing and now lives in New York with his wife. Visit him online at www.jeff-hirsch.com.